A middle-aged businessman reliving a murderous punch-up that happened in his youth; a chatter-box bar girl cheerfully describing her involvement in a customer's fantasy life; a novelist puzzling over an obsession with tree shadows; and a scholar dabbling irresponsibly in the biography of a famous modern poet.

This is the rich and varied world into which you are invited, a world of only half-solved puzzles for its inhabitants: the scholar, for example, discovers a tragedy in his own past in place of the impersonal facts he sought; the novelist, in his search for the origins of his strange preoccupation, encounters a woman who improbably claims to be his mother. It is a world of brilliant surfaces: satirical, at times to the point of parody; incisive, at times to the point of cruelty. A world also of sudden depths, the mind at last confronting truths it prefers not to acknowledge.

These two short stories and two novellas ("Tree Shadows" was awarded the 1988 Kawabata Prize) make up the second volume of Maruya's fiction to appear in English. His novel *Singular Rebellion* was acclaimed internationally as "a superb piece of urban fiction". This new collection should serve both to confirm his reputation and to give readers a better idea of the scope of his writing.

Here is a writer who not only sees the profoundly comic side of human life, but subtly reveals—without resorting to that aggressive sentimentalism which makes some Japanese literature so hard for Western readers to take—its pathos: the fact that we are all emigrants from a past we remember only too little of. It haunts us, and we try to reconstruct it, but most of what is important in it escapes us.

When *Singular Rebellion* appeared, Anthony Burgess generously hailed Maruya as a major comic novelist. With this second volume, the limitation of the word "comic" may, we believe, be dispensed with.

RAIN IN THE WIND

RAIN IN
THE WIND

Four Stories

Saiichi Maruya

Translated by Dennis Keene

91-055

KODANSHA INTERNATIONAL
Tokyo and New York

"Rain in the Wind" (*Yokoshigure*) and "The Gentle Down-hill Slope" (*Daradarazaka*) were published in Japanese in *Yokoshigure* (Kodansha, 1975); "I'll Buy That Dream" (*Yume o Kaimasu*) and "Tree Shadows" (*Jueitan*) in *Jueitan* (Bungei Shunjū, 1988).

Distributed in the United States by Kodansha International/ USA Ltd., 114 Fifth Avenue, New York, New York 10011. Published by Kodansha International Ltd., 17-14 Otowa 1-chome, Bunkyo-ku, Tokyo 112 and Kodansha International/ USA Ltd. Copyright © 1990 by Kodansha International. All rights reserved. Printed in Japan.

First edition, 1990   ISBN 4-7700-1440-6 (in Japan)

Library of Congress Cataloging-in-Publication Data
Maruya, Saiichi, 1925–
  Rain in the wind.

  Translation of: Yokoshigure.
  I. Title.
PL856.A66Y613   1990   895.6′ 35   89-45166
ISBN 0-87011-940-0 (U.S.)

CONTENTS

THE GENTLE DOWNHILL SLOPE

The great thing in a fight is to have plenty of room on both sides of you. Don't choose a place where you're hemmed in. Some of the youngsters were boasting about the punch-ups they'd had, and those were the few words I chose as my uninvited contribution to the subject. It was at some place we'd gone to drink after the firm's end-of-year party, can't quite remember when. They all just grinned, of course; couldn't associate their section manager, of all people, with any sort of rough-house. Not surprising, I suppose—not the way I look now, anyway. I kept quiet after that, but I think I could still handle myself all right if I had to. I've always felt pretty sure of myself, ever since I was a boy. Of course, the sort of fights kids have are just a muckabout, but I once got mixed up in the real thing; only once, mind. I still reckon that was what you could call a real fight, though I wouldn't want to insist on it, of course.

Funny sort of thing to have started talking about; I can't imagine how we got onto the subject in the first place. Still, it'd look even funnier if I stopped now, wouldn't it? You'd probably think I was trying to have you on. So I might as well give you the whole story.

It was five years after the war. I'd just failed the university entrance exam. That was in March. I went back home for a bit, then returned to Tokyo in May. I'd managed to persuade my parents after a very long struggle to let me go to a crammer for a year. They didn't have much money, you see.

I'd stayed at my cousin's place in Kichijōji when I'd come up for the entrance exam in March, so I just sort of ended up there

3

again. He was six or seven years older than me, and when he'd got out of the army he decided to chuck the university in right away, doing a bit in the black market, then going from one firm to another. Pretty filthy sort of flat he had. We had to eat out, of course. There were a couple of places that took ration vouchers, one near the flat and the other by the station, and we ate at those. The only difference was the soup at the one by the station was a bit thicker, but the other one had a toilet. Funny the sort of things you remember.

I call it a flat, but it only had one small room. When we put the quilts down for the night there wasn't space for anything else, so my desk had to go in the bedding cupboard. He used to come home drunk most nights, and although that didn't actually stop me working, somehow I just couldn't sort of settle down. It was all a bit awkward, you see, and I felt I wasn't doing the right thing by him, so once I'd started going to school I began to look for a place of my own. Only there weren't any. Nothing to rent, anyway. If you found anything, the sums you had to fork out as key money and deposit money and what have you were astronomical. You remember how bad the housing situation was at that time, surely?

While I was walking my feet off, the money ran out. In fact it had run out some time before, but I'd got by with selling my watch, dictionaries, shoes, and so on. I wasn't used to life in Tokyo, and what with the inflation and not having much of an allowance to start with, it was just bound to happen, I suppose. I wrote home about it, but not a murmur. So it meant I had to stop going to school, though I'd paid the fees, and find some sort of part-time work. I started off in a pin-ball parlour, but the racket got on my nerves so much I had to pack it in after three days. The next was a job in films, or rather carrying the films from one cinema to another. That was the golden age of the Japanese Cinema all right. I stayed with it for ten days, perhaps a fortnight

4

at the most; but I jacked that one in too because in the meantime some money had arrived from my mother. Of course, it wasn't all that much, though I could easily guess what a struggle she'd had to scrape even that amount together. In addition to my monthly allowance there was just enough for me to rent a cheap room somewhere.

Seeing as I'd be able to cash the money order on the following day, I emptied my purse and had a good solid meal for a change, and that night my cousin came home surprisingly early (which still only meant half past eleven). Normally when he came back early he looked pissed off, but this day he looked very pleased about something, even offering me one of the Chinese buns he'd brought back with him. Naturally I took it like a shot. They taste pretty good when they've got a bit cold. He liked them with soy sauce, and slapped plenty on. I think he even put it on the ones that didn't have a meat filling but bean curd inside. Well, everyone to his own taste, I suppose. Then I told him the money had arrived and I was going to find a room and move out, which was just fine with him, of course—though he said something a bit weird:

"If I had that much money, first thing I'd do would be to buy me a woman."

Then he went on about the good times he'd had in Shinjuku. I suppose he was just trying to have me on in a crude sort of way, but I was too busy with my bun to bother much. After all, there was I, a pure, fourteen-carat-gold virgin, just up from the country to work hard for my exams, and all I had on my mind was how I was going to find somewhere to sleep and something to eat.

I slept till around noon the next day; just didn't have the energy to get up, I suppose. Riding about on that damn bike all day I was pretty worn out, and then I was feeling really good because the money had arrived safe and sound, and the idea of sleep, just sleep, was too good to resist. Still, I wasn't yet twenty, full of energy really, and once I'd got up all the tiredness vanished just like that. Good, deep sleep, you see. Can't sleep like that any more; lie there with my eyes open; can't seem to get off. Not unless I've had quite a bit to help me on the way.

First I went to the post office, then had a combined breakfast and lunch, and just as I was finishing I remembered I'd forgotten to phone the cinema and tell them I wouldn't be in that day. But I told myself it would be all right somehow, look on the bright side and so on, until finally I decided I might as well jack in the job anyway. Once I'd made up my mind about that, I realized I hadn't been paid for the previous two days, but I thought I might as well go the whole hog and forget about that too. I was still young, you see: rash, irresponsible, not looking before I leapt, and all that. Silly, of course, because I had no idea how much money I'd have left after I rented a room, nor if I could get another job if I gave up the cinema.

The fact is I had a really lousy time after that as well. Couldn't find work no matter how hard I looked, and when I went to the Employment Exchange the man in charge was a real nasty little bugger, said they'd only got work in the docks in a sort of sneering, insinuating way, implying I wouldn't be able to handle it, and that way of talking got my back up, so half to prove something to him as well as to myself I said I'd take it. Well, being a stevedore is no joke, I can tell you. Tough stuff, believe you me. The money wasn't all that bad, though. Still, slaving away on the docks, what sort of life is that, I ask you? I could never work out how I managed to pass my exams the following year after farting around like that all the time. Must have been easier then, I suppose. Can't think of any other reason. You'd never get away with it now, of course.

Still, that all came later. To get back to the day in question, there was I all dressed up in my pepper-and-salt student's outfit, the loot safely stashed away in my inside pocket, and off I went to

6

Shibuya. My cousin had told me there were lots of estate agents with rooms to let in Dōgenzaka, just at the top of the slope. So up the slope from the station I went, but not one estate agent could I find, not a sign of one. That didn't bother me too much, though, and I just kept on walking till the shopping centre came to a sudden end, with just a lot of fields where the houses must have got burnt down during the war, though there were still one or two here and there, but nothing to speak of. So I turned back and thought I'd try the other side of the road, and there, sure enough, set a bit back from it, were five or six estate agents all lined up next to each other.

I had a look at the notices stuck on the glass door of the first place, but couldn't see anything suitable. Everything was a bit too expensive for a start. At the second place there were a couple that looked as if they might be all right, but when I asked I was told they'd already been taken. The skinny runt in charge wore a white shirt and trousers with a thick woolly waist-band over the top, so he didn't look all that trustworthy. Again, he was a bit too brisk telling me the rooms had gone and suggesting alternatives. I mean, I suppose he might just have forgotten to take the notices down, but it's more likely he was either trying to give the impression that business was really humming, or it was a fiddle to get customers inside the shop. Almost certainly that, of course, although the idea never even crossed my mind at the time, and I just felt genuinely disappointed.

I left that one, found nothing in the next, and was just standing in front of the fourth going methodically through the ads, when I noticed two people who looked like students were suddenly standing on both sides of me, and grinning for all they were worth. Either they were smiling at me, or smiling at each other about something to do with me. I didn't like it at all, right from the start. I mean, neither of them looked as if they were reading the notices.

7

Then the one on my left with a student's cap on started talking to me. Grubby sort of cap it was, too—looked as if he'd used some sort of grease on it to make it stiff. It had a university badge, but not one I recognized.

"Excuse me," he said, "but might you be looking for a room?" which was a damn silly thing to ask, it being pretty obvious that I was.

"Well. You know."

"I see. Terrible business, isn't it?" he said, with a winning smile, and then addressed himself to his mate who was standing on my right.

"Terrible, isn't it?" he said, with a nasty sly look on his face.

"Yeah, terrible, all said and done," was the pointless reply that one made. He didn't have a cap, but was wearing black trousers and a khaki army jacket. There were still men about in old army uniforms at the time, though he looked a bit too young to have been in the war. Pretty sure he couldn't have been.

After a slight pause the one in the cap said:

"Found a super room once, only I didn't have the money to put down, so someone else got it."

He seemed almost to be talking to himself, but the army jacket added sharply:

"Bloody fool you were," and started laughing.

You hardly call someone a bloody fool for something like that, and I felt myself go tense all over. This time the army jacket addressed me, jutting out his jaw as he did so.

"Now, you're no fool, are you, old man; so you'll have it on you, won't you?"

"No. I don't have any."

But my reply had been a bit too quick, too automatic. It was clear straight away that I was lying.

"No. He don't have any," said the student's cap, mimicking my voice, which they both found very funny. While they were

8

laughing they edged a bit closer to me. The army jacket's shoulder brushed against mine.

Squeezed as I now was between them and looking at the notices about "no children" and "gas and water fully laid on" (looking rather than reading, of course, seeing as everything was all sort of blurred before my eyes), I was thinking I ought to nip smartly away from here as soon as possible, wondering what I ought to say as an appropriate leave-taking, and being unable to think of anything. Either I'm just awkward in social situations of that kind, or maybe it's pride that prevents me saying the right thing.

The chap in uniform started searching through his pockets in a theatrical way, then asked:

"Got a smoke?"

" 'Fraid not," said the one in the student's cap.

He nodded, then turned to me.

"How about you, old man?"

"I don't smoke," I said.

"Don't you, now? In that case, sorry and all that, but perhaps you could lend me the money, to buy some smokes, you know," he said in a very quiet, very calm voice.

The give-and-take that followed went on for quite a while, but I'll leave that bit out. It was the usual pointless stuff: me saying I couldn't lend money to someone I didn't know, and them telling me I ought to trust them, just try them once at least; all spoken in this awful, restrained, ceremonious manner. Stupid business. Went on about five minutes, I think. All in these weird, quiet voices, though sometimes raised a bit. Theirs, of course, not mine.

While this was going on, the man in the shop next to the place next door, the one with the waist-band over his shirt, came out to have a look because he must have realized something funny was going on, but the army jacket just gave him a very hard stare, so

9

he pushed off back in again. The man whose window we were standing bang in front of never came out once the whole time. He must have heard it all, and he certainly hadn't gone out anywhere because when the phone rang he answered it. He was there all right.

Still, the upshot of this whole exchange was that the one in the cap said:

"Well, don't seem to be getting anywhere, do we? Perhaps we should go to some nice, quiet place and talk it over? I mean, somewhere like this isn't really . . ."

His eyes had narrowed. The nice, quiet place wasn't going to be any teashop; the talk wasn't going to be some pleasant chat. That would have been obvious to anyone.

"No thanks," I said. "I'm going home now."

They both seemed quite indifferent to this unsociable reply.

"Are you, now?" they said, and sniggered.

But they made no move to stop me getting away, and when I turned round and started to walk off I soon understood why. About half a dozen yards away another of them was standing. He wore a black student's uniform, but no cap, with wooden *geta* on his feet. He looked well built, looked a pretty tough customer, in fact. Had plenty of experience in any amount of punch-ups, I shouldn't be surprised.

"So it's got to be a little talk, has it?" he said to the other two, as if he blamed it all on them; and I realized then that if I didn't watch it they might really clean me out. I'd been taken in by the idea that I could probably handle just the two of them, but it was a bit different now.

The two made some kind of brief apology, then came in close and started walking, and I just sort of got carried along with them. I mean, there didn't seem anything else I could do. The tough-looking character had taken two or three steps backwards, with his eyes fixed on me all the time. He said nothing. As luck would have it, there was nobody about at all, just a kid on a bike with some heavy-looking cardboard box strapped on it who went wobbling past, but there would have been no point in asking him to do anything. So I was stuck with my two companions—or three, in fact. It never crossed my mind to shout out to the man in the estate agent's for help. The tough guy had fallen in behind us, and I knew he wasn't going to take his eyes off me for a second. I could hear the clip-clop of his *geta*.

Now that I knew I was in for something, the only thing I could think about as I walked along was what it must have cost my mother to send me that money. I wasn't going to let these bastards take it off me just like that. I got very worked up about it. They wouldn't get it without a fight. So the idea of Mum back there in the village served to rouse the old fighting spirit. Very useful. Funny way of repaying a filial obligation, though, I must say. Anyway, the more I thought about the money, the more set I was on putting up a real fight for it, and making sure I won. It wasn't any different, probably, from what a member of a street gang feels. I mean, that's what it's all about.

You know that part where the railway line starts to bend, don't you? Well, we got there and then the level-crossing barrier came down and we had to wait, marking time while that fussy little bell was clanging away. The train started to go by. As I watched the carriages passing I began planning things in a slightly more orderly way. I'd take care of one of them, and while the other two were hesitating I'd spot my chance and clear off quick. I couldn't take all three of them on in one go. I was pretty sure I could outrun them, though.

The train disappeared, and we crossed over and walked along a good paved road, though at that time of day there were never many cars about. Occasionally a schoolboy or a woman with a shopping basket went by, but I kept quiet, trying to look as if nothing was the matter, as if I was just having a stroll with some friends. Well, I don't know; that's the impression I tried to give, but it probably looked more like a lamb being led to the slaughter.

We went along this fairly wide road for a bit, then turned left, then right, and now it was a narrow lane for quite a way till we passed through a broken-down gate with stone pillars into what must have been part of a really big house destroyed in the bombing. What was left of the concrete foundations made up three sides of a square, with a wide space around it which had been the garden, just a field now with thick bunches of weeds and wild grass in places. Since the whole area was enclosed by a concrete wall it couldn't be seen from outside, so it was just the place for the job—if the job is what they call extortion. They must have spent quite a time finding somewhere as good as this. Must have had other clients here, too, before me.

I was still wedged in between the two of them. The one in the cap made a point of trampling on some bits of glass which for some reason were scattered all over one part of the concrete, and it made a really nasty sound as his shoes crunched down on it. I wonder what he thought he was up to. Probably just trying to scare me, I suppose.

We went to the middle of the field, or it might have been a bit closer to the wall than that; anyway, round about the middle, and the two of them stopped a few paces in front of a rusty brown water pump which had been badly scorched by fire. Naturally I stopped as well. I looked back over my shoulder, and there was the tough guy—the one with no cap—quite a long way off, leaning casually against what looked like the remains of the concrete wall of a bath-house. No doubt he was making sure I wouldn't run away. Having worked out where he was, I stared at the one in the army jacket.

"Look, just hand over the money, okay?" he said in a kind of depressed mumble. You can't blame him, really—I mean, it isn't an easy line to say.

12

Now . . . and this is where the action starts, so just hold tight and let me get on with it . . . the moment he asked for the money I really let him have it—bang on the jaw, with the whole weight of my body behind it. It went right home, too. Back he flew, at least a couple of yards, and there he lay stretched out on the ground. All over in a flash, and the bastard didn't move. Out cold. Reckon he must have cracked his head on the concrete base of that pump. I don't think he hit the pump itself. He must have banged his head on something hard, because one punch could hardly have done that sort of damage.

The cap was so horror-struck he just stood there. I'll admit I was a bit dumbfounded myself. I hadn't really meant to go that far. So I just stood there too, like him. Probably only lasted a split second or so, but it seemed longer. Just standing there in a sort of daze.

Now, if the one behind had rushed at me I don't know what might have happened. I mean, coming at me from the back I'd probably have been done for—almost bound to have been. But in fact the stupid bugger started screaming out "You bleeding sod", "You fucking bastard", etc., trying to get himself into the right mood, I suppose. I automatically reacted by turning round and getting the wall at my back. I completely forgot about the other one; didn't even notice him.

I crouched a bit, getting ready for him. He kicked away his *geta*, and then he had something glittering in his right hand and he rushed at me. Can't think where he'd been hiding it. He must have had it on him all the time. It gave me a hell of a shock, anyway, and I can't really describe what happened after that. I think I kept quite still up to the last moment, then jumped to my left and got hold of his right hand. Something like that.

Of course, what I was trying to do was twist his wrist to make him drop the knife, but I'd grabbed him a bit too low down, caught more of his hand than the wrist so it wasn't possible to get a proper grip on it. Couldn't get my fingers round properly. I'm not too clear on that part, though. Anyway, naturally he tried to get free. So there we stood, both with our weight on our right legs, straining with our right arms, and gradually we began slithering and sliding a bit over the ground. I was trying to keep his hand as far away from my body as possible, and he was trying to get it right in there, sweating like mad, panting away; and then suddenly I swung round behind him, quick as a flash, leaving my right hand where it was and getting my left arm round his neck, and while I was doing this I sort of paid a bit less attention to what my right hand was doing, relaxed the grip slightly or maybe it just slipped with the sweat. Anyway, he suddenly jerked his hand, and I thought I'd done it now, he'd got free, so I snatched my arm away from his neck, trying to get clear of him before he . . . you know. The fact is I'm not all that clear what I did. All I know is he let out a funny sort of groan, more like a grunt really; maybe it wasn't even the sound of his voice but something else; anyhow, he fell over in a direction I hadn't expected him to. He'd stabbed himself in the guts, and was now squirming about on the ground.

I can't remember it any better than that. When I say he fell over in a direction I hadn't expected I know it sounds a bit vague, but that was what it felt like at the time. In fact it's pretty stupid to talk about direction, since we'd been in a clinch like that and I'd suddenly turned him, so I hadn't much idea where I was, or him for that matter. Anyway, he'd been thrashing about like mad so he'd stuck it in pretty deep and couldn't get it out. I'm fairly sure he was lying there with it still in him. There was blood all over the place—"splattered" is how they'd probably describe it, though it was more like one solid stain on the ground. Yes, he was screaming all right. Like a maniac.

I just looked down at him. Didn't do anything. Just stood there. I then felt the outside of my pocket very slowly to make sure the money was still there. Then I left.

When I'd got as far as the gate, I suddenly remembered with a jolt the one in the student's cap and looked back, but there was no sign of him. He's got away, I thought, and immediately the sweat started pouring off me again. I still didn't undo my jacket buttons, though. There were four or five trees by the garden wall which had survived the fire, half burnt with the leaves sticking out in funny isolated bunches, like hands. The sun reflected off the wall onto the leaves, and they swayed in the breeze. Above them was a pale blue June sky. I looked at the scene as if I was taking a photo of it, fixing it in my memory, then went out through the gate.

I went back the way I'd come, crossing the railway line again, until I got to the area where the six estate agents lay a bit back from the road, but I only glanced in that direction. Then I came to a long, gentle slope, and as I started walking down it I soon came across people; suddenly there were crowds of them. The further I went, the more I found. Of course, it wasn't like it is now, absolutely swarming with people, but there still seemed an awful lot to me: people going down, people going up, people just standing about in the same place. And it all seemed unreal, somehow; it all felt like an enormous lie that someone had cleverly made up. There were people walking along carrying things in briefcases, in suitcases, in bags, or just wrapped up in pieces of cloth; there were people walking along carrying nothing at all. There were people with somebody; there were people with nobody; people waiting outside a cinema, people peering at the shelves sticking out into the road from one of the shops. Here was an unloaded truck; there was a man with some electric massage machine in his hand, running it along someone's shoulders, trying to make him buy one. A small crowd stood in front of a restaurant window, trying to decide what they were going to eat. The road had no pavement. Some people were on bicycles.

But nobody seemed to notice me at all. Nobody even looked at me. They weren't interested, they didn't care; they just walked. They bustled along, they hurried along, they strolled along, they wandered along. Lots of different ways you can walk, but, generally speaking, they weren't so much strolling or bustling as just keeping up a good, steady pace. Even the people just standing about didn't notice me—not one of them. It was broad daylight in an ordinary town; nothing out of the ordinary ever happened here. Yet here I was, a man who might have killed two other people, and they just didn't notice. The feeling irritated me; it irritated me all the way down that slope, that cheerful, noisy, lazy, gentle downhill slope.

What was I thinking about at the time? Well, assuming I was actually thinking about anything, I suppose I was thinking how lucky it was I hadn't lost the money, thinking I could leave those two young thugs to their friend to deal with; but it would only have been momentary, only in fits and starts. I wasn't really thinking, I was feeling; and the irritation I was feeling was not because I'd done something spectacular and been ignored, not because I'd been frustrated in some desire youngsters are supposed to have to show off in front of other people; nothing like that at all. There was none of that, not a scrap of it. If I was to work it out properly, really analyse it, then I think I'd have to say that the irritation represented a young man's reaction to the fact that, for the first time in his life, he'd been thrown right into the thick of society, been shown the whole truth of it in one long moment; and he was bewildered by what he'd suddenly seen, then made intoxicated by it, though it had a harsh, bitter taste to it. I'd found out that the world we live in is dangerous, disturbed, violent, or any other adjective you prefer to use; and yet I'd swallowed the whole thing in one gulp. I found I could take it—it didn't seem to affect me at all—and while I was being amazed at my own reaction I discovered I'd become fascinated by it all.

When I say the world, it's society in general I mean. I'm not talk-

16

ing about a country boy being overawed by the big city. The point is that the violence and danger wasn't represented by those three thugs, but by myself. I'd not only just found out what society was, I'd also discovered I could manage to get by in it. It was making these two discoveries at the same time, getting them mixed up together, that confused me. It was an odd mixture, part pleasure, part distaste, producing a sort of big-headed excitement.

That's right. I did say I wasn't thinking about anything. But if you have to force it into words, then it was something along those lines. That was how the world tasted to me as I went on down the hill, wiping the sweat off my brow, hurrying along.

Perhaps I wasn't hurrying all that much; dawdling a bit, probably. Yes, I wasn't in any hurry. Taking my time; strolling along. Nobody noticed. It was Dōgenzaka, an early afternoon in June. Nobody noticed anything suspicious about me.

I got to the station, went into the public toilet to take a leak, and noticed my left hand had blood on it. I washed my hands carefully, then my face, and wiped myself with my handkerchief. I was feeling hot, so I undid my buttons and saw there was a huge, round bloodstain on the left side of my jacket. The blood had soaked right in. It was a bit like the way the soy sauce soaked into the skin of those Chinese buns my cousin ate. How it had got there I couldn't work out, but it was certainly his blood and not mine. My left sleeve was pretty badly stained as well. My trousers were all right, though. I couldn't think why I hadn't been arrested straight away, walking about in a state like that. I felt let down, somehow; almost as if I'd been swindled.

I waited till there was no one in front of the small white basin, then tried to wash my jacket with it still on, but it didn't work. So I took it off and kept rinsing and rinsing it under the tap, and the red water kept on coming out, leaving a permanent stain in the bowl. From time to time, men who'd finished their business would come and dangle their fingers under the running water, then hurry away, showing no interest whatsoever in my laundry operations, nor in the red-stained basin. I went on washing, feeling there would never be an end to it as the red water kept oozing out of my jacket. Then my memory seems to have switched off at that point.

What I next remember is walking around the red-light area in Shinjuku. Yes, I had my jacket on all right. It was still only the afternoon, but there were a surprising number of people about, and the girls were shouting cheerfully trying to get customers to come in. There was one who looked really ancient to me, standing about with a dressing-gown on, and it struck me it was a lot like what you see at a hospital. Still, I don't really need to describe this to you, do I? You know what it was like round there in those days.

It was the first time I'd been to a place like that, and I was walking along between the rows of gaudy, gimcrack houses, when my eyes happened to meet those of a young girl who was standing quite near me in front of the pink portals of one of the knocking shops. She smiled slowly at me, and I automatically smiled back because I felt so happy. Then I went up to her.

I didn't know there could be anything as wonderful as this, although the girl didn't give me a particularly good time. But everything was a revelation—breasts, buttocks, thighs, everything —as if I'd had some rare, remarkable prize awarded to me. I didn't think about the money I was spending. When it was time and the woman got up, I was still feeling in a sort of daze, but managed to stagger off to another place, then another: four in all, one after the other, a real brothel crawl. Sounds pretty incredible now, and it was all done in a brief space of time as well. As I was being seen off by the fourth woman in the fourth place, it was just getting dark.

Well, my apologies. A weird tale of heroic exploits, particularly that last part. Still, I went through a pretty awful time afterwards. Obviously I didn't have the money to rent a room, so I had to go on being a nuisance at my cousin's place. I also had to keep on having women, so I was always short of money. Became a different person, you see. That's probably why I took that job on the docks. I blame it all on what happened to me as I walked down that slope.

But the human mind's a funny thing, you know. I mean, why should my memory have suddenly stopped working while I was staring at the red-stained water? Yet there's something even stranger than that. Those two could well have died; I knew that all right in my head, but deep down inside I couldn't give a damn. Was I trying to fool myself into believing that nothing much had happened and they'd have been all right? Had I told myself it was in self-defence anyway, so it didn't count as a crime? I mean, they say a murderer has bad dreams about his victims, don't they? And yet, you know, I've never once seen those two in any dream of mine, not these twenty years and more.

I'LL BUY
THAT DREAM

Y ou've just got to listen to this. Well, when I was working in the bar before, there was a girl called Mayumi who lived quite near, and we used to go to the same hairdresser's, and one day I'd just had my hair set and was going out and there was Mayumi waiting, so we went off together. Then the manager came running after us, just as we were going out the door, and he said all friendly and smiling:

"Oh, my word, if it isn't Rika. So sorry we never had time for a little chat, darling, but I've been absolutely rushed off my feet all day. You will come again, won't you, dear? Tomorrow or the day after would be lovely. Of course you'll come too, won't you, Mayumi?"

Naturally I was all smiles too, and said:

"Of course we will. Wouldn't go any place else, would we?"

" 'Course we wouldn't."

"Oh, the things you say."

"What's happened to Bee? Didn't see him anywhere today."

"That's because the poor thing's caught a cold."

"There's a lot of it going around nowadays."

"Well, make sure he looks after himself," I said, being really friendly, and then we waved and said goodbye. Bee's a boy who works in the shop. Nineteen, I think—or is it twenty? He lives with the manager. I met them one Sunday going for a walk, and we went to their place and played Reversi together, all three of us. Bee was terrifically good at it. I'm hopeless. Still, it was fun really. They've both been to my flat, too, a couple of times, and although we live so near they still sent me New Year cards,

23

separately as well. I suppose if you're like that it must be quite relaxing to have a friend who's a girl.

Anyway, we got on the underground and Mayumi was telling me how the manager wears a wig. Poor thing, and he's only forty. I mean, he's so pleased if you tell him he looks young it's almost embarrassing. And yet he's bald. It really is cruel.

I then invited Mayumi to come and have something to eat before we went to work. We had sandwiches, and while we were eating Mayumi told me about a dream she'd had. Normally I just hate people telling me about their dreams, but this one was quite interesting. There's a girl called Kyōko, who's quite pretty, I suppose, and she appeared in Mayumi's dream and made a confession. It was about when she'd been a fashion model, and the model agency had told her to have some plastic surgery, and she didn't want to but she couldn't refuse, so she had it and got a new face, but she really couldn't stand it and decided to stop doing this sort of work and have another operation and get the face she had before back again, because then when she passed people she knew in the street they wouldn't know it was her, and she wouldn't have to notice them. Then after she'd said that she took an egg and cracked it and poured it over a bowl of rice and ate it; and that's when Mayumi woke up.

"I expect there was something going on between Kyōko and the head of the model agency," I said without thinking.

"Um, could be, and that's why she couldn't refuse the operation."

Mayumi's a bit slow at the best of times, and getting all interested like that was silly, because it was only a dream anyway, and when we realized it we had a good laugh, because it *was* funny, wasn't it?

"Well, you don't like Kyōko, and that's why you had that dream about her," I said, but she said that wasn't true, because she liked her really, and I was amazed.

"But didn't you once say that Kyōko only looked nice because she'd had an operation?"

"Did I?"

"And you said it wasn't true she'd been a model, and she was just making it all up."

"Can't remember. Did I really?"

I thought she was just pretending she'd forgotten, but perhaps she wasn't. Perhaps it was all made up, anyway. I mean, Kyōko is quite pretty, but nothing special. It wouldn't be very nice to go through all that business just to look like her.

"Listening to people's dreams is really boring," I said.

That really surprised Mayumi, and she said it took all sorts, of course, but she'd loved hearing about dreams ever since she was a child, and she started talking about one in a fairy story, even though I'd just *told* her I didn't like hearing about them. I mean, how slow can you get? And the fairy story was a real mess, a lot of different ones that had all got mixed up together.

"You know that one about the man who was dreaming and a horse-fly flew out of his nose, don't you?" said Mayumi.

"Yes, but it's a little child having an afternoon nap, and it's a wasp that flies out."

"No it's not. It's a horse-fly."

"Then the mother swats the wasp. . . ."

"Seems to be a different story," said Mayumi.

"And the little child dies."

"Why does he die?"

"Because in his dream he'd become a wasp. The wasp was the little child's soul."

"Oh."

"That's why you mustn't kill wasps near people who're asleep."

"Mine's different," said Mayumi.

"I heard it from my granny. Every year around the beginning of summer she used to tell it me."

"That's why I expect you don't like listening to stories about dreams. You were frightened when you were small."

"Could be."

"The story I read was about a man getting rich."

"There is one about a man getting rich, and he goes by a bridge and there . . ."

"He doesn't buy a bridge. He buys a dream."

"By a bridge is the place where he is," I said. "It starts off, 'Once upon a time in the land of Hida dwelt . . .' "

"I'm sorry, Rika, but it's the land of Shinano. I read it in a book in our class library. 'Once upon a time in the land of Shinano dwelt . . .' "

Once she'd started she wouldn't stop. Like listening to a tape recording. Once upon a time in the land of Shinano dwelt two good friends, and they both used to hunt in the forest. One day they were in the forest and they sat down to have their lunch, and when they'd finished one of them had a little nap. Now, after a while, what should happen but a horse-fly comes out of the nose of the one who's asleep, flies away, then comes back a little later and goes back inside his nose. The other hunter is watching this all the time. Well, his friend wakes up and says he had a dream about being a horse-fly which flies to the mansion of a very rich man called Nibo no Gorobei on the island of Sado, and alights on a camellia tree covered with beautiful white flowers. It then tells him that if he digs a hole beneath this tree he'll find a great treasure. The hunter happens to be standing under that same camellia tree, you see, because it's all a dream, and so he digs away and finds masses and masses of gold coins. That's the dream. Now, the one who's been listening to all this then says he'll give him a hundred copper coins in exchange for the dream, and naturally the other one agrees, and he buys the dream for a hundred copper coins and goes to the island of Sado and finds work as a servant in the household of Nibo no Gorobei; and one bright moonlit night, when the whole house is asleep, he digs a hole under the camellia tree, and out come masses and masses of gold coins. He gathers them all up, and goes home a very rich man.

That was the story, but I couldn't go on chatting away like that all day because I'd be late for work, so I told Mayumi I thought she had a fantastic memory, and how interesting it had been, drank up my coffee, and took the bill to the counter. But Mayumi came after me and said:

"Let me do it this time. You paid for me only the other day."

Of course, once she'd said that, she couldn't find her purse, so I said it didn't matter, I'd get it, and she said it wasn't right I should pay again and went on fumbling in her handbag, so finally I said:

"Let's just say I'll buy that dream off you."

Naturally I only meant it as a joke. The silly little spotty thing behind the till started grinning away as well, though she didn't have a clue what I was talking about, of course.

That was on a Monday. The following Sunday evening a professor just back from America came round. He was one of the customers at the place before, and we were keeping company. I'd told the mama there all about it; I mean, I had to, because if she thought anything funny was going on she'd keep on and on at you till she found out, and you just couldn't get away with anything, she'd finally make you spit it all out. Well, of course, I always tell you, mama, don't I? I've told you about the director I'm going with now, haven't I? Yes, it's still going on.

The professor was about forty-five; a theologist. When he was a student he'd written some essay about Jesus Christ walking along the road and having sunstroke and falling over, and hearing the word of God, and he couldn't see for days after that; and it had been published in some magazine, in English of course, and he'd got a world-wide reputation. Apparently he'd used some new material in a very original way, that's what they said. This new

27

material had been found, I think, in the mountains of Judaea dozens of years ago by a boy who was looking after some sheep, and the sheep got into this cave and there were lots of old papers in pots and the sheep were munching them all up. On the bits they'd left over there were things written about Jesus Christ, and what they'd found out about the sunstroke from those bits of paper was what he'd written about in that essay of his that everybody admired. He was a university professor, and he'd already been abroad teaching twice. I heard all this from the man who first brought him to the bar. He belonged to some religious group. He said the professor was a very brilliant person.

When I heard he was a theologist I thought he couldn't have much money, because they don't invent things or anything like that, do they? Well, I was quite wrong. He was working as an adviser to this religious group in Izu, and always being asked to think about very difficult things for them. Something beginning with doc or dog—doctrine? Dogma? Anyway, it just meant he had to clue them up about things, because they didn't seem able to work it out for themselves. The professor gave some fancy reason why they were doing something, and that made it look all right. He once told me a bit about it, although he didn't go so far as to mention their name. After all, it wouldn't have looked too good if the word got out that they had to employ someone to do their thinking for them; and if people knew he was racking his brains for a new sect, working out the right relationship between their founder and the Lord's bounty and whatnot, meaning all the money they got from people, it wouldn't have done the professor's reputation much good either, would it? Particularly as he had a fair amount of cash coming in from them every month; untaxed, as well.

But he was mean as anything with it. I even asked him to put my monthly allowance up a bit, but he just wouldn't. Plain stingy, that's all. And the only thing he brought me back from America was a muumuu he'd got in Hawaii, for heaven's sake! I thought that was a bit much, so I wasn't in a very nice mood, even though it had been quite a long time.

When we'd finished he was a bit drowsy, and started talking about a dream he'd had on the plane. And I hate people talking about things like that! Anyway, he was in the garden of the house in the country where he'd been born, and there was this big, pale green animal, all covered in scales like cactus leaves, flopped out under a pear tree. It was a dragon, he said. Also—and this bit's disgusting, I'm sorry—the garden was full of some slimy white stuff because the dragon had got a bad tummy. He then happened to look up, and the pear tree was much bigger than it usually looked, and full of pears; and though normally they were only the size of ping-pong balls, now they were as big as tennis balls, and as he watched them they were getting bigger and bigger all the time. Every year the tree only had small, hard fruit, but now they weren't just big but all shiny and delicious-looking. So the professor—in the dream he was only a child and not a professor, of course—thought it must be because the dragon dung had fertilized the tree, but no matter how hard he tried he couldn't reach the fruit, so he decided to go and get a ladder, and went into the garden shed, but it was so dark in there he couldn't see a thing, I suppose because he'd suddenly gone into a dark place, and he felt lots of spiders' webs on his face, and it was an awful business trying to get them off—they were all over his nose and ears and fingers, all these fat, slimy threads like macaroni cheese sticking to him. Anyway, just as he was cleaning his fingers under his armpits on his shirt and wiping his face with his hands, there was a flapping sound outside and he rushed out to see what it was, and the dragon wasn't there any longer. It must have flown away. And then it started to pour with rain.

"So you didn't manage to eat any of the pears, I suppose?"

"That's right," he said. "It all ended there."

Then he began to wonder aloud why he'd had that dream. When he was a little boy at school they started keeping chickens at home, and because the chicken shed had been put right next to the pear tree it suddenly got great big pears on it. So this must have been lying somewhere at the back of his mind, and he went on and on about it and some drawing of a dragon by somebody in Indian ink on a scroll in the living room, so there you are, blah blah. And on he goes again—yes, wait a minute, what about that drawing he saw in some American museum by a little Indian child, of lightning that looked just like a snake?—very interesting that was, could well have been because of that. Well, I myself didn't know dragons belonged to the snake family. First I'd heard of it, and it's a bit silly if you think of a snake flying in the sky, isn't it? That's what I said, and he said cheerfully that God must have done something with solar energy to the dragon, but I couldn't make head or tail of what he was saying. Too hard for me, I suppose.

While I went on listening I was feeling a bit sick of him because of that muumuu, I expect, and I wanted to do something really wicked. So finally I thought I'd tell him a whopping lie, and that would teach him. You feel like that sometimes, don't you? But I couldn't think up any good one of my own, so I thought I'd tell him that one about Kyōko in Mayumi's dream as if it had happened to me. When I was working at the model agency, I said, the boss had made me have plastic surgery, but I just didn't like the face I had now. I liked the face I used to have much better, whatever other people might think. So I was thinking of giving up working in a bar and having an operation to get back my real face, then when I met customers in the street I could just ignore them and walk by, and nobody would know. Just thinking about it made me happy.

That was the story I told him in dribs and drabs, in a pretty sincere, gloomy voice as well. I've never been a model or anything like that. Came straight to Ginza. But while I was being so serious I half came to believe it all myself.

He lay there listening to me in the dark, but halfway through a change seemed to come over him. He edged his body away a bit and stopped making any little interruptions, becoming dead quiet. Very ponderous it all became, and when I reached the end he didn't say a thing, so I didn't either. I thought of telling him, all right, don't worry, I was only having you on, but that didn't somehow seem right, either. Then he suddenly switched on the bedside lamp and looked me in the face. Then he put the overhead light on as well and stared hard at me. I didn't like it being all dazzling like that, and he looked so sad, too. He looked at me from all sorts of angles, like he was investigating some mystery. I don't think anyone's looked at me as closely as that before, so I thought he must have seen through me and knew I'd been lying.

"Don't you believe me, then? Well, that's just great, seeing it's something I've never ever told anybody else," I said, but he just mumbled something and switched off the overhead light, turning down the bedside one as well.

So there he was lying muttering to himself—how he would never have thought it, but you had to admit . . . and things like that—in this incredibly sincere voice, since he'd swallowed the whole lot, while I was so pleased I could have hugged myself, and it was so funny I started to giggle inside. Even when I said really soppy things like, don't you think I'm beautiful any more, he took it quite seriously and said, no, of course he did. But the real trouble was still to come.

"You must have lots of photos of when you were a model. Let's have a look."

Well, I was hardly likely to have any, was I? So I got all flustered and said:

"There might be some somewhere. And then there might not.

31

It was only a tiny little agency. Not for the really big magazines, and no famous photographers. I never liked any of the pictures of me at all. The clothes were hopeless as well."

I tried to get round it like that, and he replied:

"Come to think of it, you never show me any photos of yourself, not like other girls do."

He was quite right, really, because some girls do like showing you lots of dreary pictures. Men as well, for that matter. There was one customer at the place before who'd been on some great long trip with his family all round Europe, and he brought absolutely loads of them to show us and it was just awful. I'd had enough of it before we'd even finished Italy, so I went to another table, but that customer left and I had to go back and he'd still only got as far as Germany. Then it was Switzerland, France, Scandinavia, England, and you just couldn't think of any more polite things to say.

What the professor really wanted to see, though, wasn't pictures of me as a model. Just as he was leaving—he never stays the night—he asked me in a very put-on casual voice if I had any photos of me as a schoolgirl. So that's what he's after, I thought: he wants to compare me with the way I look now. He'd suddenly become more interested in the way I used to look, you see.

Well, I said I wasn't sure but I didn't think I did, and then started getting all cute and sultry and asking when I was going to see him again, and once he'd left I laughed myself silly.

A couple of days later it was my turn to go in early that evening, and who should turn up but the professor, and on his own, too, and suddenly he says let's go, which isn't all that unusual, and I thought we were going off to eat somewhere but instead we went to my place. I mean, I was really surprised, it being the second time in only three days. He said he'd been longing to see me for the past two days; he couldn't wait; that sort of stuff.

On the way in the car we started talking about my high school days for some reason. Naturally he was the one who brought it up. He asked me what school I'd been to and when I'd graduated, but I said that'd be telling, wouldn't it, and I didn't want him to know my age; so I got out of it like that, and while I was still teasing him we arrived.

Then, when we'd finished, he asked me to show him my photo albums, but I said I'd left them with my mother. Well, we got dressed and were having a drink, when I saw him have a quick look at my key-ring which I'd left lying about. I knew what that look meant.

"Oh, by the way, perhaps I ought to have that spare key, after all. Be easier that way," he said. I mean, when I'd first offered him one he'd refused it, and now he wanted one. But I knew what his little game was.

"I left it with Mother."

"Leave everything to Mother."

"Well, there's no one else I can rely on, is there?"

"All right, then, just get it off her sometime. No great rush; any time you happen to drop in."

"Wouldn't your wife notice?"

"No problem."

"Sometime, then," I said. I'd soon worked out he meant to come here when I wasn't in and look for the photos.

After that he really started to make a nuisance of himself. First he rang me up when I was still asleep and asked me what had happened about the key. Perhaps it was because I was sleepy, but I suppose I didn't sound all that helpful, so the next thing he did was come to the bar much earlier than usual, saying he'd go back first and wait, so could he have the key? Pretty obvious he was going to look for the albums, wasn't it? I made up a story about the room being in such a mess I just couldn't. So he went off to another couple of places, then came back and we went home together, but of course I had to go in first and pretend I was tidying up, keeping him waiting ages before I let him in. Perhaps he'd had too much to drink, because we didn't do anything.

We had some tea, and while we were drinking it he started talking away cheerfully about plastic surgery. He knew an awful lot about it: operation methods, anaesthetics, lasers and all that. I thought it was a bit funny, and then he said he'd bought a book, not some paperback but a real medical book for doctors that cost a small fortune. Seemed to be pretty generous when it came to books, at least. He said Japanese books were no good, and he'd ordered this one from America by air mail.

So he asked me all sorts of questions about the operation I was supposed to have had. Naturally, I had a lot of trouble making it all up, and thought he was bound to say it was a pack of lies, but he didn't. He couldn't, I suppose, because he'd made up his mind to believe everything.

"I wish I'd been able to see your real face, Rika," he said in this really heartfelt voice, but then he asked me if I'd shown the doctor the photo of some actress I wanted to look like; and I thought it might be some sort of trick question, so I passed it back and asked him who *he* thought I was like, and then we talked about who I did or didn't look like.

Apparently it said in that expensive book of his that it's forbidden to take on any patient who comes along with the picture of an actress and says she wants a face like that. Well, it's quite right, because obviously they'd only complain like mad afterwards, wouldn't they, and the doctors would have an awful time. Still, it's no good just saying you want to be beautiful. I wonder what you are supposed to say, then. I mean, you're not allowed to use paintings or statues as models either, it said. That's only right, though. There's that painting somewhere of the Virgin Mary, and she does look lovely, but even so they say her head's not quite the right size for her body.

I made him another drink, but he hardly touched it. He just sat there twiddling the glass in his hand, staring at the cupboard. I knew he was thinking the albums were in there somewhere. And he was quite right, too. But men are so proud, you know; they won't say. He wouldn't say they're in there, aren't they, but just kept looking; and finally he started nodding off, but when I asked him if he wanted to stay, he woke up with a start and dashed off.

I was getting really worried now and, after thinking about it a lot, on Sunday morning I went round to my hairdresser's place to ask him to look after the albums for me. I wrapped them in a cloth, then put them in a paper bag from the supermarket. He had this really flash dressing-gown on, so I suppose he'd just got up, and he didn't seem all that cheerful, but of course he agreed to look after them.

"I shall cherish them, dear, treat them as my very own. If anything happens, they're the very first thing I shall rescue, I promise you. So don't you worry a teeny weeny bit. Bee's still asleep, dear. Young people do sleep a lot, don't they?"

I hadn't asked about Bee, but I suppose he just felt he had to tell me.

That evening the professor came with a camera.

"I've decided I need your present face if I'm to try to conjure up what it used to look like," he said, and took a number of shots. First face on, then profile, then front and profile again but this time with no make-up on. While I was posing, it struck me how deadly serious this had all become, so I tried to fool about a bit, with the result I just turned out looking gawky. He photographed me from the back as well. Well, I've never been taken from behind before. It was like being sucked into the camera. Made me feel creepy all over.

"I wish you'd hurry up and get those other photos," he said, sounding as if he didn't really believe they were at my mother's. So I gave him one taken the year before in a swimsuit, and said he'd have to made do with that for the time being.

Then two days later the caretaker paid a call early in the morning, saying there was something he had to talk to me about. His voice sounded quite different from usual, so I had him wait a bit and then opened the front door, and I was really amazed at what he told me. Late in the afternoon of the previous day he'd gone into the area round the back where there's a sort of shed with a coin-operated washing machine and clothes drier in it, and he saw a man just standing on the roof of the shed. The caretaker had left his ladder leaning against it, and the man must have climbed up that.

He called out to him, and the man came down and gave him his visiting card, and said he'd left something at my place and had come to get it but I was out and he was wondering if there wasn't some way in, and spied the ladder, but, well, afraid it wouldn't work, just have to give up the idea, never mind, don't bother yourself about it, etc., all spoken in a very cool, calm, and collected manner. Of course the card the caretaker showed me was the professor's. Can't have things like that going on, the caretaker had said, and the professor nodded and left. He admitted he was a very fine-looking gentleman, a university professor and all, and he thought he'd seen him once before, but he still felt I ought to be informed. Then he bowed and went away.

I don't know about a fine-looking gentleman, but it's true he didn't look all that bad. The director I'm going with now is a real flop in that respect. Looks awful. I'm ashamed to be seen walking down the street with him. Still, he's a very nice person.

Anyway, I felt really relieved he hadn't rung the police. Actually I only thought about that later. At the time I was so surprised I even forgot to thank him. I mean, the professor couldn't possibly have got in from there even if I was only up one flight of stairs. It was a good six feet from the roof of that shed. Just like a burglar, for heaven's sake! I could hardly believe it, and got so depressed I didn't feel like ringing his office to ask him what he thought he was doing.

I suppose he must have been feeling a bit awkward about it himself, because he didn't show up for a while, and I was just wondering what had happened to him when quite out of the blue the manager at my hairdresser's came to the flat. But he wouldn't come in, however much I asked, he just stood there in the entrance. He looked awful, with wrinkles at the corners of his eyes, hadn't shaved, and his trousers were all creased.

He hesitated a lot and then asked if Bee was there. I said he wasn't, and then he said, oh where can he have got to, and I thought he was going to burst into tears.

"What's happened? Are you on holiday today?"

"It's Bee. He's gone. Just a little while ago I began to think there must be something wrong, there must be. Yesterday at work he said he had a headache and was going home, but when I got back he wasn't anywhere. I've tried everywhere I could think of, but he's not there, so I thought I'd come and see if he might be here."

Really depressed he looked, so I said I was just thinking of making some coffee, but he only muttered and mumbled, so I said:

"Now don't you worry about it so much. He'll come back in a day or two. He's just young, you know. He wants to enjoy himself a bit, that's all."

But it was hopeless trying to cheer him up, and finally, with a sort of hollow groan, he said the situation was desperate, because Bee had left with all his belongings. Then, banging the door shut, he went away, though I tried to stop him.

What a business, I thought, and was watching television, wondering if I should make some proper coffee or just have instant instead, when back he comes again.

"Rika, I don't know what to say, I'm awfully sorry, really I am, but he went off with that paper bag of yours."

Bee is a real feather-brain, you know, and now he'd pushed off with my bag of photo albums instead of one with some of his own things in it. Well, it was such an unexpected thing to have happened I couldn't quite take it in at first, so I couldn't say much except things like "really" and "oh" because the words wouldn't come. The manager kept apologizing and bowing his head, and it ended up with me trying to buck him up, telling him he was bound to come back soon, and while I was doing this he went off —for good this time.

I breathed a sigh of relief, locked the door, and went back into the living room, made my coffee, turned down the television, and as I sat drinking the coffee I thought what a nuisance it all was. I mean, it was a bit more than a nuisance, really. But then suddenly it struck me that it wasn't a nuisance at all, it was a bit of incredibly good luck. Naturally I felt sorry for the manager, but that was just one of those things you can't do anything about: but I was really overjoyed those albums had disappeared somewhere, as if suddenly some huge weight had been taken off my mind. It was like Bee getting free of the manager: I was now free of my past. The fact is I was really sick to death of the person I'd been up till now, probably because the professor always bored me to tears by going on and on about it, although I just didn't like what I'd been as a child and at school anyway.

So I was watching the television where there was this big close-up of some tiny wild flowers blowing about in the wind and swaying to and fro, and I thought of my albums being thrown away with all the other rubbish, carrot peel, cabbage leaves, fish heads and bones, left-over rice, scraps of paper, and all the grey, fluffy stuff that comes out of vacuum cleaners, all loaded together into the rubbish truck and used to reclaim land in Tokyo Bay; and the rain fell on the new land and it turned into black earth and the birds brought seeds and there were lots of wild grasses and flowers, and it made me feel so happy. Silly, I know, mama, but you can see what I mean, can't you? I just felt so relieved.

But things didn't quite work out like that. The next week there was a holiday, and the professor suddenly paid a call and produced a large photograph. It was one of my graduation class at high school. Well, it was only a photocopy but exactly the same size. I was in the middle row a bit to the right, looking so bored I could die, with my face about the size of a pea.

He took off his ordinary glasses and put on his reading ones, and pointed at me and then at some freak and asked which of the two was me, and like a silly I said:

"This one, of course. You are awful. I know it's only small but surely you can tell?"

And I pointed to the real me, which was a mistake, I know, and I'd have been better off telling a lie, but it was harder saying good-bye to the old me than I thought it would be.

"That's the one I thought you were as well," he said. "As I'd imagined, you were a lovely girl without the operation."

I suppose he meant it as a compliment, but I was just thinking of the fix I was in, although the picture was so small you couldn't really make out anything, so I wasn't all that worried.

"But how did you manage to get hold of it?" I asked.

"By leaving not a single stone unturned," he said pompously and wouldn't tell me, behaving like a real tease. I said he must have met somebody who knew one of my class-mates, but he just made a silly mumbling sound in reply, and when I asked him again he made the same mumble, really irritating; and we were going on like that and looking at the photo when a special delivery came. I signed for it, thanked the man, came back into the room and opened the parcel in front of him without thinking—and what should it be but my two albums! There was a note from Bee with them.

I gave a little cry of surprise, but it was too late to do anything about it, because I could hardly hide them somewhere when he was insisting I showed them to him. So I gave in, but said I wouldn't look at them with him because the pictures were so embarrassing, and I'd read a magazine instead. So I went into the bedroom and lay on the bed. The suspense was awful, I could hear my heart beating. But in the end I decided if the worst came to the worst I could always apologize. I didn't care all that much.

About an hour passed, and then he came into the bedroom and suddenly stripped all my clothes off. When we'd finished, the first thing he said was:

"You had your lips made thinner, didn't you?"

When I knew he still didn't suspect a thing I did feel so relieved, but he'd been so athletic I just hadn't the energy to reply.

"The nostrils have been done extremely well. The eyelids could have been better," he murmured, moving his fingers over my face very gently as if he was handling a piece of broken crockery that had just been glued back together.

"I may be imagining things, but your face seems to have acquired a certain depth," he added, plus a few other flattering things. He was in a really good mood.

"There's nothing like a knowledge of the past for deepening one's emotional awareness of the present," he said in a very professor-like way, but I was so worn out I didn't say anything at all, just smiled back, sometimes looking all sort of prim when I wasn't smiling. The things I'd been worried about, like his asking me exactly which pictures had been taken before and after the operation, and why there weren't any of me as a model, I got round in the same way.

Then he said he'd take me out to eat at a French restaurant, and he rang up to reserve a table, and then we went. Up to now we'd usually eaten Chinese, or sometimes Italian, but never French, so he must have been feeling in a particularly good mood. Even ordered a bottle of expensive wine. I thought some-

thing special must have happened to cheer him up, and I was
right. A religious group in Tokyo that was in competition with
the one in Izu he was working for had talked him into coming over onto their side. They said he was just the man for the
job. Same sort of work, of course—thinking work—but this time
it was making up theories that would really mess them up in Izu.
Apparently people in that kind of business get really worked up
about things like that. It was the new group who'd found my
graduation photo for him.

"Well, they said they'd do absolutely anything for me, so I
thought I'd try them on that. Not very seriously, of course. They
soon got hold of it. Nothing like the power of the organization."
He seemed genuinely impressed as he drank his martini. "Naturally that put me under an obligation to them, and I could hardly
turn them down. So it's all your fault, you see."

Well I liked that! Making me responsible. Why didn't he ask
them for something worth a bit more?

When the hors-d'oeuvre came he asked me if I knew about
angels—the things with wings, for heaven's sake—as if he
thought I didn't. So I told him, with a smile of course as I was
eating my pâté, that I did because there was one on Morinaga
chocolates and things, and did he think I was ignorant or
something? Anyway, the point was that at first they didn't have
wings, so he said, and that was awkward because it said in the Bi-
ble that when the messenger of the Lord came down on some er-
rand or to deliver the word or whatnot, people didn't know it was
an angel and always asked him, "Who art thou?" If he'd had wings,
then people would have known straight away, wouldn't they?
Anyway, that's how we know those angels didn't have wings but
just looked like ordinary people. It was only later on, in paintings
and sculptures, that they started floating about in the sky. He said
that was the influence of Greek sculpture and the religions of
the East. There's a statue of some goddess in the Louvre, the

something Victory of somewhere, which hasn't got a head but just these huge great wings.

That's what he said, so I asked him if it was the same with Japanese spirits who had magic feather cloaks so they could fly, and he said it could be considered similar if one took a broad view of the matter, but they were Indian really anyway.

"What it means is that, behind every angel with wings there's a divine messenger without them, and then behind him a heavenly spirit with a feathered cloak. In the same way, behind the face you have now there's the face you had before your operation, and behind that the one you had as a baby. Well, it's not quite the same, perhaps," he said, and smiled.

I felt terribly flattered hearing that because I thought it meant I looked like an angel, but when I thought about it afterwards it doesn't have to mean that at all, does it? Still, I was feeling really happy as I drank my wine, and he was smiling away as he drank his, so I thought this was a good time to ask him something I'd always wanted to know.

"Which religion do you believe in yourself?"

"Well, that's a very tricky question, Rika; one I've decided never to answer, no matter who asks me. Our job as theologians, as students of religious ideas, is to give a helping hand to whatever religion we happen to be studying, and to understand the point of view of the religious believer, in whatever time or place; and then to consider all in the light of philosophical theory."

That's what he said. Get it? Well, I didn't, but I suppose he was probably right about it really.

"The thing is you've got to try your best to make believe you believe," he went on, and I'd no idea what I ought to reply so I said:

"But you try your best at everything, don't you? Look at that business with my photos."

He thought about what I'd said, then nodded, and he must

42

have been pleased with my reply because he said he'd raise my allowance by half. He ought to have done it ages ago, of course, and since he hadn't been giving me much to start with it didn't mean all that much more, but it did make a difference, I'll admit.

Still, about six months later, when I hadn't seen him for a while and thought he must have gone off on a trip somewhere, I rang up his office and was told he wasn't working at the university any more. Well, I was taken aback, I can tell you; and then an air-mail letter arrived from Germany saying it had all happened very suddenly but he'd signed a two-year contract at a place there, and that the religious group he'd been working for kept on at him about the stupidest things, so he'd broken off with them, and in fond memory of our friendship he was sending me something he'd bought in Paris. Very difficult handwriting to read. I suppose it never crossed his mind to give me any separation money. It wouldn't have, of course; that was just like him.

While I was wondering what the present was—a handbag, perhaps, or something even better—it took such a long time to arrive I began to think, ah hah, he's sent it by sea. I was right, too—economizing again—and when I opened it up I thought he must have been trying to pull my leg. All it was was just one big photograph, a statue with enormous wings stuck on its shoulders, probably that goddess something in the Louvre. It seemed a pity just to stick it away somewhere, so I took it to a shop and had it framed, then hung it on the wall. It doesn't look bad at all, really. If you ever have a very nice dream, mama, I'll buy it off you with my picture, if you like.

TREE
SHADOWS

1

Just before the Kasumigaseki exit on the Tokyo expressway there's a view of which I'm particularly fond, although it's not the sort of thing that other people, perhaps, would even notice. Normally I approach it from the Meguro interchange, since I live in that part of the world, and round about the Iigura tunnel I get myself ready, gazing expectantly to the left when the three-hundred-yard exit sign for Kasumigaseki appears. The steep bank behind the Prime Minister's house presents a large expanse of grey concrete as background to a row of ginkgo trees. It's this that I've been waiting for.

What appeals to me is the combination of that background and those trees. Neither the trees nor the concrete wall are anything remarkable in themselves. They are, after all, the kind of trees you can see by the side of any road. It must be the extraordinary clarity with which they are outlined against so plain a background that I find so compelling. They please me most under a strong sun when their shadows are projected straight onto the concrete, and yet other times and seasons, when the shadows are only faint or thrown sideways, still have their attractions. Even on cloudy days, when there are no shadows, I can still feel some satisfaction in the thought that they are really there in the deeper grey of the background. The view only lasts a few seconds, but this perhaps is all to the good, for it produces a sense of the fugitive almost painful in its intensity. Although that whole area, the hub of governmental power, has nothing to do with me, being something I merely glance at as I hurry by on the expressway, the existence of that bank and the trees has given it an importance it would otherwise not have had.

I have always been attracted by the shadows of trees, though I would find it hard to explain why. Shadows cast on the ground arouse no particular emotion, even if I don't actually dislike them. It's the vertical shadow that moves me, especially a whole group of them thrown by an avenue of trees, thrown upon a wall. Something profound is stirred in me, a sense of the inconsolable, of some lost home to which I'll never return, yet apprehended with pleasure almost, a deep warmth. The wall itself has to be quite blank, preferably of a weak, negative colour; any form of pattern totally alters the effect. I particularly dislike buildings with lots of windows, surfaces of variegated brick, and am completely put off by those white lines left in concrete when repair work has been carried out. A blank, indifferent surface is best: a view of trees projecting their long shadows onto its wide emptiness seems to reaffirm for me the solitude of all created things, for what truly belongs to any object is only the shadow it casts.

Reflections in mirrors or in water move me little, although I've no great objection to them. Some might think it strange to consider both sets of images as the same type of thing, claiming that there's something quite different about the rich foliage of trees reflected, not in water but, for example, in the glass wall of a large building in the centre of the city, where the effect is of the trees actually growing there inside the building. But though I can see what they mean, I still have to admit that such images leave me fairly cold. What I require is the black pattern created by strong light held back by trees, and this can be sunlight or moonlight, or even the light of a street lamp; and since one can rarely see this cast over a wide, unpatterned surface, I've learnt to find pleasure in only a limited area of shadow, or even in something very faint thrown on a surface already confused by the artificial, multi-coloured shadings of other objects.

Once I was staying in a hotel in Tsurugadai trying to get on with some writing, and when I'd more or less finished it I went for a walk late at night; and I remember being cheered up considerably by the sight of some tree shadows that had virtually soaked into the wall of the nearby school. The view of a row of trees reflected starkly on the wall of our local petrol station has often soothed my slightly bleary eyes on returning home half tight from Ginza. Another rather good one is the shadow of a pine tree on a bank reinforced by large stones in the garden of a biggish house, seen on a slope in Meguro during a pre-breakfast walk; but it requires the early morning sun, so I rarely encounter it. Another of these early morning displays is near our local park, the shadow of a zelkova tree on the white wall of a fairly wretched four-storey building, with a cheap restaurant and coffee shop on the ground floor, and a number of quilts hanging out of various windows to spoil the view. Then at night, on getting out of the taxi, I can always see the shadow of the arbutus in front of where I live, or at least that of the lower half of the trunk and the few leaves on it, thrown on the wall by a low light concealed in the shrubbery. Every time I'm confronted with one of these scenes, it almost takes my breath away; I stand rooted to the spot, and have to tell myself that I can't hang around all day looking at things like this before I finally manage to move away. So great is my obsession that the usual admiration for massive, ancient trees hardly affects me; whenever I look up at one, or even at just a photograph, I'm struck by a sense of lack. What I want is some huge backcloth towering up into the sky to show me its giant shadow.

Since I'm the victim of what must be a rare obsession, I should be in an excellent position to do some solid research into the fascinating question of why I have it; but I can never think of any reason at all. My father certainly didn't share it, nor have I suffered from anything like the death of a favourite dog, for instance, when, through a veil of tears, I suddenly became aware of a landscape with tree shadows in it. I have no recollection of ever having admired a painting of that kind, either. I can, for example, recall having an adolescent enthusiasm for the Parisian scenes of Utrillo, and I had a passion for his prints, which now seem to me merely incompetently crude. But at the very height of this craze, just after the war, when I went to two Utrillo exhibitions and also borrowed an enormous volume of the paintings, I don't believe I once came across any work of his with tree shadows in it. I'm told there are various famous scenes in films which make skilful use of this motif, but these all seem to be in masterpieces I happen to have missed. It's true that about a dozen years ago we used to have lace curtains in the living room with a tree pattern on them, and at dusk they threw what looked like the shadows of an avenue of trees upon the wallpaper; but these curtains had been chosen by my wife, who was well aware of this taste of mine, so they can only be considered a result, not a cause, of it.

Although I seem, then, to be unable to say where the obsession comes from, I should at least be able to say when it started, but even on this point I'm only very vague. I have tried, for example, to pin it down by asking myself if I had it in my early teens, but can't remember with any certainty. This isn't only the case with this particular question, since I've been feeling for some time now that I have pretty bad recall about almost everything; so probably the only thing I can do is try to work out, by the use of basic, theoretical principles, why I should have it. My reasoning then goes as follows.

The tree, as a totally natural phenomenon, rejects all attempts to conventionalize it, to reduce it to one basic form, and since I am a person whose principal concern is with imposing forms upon experience; trees are unable to provide me with total satisfaction in themselves. But when it comes to the shadow, we have an immediate elimination of all those irrelevant natural details, as the excrescences, the various bends and contortions the tree itself has, are straightened out when the light cast on them removes or exaggerates such aspects in complete conformity with the demands of the background on which the shadow is thrown, ignoring all differences of coloration, all irregularities, reducing it to a single, uniform quantity over which one colour alone has been applied. In other words, an artificiality is conferred on it, bringing it closer to the state of an artefact, and thereby arousing more powerfully the emotions of the beholder. Consequently it is a compromise phenomenon, a work of nature which is yet unnatural, a work of art which is still only partially contrived or not even one at all, and it is this peculiar status which appeals to me.

The obvious lyrical approach to the matter won't work, however; or at least it's a mistake to concentrate only on the imprecise, suggestive nature of the object. The attraction of a tree's shadow is not in its being feebler and more transitory than the tree itself. That may be an aspect of it, but it is certainly nothing like the whole. What matters is that the essential nature of the tree is more directly revealed as a result of this process, in much the same way as the stone columns and foundations of a ruin seem to clarify the basic reality of the original building. Ruins are, indeed, another midway stage, an intermediary between the worlds of nature and of art.

Now, even if ratiocination of this kind is considered acceptable, it remains so abstracted and generalized as to be far from providing any insight into the history of my personality as revealed in what is, after all, only a mild tendency of mine. It ignores, for example, the vital questions of why such shadows when cast on the ground should not move me, and why a row of trees should have so powerful an effect. Despite the fact that the above remarks are, indeed, my own, I must admit they strike even me as being slightly devious, an evasion of the main issues. I can't see that they give any proper theoretical account of why trees reflected in water should necessarily be irrelevant, either. Obviously a more adequate explanation would require a descent into the unconscious regions of my past, but I lack the leisure for such a quest, nor do I readily possess the means to do so, and doubt if I could find them anyway. So I can only conclude that no answer will ever be forthcoming, and that the question probably wasn't worth bothering with in the first place, assuring myself that life itself constantly presents us with minor problems of a kind that permit no conclusive interpretation. This is a conviction I have been obliged to accept so often in the past that it now comes easily to me.

One can, of course, argue that it's precisely this sort of mental irritant which provides the impetus for the creation of fiction, and, considering my profession, it wouldn't be odd if it did so in my case. I did, in fact, once spend a considerable amount of time over this, and even managed to create the outline of a story in my head. That I was finally unable to write the thing out should not be put down to sheer laziness, however, for I was just about to do so, some ten or twelve years ago, when I came across a translation of a short story, I think by Nabokov, which appeared to be almost identical in plot. So I abandoned mine, reflecting as I did so that I seemed to be doomed in many ways to following in other people's footsteps rather than forging ahead on my own.

To make a tendency of this kind serve as an excuse for the paucity of my literary production may invite the charge of eccentricity, but there have been a number of similar instances in my life. The case of the bow tie is one of them. I have always liked bow ties, and sometimes go to gatherings wearing one (to the disdain of the literary fraternity). Unfortunately I can't tie one myself, and have to get my wife to do it for me. I remember once having to go to Nagoya by myself to attend a relative's wedding, and after breakfast I decided to get in a little practice, managing to tie it with such proficiency at the first attempt that I was reluctant to undo it, and left it like that until the wedding at three o'clock. In fact it only became untied in a bar late that night when some malevolent drunkard did me this service, and I had to ask the bartender to retie it for me. But it was the first time he'd ever tied anyone else's, and he found it surprisingly difficult.

Now, it is an elementary truth about the writing of fiction that minor details like this can lead to its most striking effects, and I wasn't such a fool as to allow this particular opportunity to go by. Immediately I imagined a story beginning with a man who is unable to knot his own bow tie and who spends the night with another woman. In the morning he stands before her to have it tied (as was his custom with his wife), and when she tells him she can't he is astonished. Well, I had got the opening worked out, but before I had time to develop it I came across a story by Edna O'Brien which uses that very scene as a turning point halfway through, so I had to abandon it. No doubt some of my readers will know the story in question, so I shall refrain from inflicting any further account of it on them here, giving instead the more relevant plot, as I vaguely recall it, of the short story I thought was written by Nabokov which has tree shadows as its motif.

The hero of this tale is a middle-aged Russian emigré writer who experiences an extraordinary excitement whenever he sees the shadow of a tree on a wall. For a long time he has been concerned as to why he should have this tendency, or habit, but is unable to arrive at any answer. Then various things occur (all of which I've completely forgotten), and after many years of wandering about Europe and America he eventually, for some reason I am also unable to recall, manages to revisit the house in which he was born in Russia, and enters the bedroom he'd used as a child. Before he goes to sleep some impulse makes him open the window, and there what should he behold but a tree bathed in moonlight (in fact it may have been a number of trees, shone upon by the light in the room), casting a clear shadow on the wall.

He understands that the cause of his obsession is this view so often seen during his childhood.

I wish I could be more precise than this but, as I've already said, I have an unreliable memory, finding poetry almost impossible to learn by heart and soon confusing the plots of novels and plays. Since this has often caused me considerable embarrassment in the past, and perhaps as a result of the accumulated surprise and resentment aroused thereby, in this particular instance I am positive I gave the work a careful reading (I'm fairly sure I read it twice), and my subsequent vagueness about it is especially vexing, even if the sense of irritation can only be directed at myself.

Naturally I tried to get hold of the work in order to refresh my memory. That would have been some years ago. When, however, I looked in the volume of short stories where I felt sure it was, I couldn't find it. It wasn't in any other collection either. I then checked briefly through a few volumes in English, and again there was nothing. So, through a friend of mine, I inquired of the translator (as I thought he was), but he replied quite flatly that not only had he never translated any such story but he'd never read it either, although he did add that the plot certainly sounded very Nabokov-like. I was now finding the whole business very strange indeed, but I took heart from that final remark and decided I did have the name of the author right even if I couldn't find the actual story; which only demonstrates, I suppose, how much my confidence in my own judgement had been shaken.

I tried (this time directly) another two people who had translated Nabokov, but they knew of no such work, and suggested I might be thinking of something by some other writer. Consequently I asked another friend, a man widely acquainted with the contemporary foreign novel, but he also had no recollection of any work with such a plot. Finally, having been to two or three bookshops and gone through all the Nabokov I hadn't read so far, and still finding nothing, I began to wonder whether I might not, in fact, have dreamt the whole thing up myself.

This isn't so unlikely as it might seem. A plot only half conceived in the waking state could well have worked itself out while I was asleep, and its completed form would then have appeared as a given, and thus the work of someone else. Having decided I was remembering the story rather than creating it, seeing it as something already read, I would abandon my own writing of it. I know there's something slightly comic about all this, and it makes me look rather a fool; but if one does take the literary tradition seriously and, in particular, values the innovator, the one who makes it new, the one who does something first, then my reaction, even if misguided, isn't at all unlikely, and can hardly be dismissed as a theoretical impossibility.

One interesting thing about this is that, were it the normal kind of literary anecdote, it would take the form, for example, of encountering one of the dead in a dream and receiving, say, a poem gratis, or at least some additions to a work of one's own. Or one might write a poem in one's sleep but find it incomplete on waking up and be unable to finish it. In other words, one would actually gain something while dreaming, whereas my case was quite the opposite, for I seemed to have mislaid a work of my own while asleep.

When the idea that this had been a dream first crossed my mind, it was only a vague suspicion, and my immediate response had been just to ignore it. But as time went by, my resistance began to weaken until I reached a state of only semi-doubt; meaning, of course, that I half believed it, too. Probably the main reason for this was that one large feature of the plot was very hard to accept, and for me this counted as more conclusive evidence than the fact that I couldn't actually find the work itself in any book.

The problem was this. It is commonly accepted that the exiled Nabokov deeply regretted the demise of imperial Russia and retained a profound longing for the vanished paradise of his childhood. This is why the principal theme of his writing can be seen as a superior version of the Peter Pan complex. Yet he never once attempted to go back home. Certainly this was because he wouldn't have been allowed to anyway, but the fact remains. The hero of the story in question, however, who seems to be a fairly distinguished emigré novelist, does return. He goes to the room in which he had slept as a child and opens the window. Now, Nabakov must have been aware, given the nature of his profession, that in his own case the likelihood of this was precisely nil. The prospect that presumably confronts the hero of the story, the returned exile, is a system of censorship crueller than anything that existed under the old regime, reflecting crude literary tastes still firmly rooted in the nineteenth-century bourgeois tradition, and simple-minded ideas of social realism which deny the existence of Proust, Joyce, and Kafka; an oppressive consensus maintained by authoritarian bureaucracy working through the medium of a rigid Writers' Union. Simply to accept such conditions would require a remarkable change of heart, yet even if this took place the hoped-for renewal could hardly be expected to go all that well. Presumably he wouldn't be able to publish any fiction in any form. All he could hope for would be to have his works read via circulation in manuscript, and since no individual was allowed any kind of duplicating machine in the Soviet Union, a writer of his seriousness would have to use masses of carbon paper whenever he sat at the typewriter. Obviously it would be quite different in the case of a writer who was naturally conformist and had happily sworn allegiance to the Stalinist regime, but it's unthinkable that Nabokov should have chosen such a figure as the hero of any story of his.

Now, we might assume that my memory could have been at fault, and that the central character was not a novelist or man of letters but, say, some kind of scientist, a technician, or even an astronomer perhaps. Being a member of such a profession, he would be much less inclined to come into conflict with the authorities. But, though it isn't entirely inconceivable that a person like this should be preoccupied with the way tree shadows have always deeply impressed him, it has a degree of improbability about it that would offend most readers, and is surely unsatisfactory from the purely technical point of view. It seems most unlikely that a writer like Nabokov would have made use of such an inconveniently employed hero. I don't want to imply by this that he was inordinately fond of writing novels about literary and artistic people (even though he certainly was), but that he was a novelist who aimed at clear, even exaggerated effects.

Consequently, if this novelist hero is to return to Russia under the Stalinist regime, a number of conditions have to be met and explanations made, and Nabokov did not make them. Or perhaps he did, and I've forgotten. The whole trouble with this kind of speculation is that it ignores the fact of the inadequacy of my memory. Even so, since the work appears to be deficient in a number of aspects, is it at all plausible that Nabokov could have written anything like it? Its very incompetence suggests that some other, inferior Russian emigré writer was its author, but it would then be very odd indeed if I had confused Nabokov with someone like that, mainly because, not being a great reader, I'm insufficiently acquainted with such literature to have done so.

Taking all this into consideration, I was obliged to conclude that the whole thing had indeed been a dream, and that the various lacunae and abbreviations in my remembered account of the novelist's home-coming were quite unsuited to the logical structure of created fiction, yet showed all the caprice, the flights of fancy, that we associate with the fantasizing capacities of the mind set free in the world of sleep. So far I have failed to come across anything that contradicts this conclusion. It must all, in fact, have been a dream. Thus one short story by Vladimir Nabokov has vanished from my particular world, and you could well say it has been lost to the world of literature as a whole.

The only way I can see of objecting to the process by which I've arrived at this conclusion (although it still leaves me personally quite unshaken in my faith in it) would be to question my motive for reaching it; and the argument does have, I admit, a certain attraction. When it first occurred to me, indeed, I was half inclined to go along with it. It maintains that all my reasonings are founded on the desire that the story in outline should remain mine and not someone else's. This is certainly feasible, for it means my encounter with the work by Nabokov resulted in a reworking of it inside my own head, and this recent desire of mine to write something about tree shadows has led to my seeking out Nabokov's short story for comparative purposes. Thus my denial of its existence now, by the use of some dubious argumentation, is purely for my own convenience.

I hope, however, the story I am about to write down will not be considered an act of plagiarism, even if there should exist another work by somebody that bears certain resemblances to it. The fact that I'm prepared to take that risk is, I suppose, an indication of the way this predetermined tale weighs upon my mind, of the obligation I feel to write it out just to get rid of it. The whole thing has become a heavy burden, and I shall only be able to lower it from my shoulders when I reach the destination that awaits it, namely its completed written form. I expect to achieve some kind of emotional release in the process; although I also still have a very slight hope that one of my readers may be able to tell me of that other work, the one it resembles, the one I didn't write, and perhaps did not dream, either.

Furuya Ippei was born in 1909 in a town on the northern sea coast of west Japan. He was the third son of the principal local landowner. The eldest son of the family went into government service, managing to rise to the rank of under-secretary in one of the ministries, and then worked as president of a number of public companies before dying some ten years ago. The second son became a doctor and, after teaching at two or three universities, was made director of a large hospital in Fukuoka but died suddenly just after taking up the appointment. There were also two younger sisters who married into other households and, since none of the sons remained at home, the family house no longer exists. The neighbouring town extended its boundaries, and where the house once used to be is now a supermarket which caters mainly to a nearby housing complex for public employees of various kinds.

This third son of the Furuya family studied French at a university in Tokyo, after which he worked first in the publicity department of a film company, then as a journalist, a teacher of French at a private university, and in the editorial section of an extra-departmental government organization; all the while writing novels and criticism. Before the war he had a certain reputation as a writer, but he was unable to make a living by his pen until the post-war period. In terms of age he has to be considered a writer of the thirties, but he hardly fits into any of the categories that implies, nor does he obviously belong to any post-war school either. He has always been more or less outside the literary mainstream, but this has not prevented his being recognized for his distinctive style, and he is now respected as a grand old man of letters, still very much alive. A thirteen-volume collected works came out about fifteen years ago, and an enlarged twenty-volume edition appeared some ten years later.

It is difficult to find any single adjective that describes the way he writes. One critic has compared his style to that in vogue towards the end of the last century before naturalism took over the literary world. Another, in a book-length critical study, has stressed the ideological nature of his work, seeing him as a writer of the "social novel of ideas", although this is clearly a misreading of Sartre's dictum that the *roman à thèse* should also be a *roman de moeurs,* an idea misunderstood to the extent that he even referred to Furuya as an existentialist writer. This really won't do at all, for the tone of his novels has nothing whatsoever to do with the depressed atmosphere enveloping that post-war Parisian world. The American translator of one of his novels and a collection of short stories has made the wild claim that Furuya's writing is closer to Chinese than Japanese literature, a throwaway remark which was taken seriously enough by a Japanese critic for him to compare the novels to certain works of the Edo period that were heavily influenced by Chinese moralistic fiction (*All Men Are Brothers* in particular); but the result has been to place an excessive emphasis on the social aspects of his books, which are not really all that important. In an interview for a newspaper, Furuya himself maintained that he was writing in the broad mainstream of the novel as exemplified by the masterpieces of the eighteenth century (both East and West), though it is important to stress the fact that statements of that kind are essentially evasive in intent, even if this particular one may give some indication of what he really thought he was up to as a writer.

He has written some ten novels. The most famous of these is about the daughter of a family that runs an old-fashioned restaurant in Nagoya, who becomes a film actress, then the mistress in turn of a Western-style painter, a soldier, and a businessman, before turning into a gangster's moll, then a sensational success as a poet who uses traditional verse forms to express a most unbecoming eroticism, and eventually a professional writer who gets arrested for shop-lifting and dies in a traffic accident. Things take an even odder turn at that point, for she is transformed into a river salmon (a young, female one, all shiny and transparent) which grows up and finds its way to the sea. That is the basic plot of a book which in length is perhaps more a longish novella than an actual novel. If one omits the transmigration bit at the end (or even includes it, perhaps) the work is very reminiscent of Defoe (particularly *Moll Flanders*) and also of Saikaku's *The Woman Who Loved Love*, so that Furuya's remark about having learnt his trade from the eighteenth-century novel in both Asia and Europe does seem to make perfectly good sense. I have also heard it rumoured that the book is currently being re-evaluated as a specimen of feminist criticism (or a critique of feminism, I'm not quite sure which).

Among his critical writings perhaps the most typical is his *Akinari or Norinaga?*, which sets the erotic fiction of the former against the morally concerned scholarship of the latter as two aspects of the same eighteenth-century world. It was what one might call a highly imaginative contribution to the critical debate that was going on about those two at the time, and opens with the apparently significant aphorism that "there are some truths that can only be expressed in the form of a joke". From start to finish he takes Akinari's side, though still managing to display much more respect for Norinaga than was fashionable then. Last year a certain young critic said the book reminded him of similar writings by Borges, since in both cases it was difficult to work out if one should treat them as fictional or critical in intent, and one sympathizes with his dilemma. Personally I find it closer to some of Oscar Wilde's work, and perhaps it is best to see both Borges and Furuya as fellow disciples who have drunk at the same wellhead: an Anglo-Irish critic who was very much *fin-de-siècle*.

In one corner of Furuya's library there are about thirty volumes of scrap-books which fulfill not only the normal functions of a scrap-book but include diary entries, outlines of some of his works, and various comments about them and other things. Opening a volume at random, one dating from ten years ago, say, you first come across a photograph of a Mayan girl in a grass-coloured dress, smoking. The blue smoke drifts across her forehead and hair, completely hiding her right eye, while the other looks severely at the camera. The next item is another photograph, of a woodcut by Itō Shinsui dated 1921 and entitled "Woman in Under-Sash". The woman, a geisha, is wearing a long, white, flowing garment, and is adjusting her hair—probably just after having sex. Then there's an offset lithograph poster for an American dance company, or rather a colour photograph of it cut out of a magazine; it shows a light blue chair which has been stood upside-down, and above it a painting of another chair, black this time and the right way up, on a light blue background in a bluish green frame. This is followed by a number of cuttings from newspapers about a large sum of money found abandoned by somebody on Circular Road 7. There is also a magazine article on the same subject, which hasn't been pasted but just stapled in. Three epigraphs on the nature of money have been written in pencil. Also in pencil is a Chinese poem by Ryōkan, with some fairly arbitrary interpretative footnotes of his own. Then, written in fountain pen, come various schemes for making money, followed by a long article cut out of an English Sunday newspaper entitled "Why Do Men Sleep with Prostitutes?" The author is a woman, but Furuya has scribbled on it, "This was written by a man." On the next page we find the outline of an erotic short story in ball pen crossed out with a large X. The writing has faded, making it very hard to read; only the large cross in red pencil is brilliantly clear. Then comes a photograph of a fossilized shrimp of the Mesozoic era: a long-mustachioed, cheese-coloured shrimp swimming smartly through a cheese-coloured sea. A label off a wine bottle has a fairly long description of the state of drunkenness appended beneath it, in fountain pen. Another photograph shows a Chinese maker of *shinko* (rice flour) figures sitting by the wayside: —an old man wearing a balaclava helmet. He is making figures of characters from the novel *Monkey*: "Monkey" is one of them; another is someone fishing with a very relaxed look on his face, a fine white fish the size of his leg dangling from his line.

Since the beginning of the year, the old writer had got into the habit of frequently taking down these scrap-books. They were covered in dust and the dust made him sneeze, but he didn't let that bother him because he was looking for a photograph he was sure he had pasted in one of these scrap-books somewhere. It was a picture cut out of a French magazine, of the shadow of a tree, and it had been accompanied by a second-rate poem. It showed, in black and white, an apple tree (perhaps some other kind) with its shadow cast on the wall of a country grange, and he could clearly remember carefully cutting it out and trying to remove all trace of the poem. Of course, he could just have cut it out and forgotten to paste it in, for it didn't seem to be anywhere.

He wanted to have another look at it because he was struggling with a novel, the subplot of which dealt with a case of adultery. The hero (university professor of Latin American literature, Marxist, pederast) has a cousin who works for a trading company (quite brilliant at his job), and his friend is a photographer who works mostly for women's magazines and goes abroad a lot on commissions. The businessman becomes intimate with the photographer's wife, though obviously the photographer is supposed to know nothing about it; and since he knows nothing about it, what could be more natural than that he should invite his friend to drop in at his new cottage in Karuizawa, as the latter has to go to that part of the world to attend a business seminar? So the businessman stays the night. The next afternoon, he takes some snaps of the married couple with his cheap little camera, and the wife takes some of the two men; and finally the photographer says he'll just take one of his wife and the businessman—all this done with the same cheap little camera, and all, of course, purely for fun. The photographer has to fly off to Holland, and two days later the adulterous pair are together in a hotel in central Tokyo. In due course, the businessman produces the pictures he has just picked up from the developers. They look through them: one of Mt. Asama, one of the childish romp at the end-of-seminar party, the company president singing, Mt. Asama again, then the shots of the married couple; and they've all come out beautifully. Then there are those of the two men smiling happily, but there is no picture of the photographer's wife and the businessman. Instead they find one photo which shows a tree's shadow thrown onto a wall. It's the shadow of the tall silver birch directly behind the photographer when he took the picture. The shadow is like smoke, like a stain. How could this possibly have happened? How could a professional photographer have made this kind of blunder? Or was it a blunder? Perhaps the tree shadow is meant to be telling them something. The two people in bed together look at each other, and search for words to conceal their growing anxiety.

For Furuya, everything had begun with the mythological image of someone being transformed, not into a tree, but into the shadow of one; and this he had translated in terms of a photograph that ought to feature two people but only shows a tree's shadow. Since this functions as a revelation of the fact of adultery, the existence of the three fictional characters can be said to have developed from that single image. As he had sometimes experienced the same kind of imaginative process in himself before, he felt no need to regard it with any sort of suspicion. He knew that the key to his book lay in this photograph, that a photo showing nothing but a shadow world would, if properly scrutinized, indicate how his fiction was to continue. His in-

64

volvement in his plot, in the lives of these three people with whom he was simultaneously living, was also an investigation of his own relationship with tree shadows; and while he was struggling with this question he suddenly remembered the picture he'd cut out of that magazine.

But it was nowhere to be found. Yet the very fact that he couldn't see it with his own eyes made the image in his mind's eye even more vivid and precise, and as his nostalgia for this phantom apple (?) tree deepened he realized that his preoccupation with tree shadows was no recent thing, but something he'd always had. There was that time fifteen years ago, for example, in Bangkok.

He had been asked by a newspaper to take a trip to France and Scandinavia, though he'd forgotten why this should have meant a stopover in Thailand. Perhaps it was because the journalist who went with him had some business at the Bangkok office, and he'd agreed to go with him because it was an Asian country he had never visited. On the first night after they'd flown in from Hong Kong they were invited out to dinner by the bureau chief, and went on to a bar afterwards where Furuya seems to have got fairly drunk. He walked down the stairs from the bar out into the hot, steamy night air, and on the road outside noticed that the street lamps were casting shadows of the wayside trees onto a long grey wall. Somehow this created the illusion that he was in Kyoto, and he felt an urge to telephone a woman he'd known there some years ago (she would still be under forty), so he asked the journalist if he could see a red public telephone anywhere (the kind that litter the streets of Japanese towns). The man looked at him very hard for a moment, then began laughing and reminded him that they were in Thailand, in Bangkok. Furuya also burst out laughing, though the bureau chief agreed that the bar district here did look very like its Japanese equivalents.

The novelist (then in his late fifties) silently observed the leaves of what seemed to be willow trees, but it was the way their shadows blurred against the wall that really held his attention. The street lamps that provided the light were perfectly placed for this purpose, and when the occasional, almost imperceptible breeze stirred the air it moved the shadows of the leaves with a gentle, wave-like motion, forwards then backwards again. There was a slight rippling in places, like the movement of the folds and wrinkles of *crêpe de Chine*.

Eventually, at the urging of his two companions, he moved off into the partial darkness of the city night, although he felt a deep, inexplicable regret at having to leave. Perhaps it was a regret for Kyoto, for the woman left there; but it seemed more a simple desire to stand and watch those shadows for a little longer. . . .

Then what about that time when there was all that fuss over the amateur theatricals? Yes, he had suddenly remembered, and it was as if he were looking far off now, farther than Thailand, farther than India.

It was towards the end of August 1945. He was an old soldier (mid-thirties, private first class) stationed at Divisional Headquarters in an obscure part of southern Kyushu. He had only been called up at the beginning of that year, and people seemed to feel rather sorry for him, so he was mainly entrusted with tasks such as censoring the mail and handling the C.O.'s personal correspondence. Although the war had been lost, there was no hope of any immediate demobilization, and H.Q. had decided that one of its functions would be to provide the troops with stage entertainments in order to keep them from getting too bored. They had two professional actors in their ranks, as well as a teacher of traditional dance, and Furuya as the resident writer was asked to prepare a script. And a very odd thing it turned out to be.

The boss of a gambling racket, played by one of the professional actors (heavy Western-style drama), sets out on a journey taking with him his mistress (played by the teacher of dance) and one of his underlings, played by the other professional actor (traditional light comedy); but the boss is such a tyrant the underling feels he has had about all he can take and withdraws his pledge of loyalty. Then, just as he's about to leave, the mistress calls him back, begging him to take her with him, since she claims to have always loathed the boss, and only unavoidable circumstances had obliged her to give herself to him. The underling is delighted to hear this, confessing that he's been crazy about her for years. This leads to some fairly pantomimic slapping and tickling, and then to some more serious clinching and groping which almost goes the whole way. The underling swears he will now go straight, being ready to endure poverty in a poor hut with bamboo pillars, thatched roof, and the other trappings of the simple life. Whereupon the mistress turns all snooty, saying there seems to have been a misunderstanding and she hasn't the faintest intention of doing anything of the kind, since a brief life and a merry one, short but sweet, is her motto; and she dashes off after making this announcement. The two men are left nonplussed, gaping at each other and bringing down the curtain with the line, "Well, did you ever?"

That was the sketch as such and, despite its dramatic limitations, so remarkable was the performance of the dance teacher as the mistress (the clothes had been borrowed from the mayor's house where he was billeted, and some form of thick face powder had been found somewhere) that the whole thing was a great success, and a special ration of saké was issued that evening. Unfortunately this resulted in the actor who'd played the gambling boss turning ugly.

It began with a few roundabout complaints concerning the inadequacy of his part, which led to some criticism of the script itself, and culminated in his insisting that the whole play was an attempt to mock his Celestial Majesty, being an allegory in which the gambling boss was the Emperor, and the mistress and underling represented the common people. So carried away was he that the dance teacher, the other actor, the office worker in charge of wardrobe and stage properties, and the primary school teacher who had made the wigs out of newspaper, had their hands full trying to calm him down, with the result that finally they all trooped off to a small shrine next door to the mayor's house. Furuya went too, making his way by the pale light of the moon, and he had just begun to wonder whether it wasn't all part of some rivalry for the dance teacher's love (homosexual, of course), when he was suddenly caught in the bright beam of the duty officer's torch. The latter was doing his rounds, wearing no sword, since they'd already surrendered all their weapons, but still clearly the duty officer, and so one and all saluted him. He returned the salute and asked them what they thought they were up to. Furuya felt himself in the sudden grip of nervous tension, for this officer was a fanatic who was still crazy about the Emperor, and if *he* got in on the act the criticism of his play might take a very unpleasant turn indeed. Luckily the office worker replied quite calmly that they were all here for serious reflection on the success or otherwise of today's dramatic activities, whereupon the patriot praised the performance to the skies, saying what a splendid sketch it had been, chuckling happily at the thought of it and even making a dirty joke before suggesting they could all do with an early night. He then slowly faded away from them, flashing his torch to left and right as he continued his specious inspection of the stiflingly hot yet peaceful darkness, and thus creating, for one brief moment, a very clear shadow of a palm tree on the white wall of the storehouse.

From the very first moment Furuya had been billeted in the mayor's house he had disliked this tree. The fact that it was perpetually smothered in dust, its overall air of shabbiness, the way the long-handled leaves (or were they branches?) spread out so awkwardly, its thick bark, furled and worn-looking, was something for which he felt an almost personal hatred. He had never mentioned this to anybody, but morning and night each time he looked at the tree he was struck with loathing for it, although most palm trees left him indifferent. Yet in that moment when the torch illuminated it he received the mysterious revelation that its clean, almost classic shape profoundly attracted him. This certainly wasn't a memory he had fabricated, for when sometime in the mid-1950s he'd read (with feelings of mild disgust and amusement) on the arts page of the paper that the actor who'd played the boss had become a leading member of a left-wing drama group, he opened his scrap-book and reread a passage he'd written down ten years before on that night in August, and found its concluding lines were these:

Palm tree. Shadow. Surprised how totally different it looked. Just like a woman who normally has dreadful taste in clothes appearing one day in a perfectly stunning outfit.

Then there was that time soon after the war had ended. Quite a lot of magazines had begun to appear and there was a demand for fiction at last, but life was still difficult and it was during the worst period that his wife left him, for various reasons. He was extremely lucky to find somewhere to live, renting the upstairs room in a house belonging to an acquaintance. He moved in one summer afternoon, bringing only a few personal possessions, much like a student moving into new digs. As he recalled, he had brought less than a dozen books. With the windows of the Western-style room wide open, he lay down on the ancient iron bedstead to rest, but the springs sagged so badly in the middle it was like being in a hammock, and as he was reflecting how useful this experience would be should he ever have to write about sleeping in hammocks, he dozed off. When he woke up it was evening, and the first thing he noticed was the grey shape of a bamboo tree, just above eye level, rising straight up and then bending suddenly to one side, the tips of its branches trembling slightly. It took him a little time to work out that this was a shadow on the wall and white plaster of the ceiling. He sat up and turned his head towards the open window, and saw that the street lamp outside was shining on a clump of bamboo. He remained for thirty minutes observing those thin shadows as if he were reading a long letter from home. When he emerged sufficiently from his trance to notice the faint rustling sound the leaves were making, he began to feel annoyed with himself for this kind of lyrical indulgence (though the word "sentimental" would probably be nearer the mark); so he decided to go out to a restaurant near the station for a late dinner. . . .

Yet despite these reminiscences the old writer still didn't bother to question the existence of this habit, or inclination, in him, which may not be all that surprising. The vast majority of people tend to consider their own personal characteristics as self-evident things, and even if one becomes conscious of them there is rarely any desire to investigate their sources. In this respect novelists are no different from anybody else. But then one day, towards evening, Furuya was out on a neighbourhood stroll, and set off in a direction he normally never took, crossed over a bridge, and stood in front of a small block of flats which was set back a little from the road. On the tiny strip of land between the road and the building a row of slender elm trees had been planted, and one of them had caught the light of the setting sun, casting a thin shadow on the narrow space between two windows. He was overcome by a deep sense of pathos, and stood a long time gazing at it.

He had just placed both hands on his stick and shifted some of his weight onto them, giving himself over to his fascination, when out of the corner of his eye he noticed the face of a girl who was staring at him in obvious astonishment, and he suddenly realized he was talking to himself: he was muttering the words "tree shadows, tree shadows, tree shadows". The girl, dressed in a blouse and jeans, must have taken him for a lunatic, and hurried nervously by.

The old man moved off, with the same impassive expression on his face, but after a while he started grinning to himself, aware now that all those times in the past when he'd been moved by tree shadows he had probably been muttering a similar formula to himself. At least it seemed more than likely, and he had no evidence to contradict the assumption. Out walking or in a taxi, in the bar district of Bangkok fifteen years ago, or gazing at the ceiling of his room just after his divorce, or looking at a palm tree that August night of 1945, he had said those words; not presumably as clearly as he'd been saying them just now, but still out loud, still basically responding in the same way. He was amused to find that the concern he was feeling for an aspect of his past of which he'd been quite unaware was very much like the involvement he felt in the lives of those fictional characters he himself created.

As he went on idly wandering about, and even after he had returned home, he tried to think why an object like the perfectly ordinary shadow of a tree should have this obsessive hold on him, but he was unable to find any satisfactory answer. The house in which he'd been born was in an area known as "Three Cedars", and there had indeed been three ancient cedar trees on the crest of a nearby hill; but there was no nearby wall on which their shadows might have appeared, and they were thus cast quite pointlessly upon the ground, extending over a field, a pond, a hut, and even under the red arch of the shrine. He could certainly remember how often he had been struck by the melancholy of this view when he looked at it from his bedroom window, but it seemed highly unlikely that the gloom of childhood had been such that he had dreamt of enlivening the scene by having those shadows stand upright.

One thing he did recall was that, when he was even younger, his elder brother had once been so keen on playing with a magic lantern that he did little else, but the only pictures Furuya could remember were of flowers and butterflies, and he was fairly sure there had been no trees. There was also the fact that in his house the hanging scrolls in the living room were changed according to the season, but since the pictures were mainly in the literary style of the South China school, it was extremely unlikely that one of tree shadows should have been among them. There hadn't been one among any of the new pictures the dealer brought, either. Moreover, since coming to Tokyo, he couldn't remember being moved by any such painting at an exhibition or in a book, or by anything similar in a film or novel.

As the days went by, the direction of his interest changed. He was impressed by the fact that none of the characters in his own novels, when responding to tree shadows, ever made use of his ritual formula, neither saying it out loud nor whispering it to themselves. He did not, however, come to the obvious conclusion that since he, the author, had not been aware of it in himself he would hardly have transferred it to one of his creations. Furuya's idea of the relationship between a writer and his characters was somewhat unusual in that he believed they sometimes became independent of their creator's consciousness, behaving of their own free will; and that by observing how they spoke, thought, and behaved one could work out what was going on deep inside their creator himself. This was a discovery he had made when he was quite young, and repeated experience had made it a part of his novelistic creed. Thus the lives of the characters revealed the writer's dreams, and since dreams made their own kind of sense it was only the act of reading that could reveal the true connecting process that was going on, which meant the interpretative act itself could only be left to the reader. Furuya believed this, so it was inevitable he should always have tried his hardest, as a novelist, to avoid any systematic knowledge of his own past, any attempt to create a precise map of the paths his life had taken.

This failure to make use of the formula looked as if it were going to be true of the businessman (the one having an affair with the photographer's wife) in the novel he was now writing, and he could also think of another two instances in other novels. The first was in the subplot of a work written in the late 1950s, *The Ocean Current Bottle*, whose main hero is a scholar of ancient Japanese literature, while the subplot is about a young delinquent, the scholar's illegitimate younger brother, who has got out of prison so recently his hair hasn't yet had time to grow. This youth is in his early twenties and lives with his mother in the western suburbs of Tokyo, somewhere along the Central Line. His two elder brothers are both married and living elsewhere. The little money earned in prison was all spent on the day he got out, and his mother is not prepared to give him any more, making quite sure he can't steal anything from her as well. He spends his days playing games of *shōgi* with himself out of a book, and reading detective stories borrowed from the library; and sleeping. Since he sleeps during the day, naturally he can't sleep much at night.

Quite late one night when he is awake in his room upstairs, he hears voices approaching on the road almost immediately below his window. He automatically switches off the light and opens the window a fraction to hear better, because not only is it a man with a woman, but the woman's voice sounds more than ordinarily flirtatious. His premonition that something unusual is about to take place turns out to be dead right, for when they reach the spot just below him the man whispers something to the woman, who then places her hands fairly low down on the fence of the house opposite with her arms outstretched. The man drops his trousers and gets on the job straight away. There is one street lamp, but at some distance, and the only nearby light is that above the doorway of a house. Tantalized by the fact that he can see almost nothing, he finds the sounds inflammatory in their effect on his imagination. As he pricks up his ears and squints eagerly into the darkness, the thought crosses his mind that if he accosts them he should be able to get some money out of the man; and if he plays his cards right he might enjoy the woman as well—at least according to the information he'd received on such matters in prison.

Confident in what seems a genuine revelation as to how things will be, he tiptoes downstairs so as not to wake his mother, takes a carving knife from the kitchen, and goes out through the back door. He has decided to leave via the rear gate and approach the front in a roundabout way to give the impression of just passing by. The man has apparently just finished, and is standing back. He is much bigger than imagined, with broad shoulders. The youth plucks up his courage, however, and calls out to him, but the result is nothing like the experience he'd been told (or lied) about in gaol.

First of all the woman lets out a fantastic scream and dashes away. The man glares viciously at him, squares up, then throws something white he had in his right hand. It travels lazily through the air but still hits the youth full in the face, and, overcome by its foul stench, he staggers. When he picks it up much later it turns out to be a crude loin-cloth, but at the time the thing is merely a white, smelly blindfold. The large man takes a pace forward, and the youth runs.

Since he knows the area well he slips smartly right, then nimbly left, disposing of the knife by throwing it over a hedge; but the man in pursuit seems to know the road pretty well too, and can also run fast. The youth's idea is to run from one dark place to even darker ones, but he manages to come out at a downward slope which is brightly lit by street lamps. He can hear the man yelling only a little way behind. There is no place to hide. Just as he decides he's done for, the whole area goes dark. There has been a power cut. He draws back to one side of the road and hears the man's heavy breathing as he races past and on down the hill. The youth sits down amid the shrubbery of some large house to recover his breath, and realizes the man must have been a gangster. "God, what a fool I've been," he groans, "trying a dirty trick like that in front of our own house. What would Mother think if she ever heard about it?"

When he grows tired of feeling sorry, he starts thinking about what he's going to do in the future. He decides to get a decent job. He'll force himself to ask his brothers for help, although he can't stand either of them. He tells himself he has to go straight, earn a proper living, even if it only means very little money. He finds this honourable decision quite easy to arrive at since he has already done so a number of times before; but just at the point where his mind is made up all the lights come on again. He is in front of a Western-style house with a white façade. The light from a street lamp throws the shadow of a ginkgo tree onto the white building. This spectacle, appearing abruptly out of the dark, intrigues him. Here is a world of real style, of fascinating beauty; and as he marvels at it he has the sudden intuition that he'll have to join an organization and become a gangster himself. It is a genuine revelation of what the future holds.

The second instance was from a novel entitled *Shooting a Butterfly*, which contains an episode that occurs during the last year of the life of a great politician. This is a man who has served any number of times in the government, has his own faction, and yet has hardly any hope of ever becoming Prime Minister. His wife comes from a powerful business family, and keeps a strict eye on him, so he has the reputation of being a man of irreproachable character; but during his late sixties he formed a liaison with a young woman, and set her up in a house of her own. The young woman has a lover, a Kabuki actor (whom we can ignore, though

75

he does have a major role in the novel). Anyway, all communication between the elderly politician and his young mistress is entrusted to a very discreet secretary, but one day this secretary dies, and at almost the same time the politician is taken ill and has to go into hospital. He leaves hospital after two months and, cleverly evading both wife and nurse one afternoon, manages to get out of the house. It is the rainy season, but the sun is shining. While he is walking along trying to find a taxi he notices some hydrangeas in bloom in the garden of a house nearby, and this creates the illusion that the house is the one his mistress lives in. Her garden also has a lot of hydrangeas growing in it, planted by its former owner. As he stumbles onwards, this illusion leads into another, that one white blossom-laden bush is the woman herself, and he approaches it, trips over a root, and falls down.

He wants to call out to the woman in the house, but is quite unable to remember her name. At this point a professional reflex comes into action, a device he used whenever he forgot the name of some member of his constituency, being a laborious plodding through the Japanese syllabary until the relevant sounds seemed to click. But even this effort turns out to be of no avail, and he loses consciousness. He comes to a couple of hours later, raises his head, and looks out through the iron railings. The house across the road is being rebuilt, and is surrounded by a high, wide expanse of dirty white canvas on which the shadows of two trees appear. The canvas flaps, billows, and fades with the wind. The shadow on the right is weak; that on the left is strong. He now suffers his third illusion. He thinks he is at an outdoor cinema, watching a film on the screen.

3

Furuya hadn't done any lecturing for ten years or so, but he had agreed to perform at a function in his home town celebrating its establishment as a municipal borough umpteen years ago, because the present mayor had been in the same class at school. They had not been particularly close friends, though Furuya had always found him congenial, and since he had written to say he was now in his final term of office and for years had wanted to invite him but refrained from doing so, Furuya could hardly refuse.

He wrote back accepting towards the end of that summer. The lecture was scheduled for the end of October so he still had plenty of time, but since he already knew what he was going to talk about he began work on a draft. All it really meant was writing, somewhat earlier than planned, a critical article commissioned by a literary magazine for their New Year number. He would use the manuscript for his lecture, then send it on to the magazine. The subject matter wasn't really suitable for a popular audience, but that couldn't be helped. Nevertheless, it would mean putting aside his novel for a while, the greater part of which was written though it still lacked a title.

What is given here is only his draft of the published article. The predominance, in places, of a conversational tone presumably indicates how much he had a live audience in mind.

A certain French woman critic has written thus: the origin of the novel lies in a child's suspicion that it is not the real child of its parents.

Why do children fantasize in this way? When the child is small it dwells in the enclosed Eden of the family; it feels itself to be at the family's very centre, loved and cherished. But as it grows up it finds that the family has lost interest in it, that its parents' love and concern in particular have grown less. As a result it begins to embrace the idea that it has different parents elsewhere; that these parents with whom it lives merely found it somewhere and brought it up. Even if it doesn't go this far, it still fantasizes that one of them is not its real parent. Hence the tales of the abandoned child, of the foster child, of the step-mother or stepfather: tales of the child of misfortune, which are created with relish and greeted with joy. Both writer and reader are secretly acquainted with this kind of story from their earliest years, since it merely reflects their own fantasies of that time, or provides variations on an oft-repeated personal theme; emotionally they are prepared for it, so it is easy to create and also to respond to. Thus in the case of Oedipus (the abandoned child) the themes of exile, of the claiming of the proper inheritance, then exile again, are given tragic expression; while in Cinderella (the foster child) we have a simple progression from the life of misery to the triumph of the ball. One hardly needs to point out how often this narrative pattern occurs in legends and fairy tales.

The basic impulse behind this sort of tale is an unconscious desire to satisfy the self, the self that despises its commonplace parents and vulgar environment, dreams that it may be the illegitimate offspring of royalty, and creates a fantasy to explain why such an essentially aristocratic being should have been subjected by the machinations of fate to these unnatural humiliations. The insults and persecutions it now sees itself enduring only increase its awareness of its own absolute sanctity.

So what does Furuya say? He says that this isn't a bad way of starting off, because if one begins like this then the more dubious aspects of the anomalous (monstrous?) art of the novel—its unwholesome, morbid characteristics—are properly highlighted. The novel has always tended to be looked down on as mere make-believe, or suspected of being little more than personal confession. This was a source of annoyance to novelists until the second half of the nineteenth century, when most of them split into two groups. Group A decided they didn't give a damn anyway and became fully fledged writers of popular fic-

78

tion; Group B went all out for the autobiographical novel.

Examples:

France: Group A: *Alexandre Dumas Père*, Le Comte de
Monte Cristo
Eugène Sue: Les Mystères de Paris
Group B: *Alfred de Musset:* Les Confessions
d'un Enfant du Siècle
George Sand: Elle et Lui
England: Group A: *A. Conan Doyle:* The Adventures of
Sherlock Holmes
Rider Haggard: King Solomon's Mines
Group B: *George Gissing:* New Grub Street
Edmund Gosse: Father and Son

*In Scandinavia, there are still more remarkable contrasts,
such as that between Quo Vadis and Strindberg's Inferno,
while the autobiographical novel in its extreme form can be
seen in the twentieth-century Japanese "I-novel". One should
add, however, that in Europe even the most aggressively
popular novels maintain a logical structure of some kind, and
the most confessional of autobiographical works are still written with a certain objectivity (unlike their Japanese counter-
parts).*

*The novel having arranged itself more or less discretely (or
perhaps indiscreetly) into two groups, what about the writers
who felt they belonged to neither: those of Group C, who had
doubts about both the popular and the autobiographical novel?
Well, obviously the whole situation must have been very annoying for them, but they would have been used to that, for the
books they wrote would inevitably have laid them open to the
suspicion of belonging to one (or both) of the rival camps. The
novel is, by its very nature, not only a form of unrestrained*

dreaming, but also a confession, a confession (and this is the important point) of what has been experienced by the soul. The Group C novel therefore embodies both the imaginative extravagance of the popular novel and the soul confessions of the autobiographical type. It can be likened, in fact, to a somnambulist wandering the night-time of the spirit.

That at least is my brief account of the matter, and from this point of view the French critic's interpretation seems to fit the nature of the novel as I experience it very well. She is obviously clever, and she goes on to examine Robinson Crusoe and Don Quixote in the same terms. In my case, however, it is a work of Japanese literature that comes to mind—one that was hailed as a veritable masterpiece, as one of the major achievements of the pre-war era—by a writer whom I shall allow to remain anonymous. I myself never managed to like the work at all, and found the feelings of antipathy it aroused in me a genuine embarrassment in company; but if one applies our French critic's theories it becomes pretty clear why it should have been such a great success.

The hero of the novel discovers that he is the child of a union between his mother and his grandfather, and the narrative describes the mental suffering he endures because of this. The author himself has confessed in some reminiscences that during his boyhood (or so one assumes) he once—but only once, he insists—spent a whole night brooding about the idea that he might have been the offspring of just such a relationship. It also transpired that he hated his father and felt deep respect for his grandfather, so his case bears out perfectly what the French critic has to say.

I remember another case, too, that of a man (a folklorist) said to be the greatest modern scholar of Japanese literature. During his childhood he was obsessed by the idea that his real mother might be someone else, and may even have come to believe it was true, which suggests that he thought she was really some queen or princess. I suppose this obsession with the mother rather than the father may have been a result of the fact that the great scholar was homosexual, although I'm not all that sure about that. Still, it is certainly of profound interest that two men of letters whose childhood and youth coincided (around the turn of the century) should both have been preoccupied with a similar fantasy. One can assume from these two examples (since both were, after all, major intellectual figures) that there must have been an awful lot of people in this country at the time who also believed they were children of misfortune and that their misfortune actually enhanced their superiority as people. Here, indeed, might well be an unlooked-for clue to the real truth of the psychological history of the whole period.

It was a period when a sudden inrush of Western culture flooded the country, when sensitive souls watched the last vestiges of the old Edo civilization vanishing one by one before their eyes. So they searched for the roots of their own identities, which for the novelist meant something to do with the ancient military virtues as exemplified in his grandfather; while for the scholar, the folklorist, it was . . . What was it? Some vanished water nymph, some ondine? Heaven only knows. Anyway, let us forget about him and return to our anonymous novelist, who is normally considered a practitioner of the confessional "I-novel". The "I-novel" itself, we should remind ourselves, is usually seen as an expression of the modern idea of the self, of some alleged twentieth-century Japanese obsession with the individual personality. Well, that may or may not be so, but the point is whether the particular novel under discussion can be seen in such terms. Surely what is central to that work is a much more ancient, primitive literary function: literature not as personal catharsis but as a form of incantation, the appease-

ment of the spirits of the dead. In pre-war Japan (even now, for that matter) such primitive ritualism was rampant in society, yet every effort was made to ensure that modern Japanese people would be unable to recognize it as such, even while their lives were being controlled by it. The novel in question is a precise, curious blending of the primitive and the modern, and it appealed to people at the time because it was in harmony with the way their minds were essentially structured. They thought this was because the sensibility expressed in the book was purely modern, but they were wrong.

You can see the same thing in the Japanese-style poetry of the time, the kind that is supposed to be experimental in nature yet is the same mixture of pre-modern and modern sensibilities, a fact of which the poets themselves seemed quite unaware. You can see it in the Kabuki of the time, in the acting of Kikugoro VI, for example, which so astounded people with its "realism" yet was the same old incantatory art of the Edo period covered by a very thin layer of imported Western theatrical mannerisms.

If one re-examines this particular novel in such terms, one can find primitive modes of thought scattered throughout it. The opening (?) lines where the hero questions the nature of his birth are an obvious case in point, and the part halfway through where he squeezes the woman's breasts and cries out "a rich harvest, a rich harvest!" is straight fertility ritual. The ending of the book is mountain-worship. Every day as a boy I used to see that very mountain he travels up, the mountain by whose divine spirit he is ultimately saved, as I understand it. Even the episode where the hero, when he's a little boy, climbs onto the roof of his home could surely be interpreted as a form of homage paid to the gods and spirits of the mountain, which would link up nicely with the ending. The French critic cites two scenes, from Kafka and Claudel, in which a child climbs up an apple tree until he can see far away to the horizon. . . .

Furuya had got this far when a fat missive arrived by express delivery. The woman's name on the back of the envelope was one he couldn't place, but it had been sent from his home district, though from a village some distance from where he used to live. The envelope was of hand-made paper, the letter written on one long, scroll-like piece of paper in the old style, in correctly abbreviated, flowing characters (not the arbitrary scribble employed by so many people nowadays) and in a Japanese ink that had been chosen with obvious taste.

It began with some old-fashioned rigmarole about fire-flies among the reeds and the cool autumn breeze at morn and eve, then apologized for the dreadful rudeness of a perfect stranger making a sudden intrusion of this kind, before beginning the task of self-introduction. According to this the woman was an old lady, head of one of the leading families in the county (the Funakis). Her nephew and his wife, she said, were now living a long way off in Ashiya (in comfortable retirement, no doubt, since Ashiya is that sort of place), so she must have been asked to look after the family home for them. She seemed pretty ancient, and presumably had a housekeeper or someone to help her.

As a young girl, she had loved literature and written some poetry herself, and in her twenties had been awarded second prize in a short-story competition sponsored by an Osaka newspaper; but though she had talked to one of the people on the selection committee, for one reason or another she hadn't felt like following it up and so had missed her chance of making an appearance on the literary scene. (The impression Furuya got from this was that the jury member had made a pass at her which she declined, and he wondered who it might have been.) "You would obviously know nothing of this, but I have always felt a deep sense of affinity with your writings" (meaning they both came from the same part of the world, Furuya assumed) "and have long been a devoted reader." She particularly liked his novella about the poet who turned into a salmon, but there were many others she loved as well, and though there were parts of his critical works she was unable to follow owing to her own lack of learning, she still possessed all of them. Naturally she had all his essays and occasional writings. She had always hoped that one day she might enjoy the opportunity of conversation with him, but somehow the years had passed and she had never been able to. Now, however, she had read in her local newspaper that they were to be privileged to hear him lecture there towards the end of October. She could only marvel at the workings of chance (and of her own karma) which were now sending him to her, and felt she must write and beg him to comply with her desire that they should meet. It would, of course, be only right and proper that she should attend his lecture and pay her respects afterwards, but she was in her late eighties and her condition did not permit her to travel. This left her with no alternative but to humbly entreat him to call on her at her house, for which purpose she would of course have a car ready for his use. She trusted that her request might meet with his approval. "I must apologize in advance for the poor hospitality that is all I can offer, but hope you will be oblige me by partaking, at least to some small extent, of the inferior wine that we have here. Thanks to recent advances in science I now have an excellent deaf aid which allows me to hear in some detail, so I am pleased to say there will be no need for you to raise your voice excessively when you speak. I am perfectly able to hear everything that I want to. Finally, I hope you will excuse me if I say that for certain minor reasons I wish this all to remain a secret between the two of us, and would be most grateful if you were so kind as to bear that in mind."

Furuya clicked his tongue in exasperation, wondering what on earth the woman thought she was on about, and immediately

84

wrote a reply on a postcard, expressing his regret that he would be unable to accept her kind invitation since he was only staying in the area for a very short time; he hoped she would understand. He sent this reply, of course, by express.

Receiving odd letters was an unavoidable aspect of his profession and he was quite used to it, but this one seemed to have gone a little too far, and the ghastly politeness of the style only made it worse. He was beginning to wonder whether the sense of closeness one felt for people from the same district wasn't just an example of mindless clannishness, when his reflections were interrupted by a telephone call from a lawyer friend of his. The latter was a retired professor emeritus with nothing to do, so the conversation went on for a long time, at the end of which he asked Furuya if he'd like a game of *go*. Furuya replied cheerfully that he would make sure the other had to stand him dinner afterwards, then told his wife to get his going-out clothes ready. She was his second wife; when he'd married her there had been quite an age difference between them, but by now she seemed to look much the same as himself.

Next morning he lay in bed thinking about his childhood, and found himself concluding, unexpectedly, that he personally had never indulged in any fantasies about being either an abandoned or a foster child. There had been five children, and his parents had treated them all equally; or rather, his father had had virtually nothing to do with them, while his mother had been so busy that she treated them all with equal unfairness, as each different situation demanded. Being the youngest son, he had regarded any preferential treatment given his two elder brothers as perfectly natural considering how well they did at school, and his two younger sisters were sweet little girls, so of course they were given more attention than he, as a boy, required. He certainly couldn't remember ever being bothered by any of this. Perhaps he'd never fantasized about being the child of anybody else but his parents because he was told so often how much he took after both of them.

It was possible, of course, that he had been an unimaginative child, lacking the ability to make up such stories; in which case the French critic's account of the origin of the novel would virtually disqualify him as a novelist. The idea half amused and half worried him; he even considered asking the older of his sisters (who had married a neighbour and still lived in the area) what she remembered about it, during this trip back home. But it was only a half-serious idea, and he assumed he'd probably be too busy with other things.

About ten days later another letter arrived by express from the same address, but from another unknown woman. It was written with a fountain pen on ordinary paper, and the writer appeared to be the old woman's niece, probably unmarried since she too had the surname Funaki. It began with profuse apologies for her aunt's impoliteness in sending him so improper a letter, but claimed that the responsibility was really all her own. Her aunt had in fact shown her a draft of the letter, and she'd decided it would be all right to send it because her aunt was so set on the idea, and she wasn't all that clear just what sort of request she was making as there were parts she couldn't understand and the handwriting was difficult to work out in places, so finally she just decided it couldn't do any harm and allowed her to post it. When she thought about it now, though, the sheer impertinence of it made her blush with shame, and she quite understood how very annoyed he must have been . . . and so on. But the upshot of it all was that she repeated the same request, since her poor old aunt, who was shy and retiring by nature, had become terribly despondent on receiving the reply to her bold letter, being overwhelmed by feelings of shame as it dawned on her how rude she had been; and finally she'd had a relapse and taken to her bed. The doctor said it was only a mild form of mental distress, but she had no appetite at all and it was worrying to think what might become of her, and as the one who had to nurse her she couldn't help feeling sorry for her, etc.; in short, though she was very reluctant to make such an impudent request, could he possibly change his mind and pay them a visit, because she was quite sure the old lady would perk up wonderfully if she were to hear the happy news? "My aunt has long hoped to be able to meet the revered author of books that have been her constant companions, and has convinced herself that she mustn't let this one opportunity pass her by, and I can only appeal to you to be so good as to consider her unfortunate plight. I am keeping this letter a secret from her."

The revered author muttered to himself that this was pure blackmail. What had it to do with him if the odd book-loving lady should be taken ill? Nevertheless, he scribbled a postcard (addressed to the old lady, of course), saying: "Please have a car ready for me when the lecture ends. I can spare you thirty minutes for tea (nothing else) but will then be obliged to leave. Those are my conditions."

One reason for his insisting on such conditions was an awareness that a late night would not do the old woman's health much good, and he did have a very tight schedule (which made it genuinely difficult to fit this visit in). But that was only half his motive, the other being little more than pure spite on his part, or at least a desire to get the whole business over and done with good and early. He certainly felt better disposed towards the niece than the old woman herself, and when his wife laughed at him and accused him of becoming a quite different person when dealing with young people, especially a young woman, there was probably quite a lot of truth in what she said.

It was strange that Furuya didn't give any serious attention to the question of why the old lady should be so desperate to meet him. While he certainly felt that parts of her letter were peculiar, he'd simply gone on reading without thinking any more about them. Perhaps he just assumed that it was the normal desire to meet the author that some book lovers have; most well-known writers, after all, have to learn to put up with that sort of thing. Here, though, it is probably truer to say that he had become too absorbed again in his novel, now that it was all quite clear in his head, to really think about anything else. This is borne out by the fact that he made no attempt to find out anything about the situation in the Funaki household, or about the two women who were apparently custodians of the house, even though under normal circumstances he had a passion for investigating things like this. Nor was his failure to make such simple inquiries of his sister, who lived in the area, due to the fact that he'd been asked to keep the matter a secret, for in practice he'd completely forgotten about it. He didn't even ask any of his journalist friends, although it would have been easy enough to have done so.

Eventually a reply came from the old woman, written by the niece. Another letter of thanks came from the niece herself. According to this, the day after his postcard arrived the old woman had become much better, and if she went on like this she should be able to get up in two or three days. It all seemed to Furuya like something taking place on another planet, the real world in which he was living being that of his novel, with its subplot about the businessman, the photographer, and his wife, and its main character the professor of Latin American literature whose elder brother (the second lead) was a confirmed matrimonial swindler. It was due to begin serialization in a magazine at the beginning of the year.

The last days of October arrived. His wife disliked flying, so she didn't go with him. On the evening before the lecture, he attended a reception given for him by the mayor, and also put in an appearance at a get-together of a dozen or so of his old school friends at the same restaurant. On the afternoon of the following day he went with his sister to visit the family grave, then had an early meal at her house, but, rather as he'd expected, he quite forgot to ask her whether any of them had ever indulged in childhood fantasies about being abandoned or foster children. He didn't mention that he was going to visit the Funaki house. The lecture was that evening.

When it was over and he had retired to the ante-room, he was informed that a car was waiting for him. The sponsor of the lecture meeting came in and thanked him profusely. A journalist entered and asked a few questions. After a short rest he went out and got in the car. The driver said it would take about an hour and a half; he had clearly been told to behave in a very deferential manner, and didn't even switch on the radio. The car's heating was working nicely, and Furuya must have dozed off.

When he came to he noticed a single point of light in the surrounding darkness, towards which they were travelling. On reaching the light, the driver sounded his horn and three women trotted out of the shadows and lined up by the car. When he got out, one of them, a middle-aged woman in a kimono, bowed repeatedly and introduced herself at great length. She was the niece. The other two appeared to be servants. With his stick in one hand, Furuya crossed a bridge over a stream and came to a very large entrance gate, then walked slowly along a stone-paved path. It was illuminated by electric lights here and there, but was still mostly a grey darkness, and the woman lit his way with a torch.

The entrance hall was a splendid affair, but obviously there weren't enough servants to look after the place properly, and the air of shabbiness was reinforced by the addition of fluorescent lighting which destroyed the classic harmony it must once have had. The niece wore a kimono of dark, almost black pongee, with a mauve sash. She appeared to be in her late thirties, tall, of pale complexion, with a modern-looking face. She said the main reception room was too large to heat properly, and she would

89

show him to the ordinary living room. It turned out to be a longish trek down the corridor to get there.

The room he entered was still quite big, about twenty foot square, with a high ceiling. There was no table, just cushions placed on the tatami. Slightly to one side of what he assumed was the empty seat of honour sat an old woman quite muffled up in clothes. Instead of kneeling in the required manner she sat with her legs thrust out in front of her, her back leaning against a support. The ceiling, the thick pillars, and the wooden frames of the sliding screens were black with age, making a harsh contrast with the stark white paper of the screens. The room was heated by three gas stoves, but since most of the warmth must have escaped through various cracks and crevices there was no prospect of any sort of fug.

The old woman, still reclining against her back support, smiled at him. Furuya, however, only nodded curtly, then went immediately to the huge family shrine (at least half as big again as the one they'd had in his old home) and knelt before it, having taken the fact that it was open and the electric taper lit as a mild hint that he should do so. On both sides of the main image the shelves were crammed with small framed portrait photos, about fifteen or twenty of them in all. It was like looking at some kind of exhibition. He gave the bell a clear tinkle, bowed deeply, then returned to his place, and formalities were exchanged.

The old lady had on a kimono of deep blue pongee with a brown, one-piece sash. Her features were well shaped but, probably because her complexion was so dark, she looked rather fierce. Her slightly off-white hair was held in place by an enormous tortoise-shell comb, and perhaps for that reason her hearing aid did not attract his attention. On her feet she wore blue woollen socks, not the usual white *tabi*. She apologized for sitting with her legs stretched out in this uncouth fashion, and gave a tedious account of why she found it necessary to do so. Then she

90

thanked him for praying for the family's departed, and expressed her gratitude, calmly and at great length again, for his kindness in complying with her request.

The elderly writer made brief responses at the appropriate places, gazing meanwhile unconcernedly about the room, noting that the single-leaf screen was genuine eighteenth century, by Maruyama Ōkyo. In the left-hand corner of the room, in front of him, was a really ancient-looking two-leaf silver folding screen.

Tea and cakes were served. The cakes were a local product and he remembered the taste. It was clear at a glance that the cups were early Rokubei, but he wasn't quite sure if the beautifully worked tray was Risai or not.

The room as a whole, however, was very far removed from the ideals of taste implied by these elegant utensils. On top of the enormous television set, for example, stood a cheap money-box obviously given away by some bank. The picture on the calendar was a poorly printed reproduction of a nude. Though a specimen of calligraphy hung on the pillar behind the old lady, unfortunately it was only a schoolchild's exercise, "Autumn Leaves on a Mountain", where the simple character for "mountain" had been marked with two circles but the rest had been given only one each—nothing to be proud of even by fairly modest standards. Furuya reflected that even if the real master and mistress of the house had been in residence, things wouldn't have been much different. He also assumed that the crude piece of calligraphy had been done by a child of the niece, now already in bed.

Asked by the old lady whether the tea hadn't made him sleepy, Furuya replied that he was feeling quite all right and that physically he wasn't so sensitive anyway; if ever he did feel like that, whisky would soon put things right. She then immediately made the formal offer of alcohol, but he declined, gathering from the swiftness of her response that she could hear perfectly well. The old lady went on to give a leisurely account of her memories of reading his books, to which he listened without any visible signs of embarrassment. She had certainly read some unexpected things of his, and occasionally showed something like real insight, but on the whole her interpretations seemed remarkably misguided, and in some cases he had the impression she could well be confusing his works with someone else's.

She'd just reached the point where he expected her to launch into an attack on that member of the selection committee who had thwarted her literary ambitions, or perhaps some more general lament on the subject, when instead she told her niece to get something out of the little chest of drawers. The niece handed a square white envelope to Furuya and went back to her place. There was an ancient photograph inside; it did not look like the work of a professional.

It was of a small child, two or three years old, sitting on the lap of a woman on a sunlit veranda. The little boy was wearing a yukata and was smiling, though the face was rather blurred and not all that easy to make out. The face of the woman did not appear in it. As he took the bulky print in his hand, his first response was that it must be a photo of himself when small, and the woman was the old lady, taken on some occasion when she'd come to visit them at his home. Yet the woman in the picture was obviously grown up, and as there was only about a ten-year age difference between himself and his host, that interpretation wouldn't work. Nor did the veranda seem to be the one at home, the large stone for taking off one's footwear being quite different. Besides, he had never gathered from anything anybody had said that they were on close enough terms with the Funaki family to warrant a visit from any of them. He looked at her questioningly, and she said in a meaningful kind of way that she wanted him to keep the photograph.

"By which you mean that this is . . . ?"

"A photograph of yourself taken when you were small. In this house."

He looked intently at the picture again, then suddenly remembered something very odd. In the family album at home there had been photos of all his brothers and sisters taken when they were quite small, but none of himself before the age of six. There are, of course, periods in any family when photographs simply don't get taken, and as a boy he had derived some comfort from this sort of explanation; so, even if he had felt sad about the absence of such things, he'd never really questioned it at any later stage in life. It might of course be that he had suffered, then repressed the memory, trying to forget and eventually succeeding in doing so. If that were the case, then there could well be a few other things he had forgotten as well. But he didn't think so; in the first place, he simply found it very hard to believe that this really was a photo of himself. He decided to press the point.

"It couldn't be one of my two brothers?"

"No."

"And it was definitely taken here?"

"Yes."

"Who's that holding me?"

The old woman looked down, then replied:

"Your real mother."

"My *real* mother?"

"Yes."

Mysteriously he felt a sense of inevitability about the direction the conversation had suddenly taken. After all, the general public loves stories about unhappy children. If one readily imagines oneself as such a child, then one can imagine others in the same situation. The massive production, circulation, and consumption of tales of abandoned and foster children are made possible by this tendency. Thus a woman frustrated in her novelistic ambitions chooses a novelist from her own district as the object on which to focus her unrealized dreams and, freely availing herself of the privilege that she believes her status as his devoted reader bestows on her, decides to confer on him the honour of a cruel, hidden fate, so as to link herself the more closely to him. The fact that the plain word "mother", rather than a politer form, had been used suggested that the woman in question belonged to the Funaki household.

That Furuya should have jumped so quickly to this conclusion was the result of other experiences as a man of letters. Most members of his profession probably had similar things happen to them, but he still felt he had suffered particularly badly from the attentions of some of his readers. There was one time when a woman he'd never seen in his life suddenly decided to get in a taxi and visit him, carrying a very fat, ugly baby she insisted was his. He got rid of her by calling the local policeman. There were freaks among the men as well. A young man had telephoned all the way from Hokkaido, saying he wanted to marry a girl with the same surname as Furuya, so he knew she was a secret child of his, but she had turned him down, and he wanted Furuya to talk to her on his behalf and make her change her mind. He even burst into tears in the end. He kept on ringing so often that Furuya had his telephone number changed to a new, unlisted one. In the same way, this mad woman (as he now judged her to be) had created a fantasy in which her sister or aunt or cousin, in whose arms the young Furuya Ippei was being held, became the mother of the novelist of later years; a prime case of poking one's nose into someone else's affairs, displaying a veritable genius for making a nuisance of herself. Although it was certainly a curious coincidence that there should be no photos of him taken before the age of five or six, presumably it was nothing more than that.

"So you're saying that my mother was not my real mother? Interesting," Furuya muttered, having already worked out to his

94

own satisfaction what she was up to, and casting a fairly osten-
tatious glance at the clock—a gesture which the old woman chose
to ignore.

"Yes. You were born in this house."

"And I'd always thought I'd been born at home."

"Born in the Year of the Bird, and you were here for two years,
certainly until the Year of the Boar—or was it the next year
perhaps?"

"First *I've* heard of it."

"It was kept a complete secret."

"But the family register has me down as the third son, not as an
illegitimate child."

"Such things can be arranged."

"My mother and father never said anything to me about it. Nor
did my brothers."

"You were much smaller than they were."

"Nor did the servants."

"They wouldn't, of course. Even if you had heard something,
it would probably have meant nothing to you either."

She responded easily to all his objections, and Furuya began
almost to enjoy himself. After all, it was untrue, so what did it matter? It was a private fantasy of hers—he'd made up his mind
about that—a joke; a joke in rather bad taste.

"If you consider the matter carefully, I am quite sure you will
find that it all hangs together perfectly well."

"Do you really think so? I'm afraid that isn't at all how it looks
to me," he replied, deciding to conceal the fact that as a boy he'd
been distressed by the lack of photos of him as a small child. He
presumed this decision was because he didn't want the mad
woman to gain any sort of upper hand in the discussion, though
his overall attitude was ambivalent. Partly he was just making a
gesture of self-defence, like a man before a fire trying to keep the
sparks out of his eyes; but there was also a strong professional in-

terest in observing the workings of this lunatic's imagination, and it was a heaven-sent opportunity to do so. So he kept the conversation going.

"But you will admit that my father was my real father?"

"Yes."

"So some member of this household was . . . ?"

He hesitated, not quite knowing what word to use; but the old woman said nothing, perhaps because he had spoken a little too softly, so he went on:

"What you've just said implies, of course, a considerable moral misdemeanour, and I'm wondering if it could possibly have taken place. In fact I'd say that an illicit liaison with a young lady of good family at that time was almost out of the question. The only women available to my father would have been professionals, and that was true of all men in the upper classes."

"I never expected a novelist to say that something was impossible."

"All right, then," said Furuya, accepting the reproach. "But where could they have got to know each other? Remember, this was an age when a man and a woman were whispered about if they were so much as seen walking with each other."

"That was so, of course; but there were various ways."

"Particularly as the two families were not on close terms."

"Something can always be arranged."

"Exactly what, may I ask? And where?"

"Well . . ."

"Yes?"

"Imagine, for example—I am not saying this was how it actually happened, but just making a suggestion—that they met at a hot-spring resort."

"That's a possibility," Furuya admitted frankly, for it was true that in hotels at such places members of the same class did come into contact with each other; they would have had time on their hands, and a man and a woman could easily have been carried away and committed such a misdemeanour. This seemed all the more likely when one recalled that the rooms had only flimsy sliding partitions between them which couldn't be locked. He could remember, on a visit to a hot spring with his family when he was about seven years old, going into the wrong room by mistake at night and being astonished to see a man and a woman fooling around there. Once, during the day-time, too, when all the rooms were left wide open, a young lady of very distinguished family, who must have been three or four years older than he, had invited him to play cards with her, and he still recalled how mortified he felt when his little sister suddenly appeared on the scene. What the old woman had suggested thus made perfectly good sense; but that didn't mean he was obliged to believe this fairy tale about his birth. He was merely amusing himself by taking some passing interest in a not very well written short story he happened to have come across.

"That certainly seems to follow, anyway," he admitted. "Let's assume, then, that my father happened to be staying at the same hotel as your family."

"I said I was only giving one possible example."

"Of course. Still, let's make that assumption. So my father became intimate with the lady in question. By the way, who *was* the lady in question?"

The old woman made no reply.

"I'm asking who she was. Who was my real mother? If she's alive, I must go and find her."

She still said nothing. He assumed she'd grown tired and wasn't hearing him too well, so he raised his voice:

"Was it your elder sister? Your aunt? A cousin, perhaps?"

She turned her face away a little and said:

"If I were to say it was myself, could you believe that?"

As he looked at her face in profile, he was struck again by the inevitability of all this, by the feeling that of course she'd been bound to say this eventually. After all, what pleased the public more than that mother and child should finally meet again after so many years? It was the grand finale that an insane imagination must inevitably produce, the fantasizing mind forced at last to tread the most obvious of well-worn paths.

"Still, surely you would have been too young to be my mother? One can't dismiss the idea as totally untenable, but it still seems highly unlikely," he declared, rather as if he were pontificating in the columns of some literary journal. But she remained quite unshaken.

"All sorts of things can and do happen in this world, as you very well know."

There was nothing for it now but to be openly sceptical.

"Sorry, but I just can't swallow it. After all, this is a very peculiar reunion between mother and child, for a start. Neither of us seems particularly excited by it, do we? That's a bit odd, surely?"

But even this didn't disturb her composure.

"I have not said that I actually am your mother. I have simply said enough to make you say so. I can't even say that she was a member of the Funaki family."

"Well, that's certainly a major retraction."

"All I can say is that you were born in this house. No more than that."

"Why?" he asked, but she said nothing. He asked her a number of times, but still she said nothing. Finally, in a tone ill suited to this sensitive occasion, he burst out:

"Look. I really want to know. I want to know what sort of woman my mother was, where she lived and what she did. Do you get me?"

"I can't tell you," she said, and hastily took out her handkerchief. She was crying. The woman in her thirties became very flustered, half getting up then sitting down again, but there was nothing she could do.

"Why?" Furuya addressed the weeping woman again with a cold smile on his face, intending to get to the bottom of this thing by nagging away at the obvious inconsistencies in her story. But at this point a compassionate smile passed across her face like a shadow, and in a rather strained but quiet voice she replied:

"It involves the honour of the Funaki family name."

This wonderfully old-fashioned line, reminiscent of the grand old days beyond recall, could easily have been laughed to scorn, but Furuya refrained from doing so, feeling that what she'd said made sense insofar as it was consistent with what she was herself. It didn't mean he had changed his mind and decided she was not insane (for he still believed she was), but that he found her concern with the family's reputation quite convincing. It may well have been that once he'd entered the room and paid his respects at the family shrine, the whole system of values that governed his life as a writer in Tokyo began to give way, to be replaced by the network of customs and conventions that had dominated his life as a boy: the various ceremonies of the year's end and New Year; the festival when the portable shrine stopped in front of their gate and there was a great dispensing of saké; the festival of lanterns; the feast of the dead; the occasions when the whole family, including the children of minor relatives, would suddenly assemble in huge numbers to take their long, solemn farewell of someone who was dying; the enormous amount of time people spent bowing to each other; the intricacies of the greeting system; the exchanging of gifts; long-winded interviews with the farm-hands; the full-moon viewing when there was always something different to eat, potatoes one time, chestnuts the next—in short, the whole system of shared, communal habits and beliefs which, he was aware, had suddenly reappeared and taken control of him, making him accept in her the necessity for concealment.

The niece approached to pour him a second cup of tea, then, having done so, did not withdraw but asked his permission to look at the photograph. She took it in her hand and stared intently at it, apparently seeing it for the very first time. She then whispered:

"It looks like little Masashige."

"Like little Masashige?" said Furuya, in a voice as low as hers. She remained silent, merely indicating the family shrine with her eyes.

"Excuse me," he said. He stood up and walked over to it, then crouched down to peer inside, straining his eyes until he saw in the first row on the right the photograph of a boy three or four years old. He picked up the framed picture and went back to his seat, comparing this one behind its glass stained by years of incense smoke, and the other which he held in his hand. He made no reply to any of the remarks the old woman directed at him.

He was a fat little boy wearing a padded kimono of what seemed to be silk, and he was seated on a chair in a photographer's studio. His face was swollen and ugly, reminiscent of the baby that other lunatic had tried to foist on him as his own. It was hard to say with any certainty if this Masashige was the same child as the one in a yukata that was supposed to be him, but their physique seemed pretty much the same, and if the face of one of them had not been so blurred he felt there would have been a definite resemblance. Anyway, nobody could say for sure that they were not the same person.

An explanation suddenly occurred to him. When the old lady had been young, she had been asked to look after this Masashige, and had been responsible in some way for his death; or maybe she had just been present when he died, drowning in a stream, perhaps, or choking to death on a rice-cake. This wild surmise appeared before him in the way that some brilliantly coloured butterfly might waver across one's path, and was immediately followed by another, just as vivid: a direct intuition that sometime later she had been raped by some man (presumably not his father) in a back room of a hotel at some hot spring. He was aware that an objective outsider might simply dismiss this as pure fiction, but he persisted in his deductions with a strong sense of confidence in their general accuracy. For example, it could have been that the child was her own and, as a teen-age mother, she had been responsible for its accidental death. This accident would have left a deep psychological wound, something which lay hidden for years and was then reopened by a combination of other events, with the result that she became mentally unbalanced, and was now causing a novelist whom she considered to be related to her in various ways all this trouble simply because he had the misfortune to come from the same part of the world. It all struck Furuya as only too likely, though as a man who'd spent the best part of his life making a living by stimulating the unhealthy imaginations of his readers, he was hardly in a position to be annoyed by events of this kind.

Having now grasped the situation to his own satisfaction, he could see little point in any further quibbling over details, and made up his mind to leave without expounding his psychoanalytical view of the matter; so he merely handed the photograph back to the niece, who took it over to the family shrine and replaced it. The old lady quietly asked her to put out the light, and she switched off the small one inside the shrine. Then, just as he was about to start taking his leave, she also switched off the main light on the way back to her seat, and Furuya found himself sitting in a room lit only by the flames of three gas fires. He assumed the old woman was now going to do something really mad, but she seemed to remain perfectly calm, doing nothing more eccentric than clap her hands.

This was a signal to the servants, for a voice answered and the sliding door opened. Furuya thought he noticed a faint odour of incense drifting in, but this was an illusion; it was, in fact, the smell of paraffin. A young woman came in holding an old-fash-ioned paraffin lamp and placed it about three feet in front of the ancient silver folding screen. It had a bamboo base and, above the glass container which allowed one to see the amount of paraffin inside, was not the usual tall chimney but a large globe enclosing the lemon-coloured flame. The bamboo base seemed to have a landscape of some kind carved on it. In the dull light from the lamp the screen appeared grey rather than silver, and the places where it had been repaired stood out. The screen was clearly one of an original pair, and Furuya assumed she had some particular reason for wanting to show him this as well as the photo; she said, in fact, that they had "got just one out of the storehouse, especial-ly for him", but it transpired that she was talking about the lamp.

"The electricity was put in in 1914. It was the Year of the Dragon."

"Ah."

"Although that didn't mean a light in every room. For quite a long time we still went on using lamps."

"I expect it was the same in our house."

"Before that, of course, it was all lamps. You can still see the hook in the ceiling in this room."

She made a gesture towards where it was, though naturally nothing was visible.

"The lamp used to hang from the ceiling. But then one day in the early evening, before that lamp was lit, someone was taking one of the table lamps to another room, and set it down here for a moment. . . ."

At this point the young servant placed a small table of mulberry wood in front of the screen, then another woman brought in a potted plant and set it on the table. The two withdrew, and Furuya found himself holding his breath. On the plain back-ground of the double-leafed screen, towards the right side of it and exactly in front of him, the shadow of the plant appeared quite clearly. The square pot was of a smooth, glazed brick colour, and in it, slightly to the left, grew an ancient dwarf tree, a zelkova which had still not lost its leaves, with a tangle of powerfully spreading roots below five trunks, thick and erect; and it was these that intertwined their black shadows on the screen, drawing sharp-etched lines upon that silver night sky, somewhat larger than life and the more splendid for that reason.

The old woman went on:

"It was such a surprise to find the shadows on the screen. Such a joy for you. You loved making the shadow of a fox with your fingers, too—you were always doing it."

"By 'you' you mean me, do you?"

"Of course. It was certainly the same screen, though the plant may have been a different one."

The old woman proceeded to talk at some length about somebody's passion for *bonsai* trees; she never made it clear who this person was, but it seemed to be her grandfather. Apparently, he particularly liked finding young saplings growing wild, and often went in search of them in the forest on his own estate, wrapping their roots all round with damp rags and putting oil-paper over the top. How convenient he would have found the plastic bags we have nowadays. He always used to joke that whenever his leather gloves wore out he could still use them in his forest. Actually, of course, it was to make sure he didn't cut his hand with the billhook or the pruning shears. He didn't like using wire to bend the plants, so he just relied on a Chinese book he had on the subject, looking at the illustrations in it or at picture postcards of the Fine Arts Exhibition, and trying to let them be as natural as possible.

As he sat in the semi-darkness listening to these reminiscences and looking at the shadow of the dwarf zelkova, the novelist wondered what was really going on at the back of this woman's mind. Why should she have taken all this trouble to show him this? How could she possibly know about his secret fascination with tree shadows? Yet plainly she did know, as became obvious when she left the subject of her grandfather's favourite pastime and moved on to something else, again not making it at all clear at the beginning whom she was talking about.

"The child is father to the man, they say. I have always thought how very true that is."

Furuya's face was an expressionless mask, so she continued, surprising him by referring to a work he hadn't expected her to have read:

"In the novel about Shanghai during the last years of the Shogunate . . ."

This was a book he'd written during the war, *Shanghai 1862*, and was his only historical novel, so clearly she was referring to that. After the war, a certain critic had praised it as a unique example of the anti-war novel, and had constantly urged its republication; but Furuya, ashamed of its incompetence, hadn't included it among his collected works. It was based on an account by Takasugi Shinsaku of Shanghai six years before the Meiji Restoration. Takasugi, who had crossed from Nagasaki in 1862, described the culture shock he received on his first contact with a Europeanized city. Furuya also made use of contemporary Chinese, English, and French accounts of life in Shanghai, as well as the three months he himself had spent in the city at the bidding of a film company. In the novel, Takasugi suffers from constant diarrhoea because of the bad drinking water, is astonished by the boom of the noonday guns from the battleships, and stares open-mouthed at the sheer height of the flagpoles outside the various legations, which seem to pierce the very clouds. He hears rumours of how the American adventurer General Ward means to recover the town of Tsingpu from the Taipings, with his "ever-victorious force" of trained Chinese, and of the previous successes he has enjoyed. If the foreigners can do what they like in China, what may not happen, quite soon, in his own country? To restore his spirits he spends the night at a bawdy house where, awaking before dawn and thinking sad thoughts about the plight his country faces, he hears the sound of thunder. He peers out through the round, emerald window and sees a flash of lightning throw the shadow of a tree upon the wall of the brothel next door. It is a willow tree, tossed by the wind and beaten by the rain, the ultimate in pathos, in fleeting beauty. So attracted is he by the sight that he looks out again into the night, hoping to experience this transitory joy once more; but in vain. Another thought crosses his mind, however, which provides some compensation for the loss of this eternally vanished sight. Why not take a page out of Ward's own book and create soldiers out of ordinary peasants and townspeople? Thus the concept of a band of irregulars, to be formed in the following year back home in Chōshū by this same Takasugi Shinsaku, first sees the light in this quite unexpected manner.

This meant, of course, that Furuya's obsession with tree shadows was undoubtedly present before August 1945. Muttering to himself that he'd forgotten about Takasugi Shinsaku, he began to wonder what the woman would produce next; and, sure enough, she mentioned two scenes in other works, one in the novel about the great politician's last romance, and the other describing how the youth just out of prison is saved from imminent disaster by a power cut. None of this surprised him. What he did feel was a sense of mortification at his own facile use of the same scene in so many novels, and while savouring the slight bitterness of this he watched the shadows of the five tree trunks expanding and contracting on the silver screen, almost as if they were alive.

"You know," she said, "my memory recently has become so bad. I don't remember it all that well, but I think part of it went like this:·

And I, in my undress,
Perchance like to a tree,
The shadow of a tree.

Now how did the opening go?"

His first response was to remind himself that weird people can only be expected to say weird things. The second was that he seemed to have heard the lines somewhere before.

"Sounds very turn-of-the-century. A woman poet, of course. Yosano Akiko, or one of her imitators?"

The old woman smiled sympathetically and told him in a slightly embarrassed voice that he had written it himself. He then remembered. In the novel about the girl who becomes a film actress, the mistress in turn of a painter, a soldier, and a businessman, then a gangster's moll, a poet, a writer, and finally a salmon, he'd been obliged to write ten specimens of her poetic work, and this must be one of them. Of the ten, two or three were at least not explicitly about the sexual act, and this seemed to belong to that minority. He tried saying the lines to himself, hoping that if he got the rhythm running in his head the lost opening lines might turn up, but nothing did.

"Since I've completely forgotten the ending, I really do wish I could remember the opening," he said with a wry smile. "What you're saying," he went on, "is that I have an *idée fixe* about the shadows of trees, and that I first developed it when I was a little child watching the shadows of a dwarf tree in this house?"

"Yes."

"And I've managed to forget entirely about it, in just the same way that I've forgotten that awful poem of mine."

"You are too modest about your poem, and the quality of your memory. After all, you were only two or three years old, so it's quite natural that you should not remember. There were other places as well. . . ."

"Places where tree shadows appeared?"

"Yes. At least, I feel there were."

Furuya decided to argue no further. Discussion was hardly possible with a woman who wasn't in her right mind, and he had already worked things out to his own satisfaction. Here was a reader, well acquainted with his writings, who had managed to find a number of scenes dealing with the shadows of trees, and had allowed it to stimulate her imagination until she'd arrived at this preposterous, yet consistent, fantasy. Perhaps little Masashige really had been interested in shadow pictures, and the reality and fantasy had become interwoven into a more convincing illusion. This assumption certainly fitted the facts beautifully, and he had no compunction whatsoever about accepting it. With no doubts remaining, he went on gazing at the dance of shadows on the screen, deep black in the centre, but drifting to a fainter, greyish colour at the edges.

"It seems just like yesterday," the old woman said. "So late learning to speak. Two and a half and still not a word. Then, quite suddenly . . ."

Furuya realized she was talking about Masashige.

". . . quite out of the blue you started talking. Not baby talk, either, but real words."

The old lady smiled quietly to herself, then went on:

"Ever since the lamp was put here and you'd seen the shadows, we used to have it for a while every evening. Of course it was before the overhead lamp was lit. You loved it and looked forward to it so much. Then one day, at exactly that moment, you started talking. The lamp had been left here as it always was, and you said 'tree shadows', quite distinctly. You said it three times."

"Three times?"

He repeated the words involuntarily, and looked at her as she sat there with her legs stretched out in the partial darkness. She did not return his look. She was imitating, with some skill, a person who has just learnt to talk, in a voice that sounded hardly human, like the chirruping of birds perhaps, or a priestess chanting a spell:

"Tree shadows. Tree shadows. Tree shadows."

Furuya looked back at the screen. The flame from the lamp trembled, and the shadows of the five trunks of the tree swayed as if moved by the wind, widening and contracting. The shadows recomposed themselves, then shook into disorder again. His thoughts were not occupied with the idea that a line of dialogue in one of his books might have caught the attention of this old woman, who now recalled it, so that it provoked her unbalanced mind into yet another false reminiscence of an unreal past. Nor was he wondering who his mother was, or thinking that this woman might indeed be her. All he felt was that time had turned round upon itself, that it flowed and trembled with these restless shadows, flowed back more than seventy years to when he was a child of two and a half; then beyond that, accelerating now, hurtling backwards to lives before this one, to previous and other worlds, unknown worlds, lives he could never remember.

RAIN IN
THE WIND

1

After his health failed, my father only talked about the old days. This was a particularly disturbing change in someone so obsessed by his work that he hardly ever seemed to have time for any kind of reminiscence, and although I don't know how my mother reacted, it certainly scared my brother and his wife, as well as me. Admittedly I didn't go home all that often; just the occasional visit of a few days.

When he was feeling relatively well he would talk, slowly and bit by bit, about his boyhood, for example: how he'd grown up in a small country brewery, the youngest of three sons, and how it took him two hours walking through the snow to get to school in winter. Then it was his student days when he first lived in Tokyo, or the hospital in Korea where he'd worked, right on top of a hill, and just walking up that hill in summer had been enough to leave him bathed in sweat. There was the day he opened his practice: only three patients had turned up, and with complaints that weren't really within his scope at all; but late that night there was an emergency call asking him to handle a difficult birth, and he'd ridden on the horse the man had brought with him from his village, far off through the mountains by moonlit roads.

All his stories were about the distant past, as if he could only remember things that had happened before my brother and I were born. But there was one exception, something which had taken place just before the war started, in Shikoku, and he spoke about it with real pleasure.

Father was a local G.P. of the old school, so concerned about his patients he held surgeries even on Sundays and national holidays, and he found it almost impossible to leave home. He hardly had time to attend medical conferences in Tokyo, though it was only two hours away, and probably went there about once every four or five years—for just a few days even then. So I couldn't work out quite how he'd managed to take this leisurely trip to Shikoku, remarkable not only for its apparent length but for the fact that he hadn't gone alone. His companion had been an old and in some ways unlikely friend, a man called Kurokawa who taught at the high school in the town of Mito where my father had his practice, and where I was born and grew up. It was a state school, and I assume I don't really need to point out that, since this was before the war, it was in some ways rather like a post-war university. Kurokawa taught Japanese literature, being a specialist in Saikaku, Akinari, and other erotic writers of the early Edo period, so it was a bit weird that he should be a devout Christian going to church every Sunday without fail. He was also a remarkably heavy drinker; a genuine eccentric, in fact. My father had quite different tastes, since he read nothing except medical journals, hated all forms of religion, and only drank when social demands obliged him to; and yet the two of them were close friends. The one amusement they shared was *go*, but since neither was much good at it, or even all that interested, this wasn't what brought them together. Presumably all one can say is that they just got on with each other. Anyway, as a result of that friendship, when my brother and I went to high school Kurokawa was asked to be our guarantor, and because I took arts subjects he gave me in particular a lot of attention. I think he must have had a considerable influence on my decision to study Japanese literature at university, although I didn't actually specialize in the Edo novel but in the poetry of the medieval period instead.

Kurokawa had been born in Shikoku, so I assumed he had some

personal reason for going home and invited my father along with him. I never found out what this was since the one thing Father talked about when he was ill, as if it were a memory he particularly treasured, was what had happened in the town of Matsuyama or, more precisely, in a tea-house at Dōgo, the popular hot spring in the suburbs. The two of them met up with a priest who quite unceremoniously engaged them in conversation, and all three started drinking together, the upshot being that they spent a good part of the afternoon in a place where they'd only expected to stay a short while.

"The priest cadged drinks off you?"

"Well, I suppose you could say that," my father said with a smile. "He kept on sipping away. Certainly knew how to put it down. He wasn't an ordinary priest—the mendicant kind, trudging about with a begging bowl. But he could really tell a story—kept producing a whole string of them. Wonderful stuff; never heard so many at one and the same time. There was one about a *shōgi* player and his towel that had me in stitches."

Father chuckled at the memory, but didn't see fit to let me in on the joke.

"Knew how to tell a good dirty story as well."

I remember thinking how odd that remark was, since I'd never actually heard the words "dirty story" from my father's lips before; but my reaction was not that I was at last being treated as a grown-up: it was an unbearable, unforgettable sense of certainty that he was going to die. He remained unaffected, however, by the melancholy feelings stirring in the breast of his academic son, and went on quite cheerfully:

"We must have spent a good three hours drinking. Longer, maybe. He was a lot older than me, but he knew how to hold it. Didn't bat an eyelid, but just kept knocking it back."

"Mr Kurokawa likes his drink as well."

"He does. Still, right at the end, the two of them started having a row. That brought the party to a close. Not so much a row, I suppose, as a difference of opinion."

"What about?"

"The priest seemed to be all in favour of what was going on in China. That put Kurokawa's back up. He can't stand war in any form."

Kurokawa's anti-war attitude had been notorious. Anyone who'd gone to the high school would have been aware of it, as perhaps was also the case with anyone who had just been living in Mito at the time. He was on record as having been investigated by the Military Police for his views, which made him the subject of endless gossip, and people looked on him with an emotion close to awe. What seems strange to me now is that almost nobody criticized him for this, with even the right-wing students who got so much pleasure from keeping other people up to the mark apparently deciding that Kurokawa should be treated as a special case. This may have had something to do with the fact that the whole tone of the pre-war high schools was rather different from what it is now, so Kurokawa was accepted as an unworldly sort of person. He was also careful about appearances and made sure no suspect phrases ever issued from his lips on public occasions. But I think the main reason was that everyone knew his pacifism arose from profound religious conviction. I don't mean that people had any particular understanding of or sympathy with Christian beliefs, but rather that . . . well, they regarded him as a kind of sincere, minor freak.

The problem the police investigated him about occurred just after the outbreak of the war with China, and arose from a proposal made by the local vicar that the national flag be flown in front of the church, with a special flagpole and dais erected for the purpose. Kurokawa had so violently disagreed that somebody must have told the local police, and this eventually led to the M.P.'s at Utsunomiya and finally Tokyo itself deciding to look into the matter. The investigation he underwent didn't entail any actual beating up in a detention cell, but took the form of an appeal to the education authorities that his case be carefully scrutinized, and even the suggestion that he be asked to resign his post. But the headmaster was a man of some understanding, so everything was eventually brought under control, with nothing disastrous happening, or at least that was how the story went. By the time the Pacific War was drawing to a close the whole incident had taken on virtually legendary proportions, almost in the same class as that of the female ghost who was supposed to appear in the dormitory corridor.

Either because he was sick of the whole business, or because it encouraged his natural tendency as a teacher to stick to the text and not wander off into irrelevancies, Kurokawa became less inclined to open his mouth on matters unrelated to what he was actually teaching, and on the rare occasions when he did he never mentioned the military or the war. On national holidays, for example, when the whole school had to bow before the imperial portraits, he was said to have bent much lower than anybody else on the staff, and yet even this respectful posture was interpreted as an anti-war gesture, a heroic raspberry aimed at the militaristic state. No doubt young people living under a repressive regime tend to keep a close look-out for the slightest sign of a rebellious attitude in their elders, but judging from the invariably cynical opinions about the progress of the war that Kurokawa expressed when talking to my father, or to a young geography teacher called Yagizawa who was always thrashing him at *go*, or to those of his students and former students he felt he could trust, such an interpretation of his behaviour could hardly be called too deep a reading of the matter.

Now, this tendency to have a blind eye turned, as it were, to be forgiven his un-Japanese attitudes, was something Kurokawa might be able to rely on in his position as a teacher at school, but would hardly be the case when away from home ground, travelling in a place like Shikoku.

"Surely it was a bit unwise to say something like that to a priest? Or did he look particularly trustworthy?"

"Exactly. That's what I was worried about. After all, we didn't know the slightest thing about him. I suppose old Kurokawa, having had a sight too much to drink and being away from home, just got carried away."

Father began chuckling to himself again, so I asked him what eventually happened.

"The weather changed for the worse. That sort of brought things to an end. Then the priest went off. In the rain."

"Without paying his bill?"

"That's right. He just pushed off."

"You two stayed there, out of the rain?"

"Of course we did."

"So you had to pay up."

"Right."

I laughed. I can't remember if Father laughed or not.

"Anyway, there wasn't any trouble after that?" I persisted. "He didn't report you?"

"No, nothing of the kind."

"That was lucky."

"Yes."

Father's responses had gradually been getting briefer, but I hadn't paid much attention so I went on:

"Was all this before the trouble with the Military Police, or after?"

Father made no reply at all, having drifted into silence, not because he was displeased, I think, but only because he was tired. My sister-in-law came in at that moment with some melon. I soon polished mine off, but Father only took a couple of mouthfuls, then closed his eyes. I sat beside him as he slept, fanning him for a while. A large dragonfly came into the living room, but soon went out again.

2

That conversation took place in the summer of 1952, and Father died in the spring of the following year. He was sixty-seven. My brother had taken over the practice, and I had achieved a position as a research assistant in a university department of Japanese, so the funeral guests, or those who were unaware how low a salary I was getting, whispered to one another that the departed had nothing to worry about in this world at least.

Towards the end of the vigil, late at night when most people had left, I decided to ask Kurokawa about the trip to Shikoku. Sixty-two years old, five years younger than my father, he had already retired from school, and was now doing some lecturing at one of the new universities. He told me he was feeling perfectly fit, except that he had to limit his intake of alcohol, though from what I saw of his performance that night it didn't seem much different from what it had always been.

Kurokawa's response to my question was to put down his saké cup and grin at me.

"Yes. Shikoku. Did you hear about what happened at Dōgo? That was marvellous, offering Shinto sacred wine to a Buddhist priest in a tea-house. And he didn't have any qualms about knocking it back, either. Those were the days."

He directed this last remark at the photograph of my father set up on the small altar, then went on as if talking to himself:

"There are some terrible heavy drinkers in this world."

He heaved a deep sigh, but was then so overcome by the inappropriateness of his remark that the people around him, despite their awareness of what this solemn occasion demanded, could hardly help grinning along with him. I poured him another drink, hoping to find out more about this priest.

"He seems to have had plenty of good stories."

"He did. More like a professional story-teller than a priest. More like a court jester perhaps. A constant supply of them, one running on into another. . . ."

Kurokawa took another sip before continuing.

"A tremendous performer, that's all I can say. A real talent. Of course, it was all a bit crude, though it was bound to be since he was only a sort of provincial touring artist. That's what it comes down to, so it wouldn't be fair to compare him with any real professional, but still. . . ."

"My father seems to have particularly enjoyed some story about a *shōgi* player and his towel, though he didn't tell me what it was. Just laughed about it to himself, and in a surprisingly sly sort of way as well. . . ."

The story Kurokawa told was this. The priest was on one of his begging tours, and one afternoon, just before he arrived at the town that was his destination for that night, he came across a young man sleeping by the side of a river. He seemed to recognize the young man's face, and it turned out that they'd both stayed at the same cheap lodging house only some ten days before, spending the night in the same room. The young man was a professional *shōgi* player. He seemed to have fallen asleep after washing his underwear and setting it out to dry, for beside him was an old-fashioned loin-cloth, held down at each corner by pebbles so that it wouldn't blow away. The young man got up cheerfully when addressed, but then started complaining, not about his habitual lack of funds, to which he was more or less accustomed, but that he'd lost his hand towel. Now, a travelling *shōgi* player's most important possession is, naturally, his handbook with all the game records in it, but the second is his hand towel. You see, he visits a town, and goes to a certain house which he's heard from someone should be all right, and when he introduces himself to the local *shōgi* enthusiast whose house it is, he says he's from Tokyo or Osaka as the case may be, gives his name, pays his respects, and then, as a gesture of goodwill or sincerity or what have you, produces his hand towel (politely wrapped in paper, of course) and slides it across. The other person, naturally enough, accepts this, a symbolic bond has been formed, and so the *shōgi* player is able to stay the night, knowing his needs will be catered for; and when he takes his leave in the morning his towel will be returned to him, still in its paper wrapping, accompanied by a certain sum of money due to him from his host, also politely wrapped in paper. A similar ritual is gone through in the case of a refusal (should the person in question be busy or something), when inevitably he will suggest somewhere else to go, the obligation to do so having been established by the offer of the towel, which will also be returned immediately, so allowing the *shōgi* player to move on. The whole thing is a firmly established convention, and thus the hand towel is one of the marks, even one of the tricks, of the chess player's trade, a kind of lifeline for him.

The priest had lodged with enough *shōgi* players to know all this, so naturally he was aware how important an object it was and asked him rather anxiously what he was going to do about it. The young man indicated with a jerk of his head the half-dry white object flapping in the wind, saying that it should serve the purpose well enough. After all, it would be wrapped in paper and, if one offered it with the proper reverence, nobody would notice the difference. The idea of presenting, "with the proper reverence", a primitive piece of underwear instead of a neat little towel struck the priest as wonderfully funny, and he roared with laughter. Then, after only a month or so had passed, he ran into the young man again in another town. He appeared to be in funds now and even stood the priest a drink; but it was with an expression of genuine embarrassment that he admitted he'd met with a most peculiar disaster on the very day they'd parted a month before.

He'd gone to the house of a certain elderly dentist, well known as an aficionado of the game, only to be greeted by a young lady who had obviously just married him and was consequently quite ignorant of what the proper form was on such occasions. Having listened sympathetically to him introduce himself, she assured him that she would tell her husband all about it when he came back, and promptly accepted the wrapped object he'd hesitantly slid in her direction. Since there was no way he could let her know that she ought to slide it back, nor that the return of it might legitimately be accompanied by some appropriate sum appropriately wrapped, he was obliged to leave the embarrassing object with her and depart. Exit of crestfallen party.

The various mourners were obviously amused by Kurokawa's story, although each managed to keep the laughter down to a half-suppressed snigger. Just at that point my brother returned from some emergency call he'd had to make, so Kurokawa told the whole story again for his benefit. My brother chuckled over it a long time, reminding me of the way my father used to laugh. I felt the atmosphere of the vigil was becoming rather lax, and that I should change the subject slightly.

"Still, didn't the priest also have a very different side to his character? I mean, I heard he really lost his temper in some debate he had with you, and . . ."

"Well, it wasn't much of a debate, you know. We just exchanged a few words."

"I heard you had a serious clash about the war in China."

"No, no. Just a little discussion of the situation over there. Your father always exaggerated things. A clash, indeed."

"I see."

"Then the weather suddenly broke. A late autumn shower, with a strong wind. I muttered a few phrases to myself, wondering which of them would be right: 'rain in the wind', 'driving rain', and so on, and finally something a bit old-fashioned, 'driven rain'. The priest was greatly taken with that last one ...."

"Being a person of refined taste ...."

"... and he kept nodding and repeating it. Exactly right, he said, that's it, exactly, the perfect description, the final word on the subject. Things like that."

"I'm not surprised. It does describe that sort of weather very well. 'Driven rain.' It's nice."

Kurokawa nodded in satisfaction at my response, but added:

"Perhaps it was all just an act he put on. A few enthusiastic words of appreciation, and then he's back on the drink again. In the end he just says thank-you and pushes off. I was fairly taken aback, I can tell you. Had to pay for his drinks. Couldn't be helped. Wait a moment—I didn't pay; your father did. The one who drank the least footed the bill."

He turned towards my father's photograph and raised his cup in salutation.

"Let's take another trip together, shall we? You worked hard enough all your life. You deserve a rest. I'll soon be coming to join you, anyway."

3

An Anthology of Contemporary Haiku, the ninety-first volume in the Chikuma Shobō *Contemporary Japanese Literature* series, appeared in April 1957. I first came across it probably in the following year, and certainly no later than the spring of 1959, which means it was five or six years after my father died. At the time I was an assistant professor at a women's college, and because one of the graduation theses I was supervising was on modern poetry I had a look at the long appendix to the book, "A Short History of Contemporary Haiku" by Kanda Shigeo, and then dipped into the main text, reading here and there at random.

The big names of twentieth-century haiku, Masaoka Shiki, Takahama Kyoshi, and so on, were in a separate volume, and this one consisted of the work of seventy-three fairly minor figures, from Naitō Meisetsu onwards. As I read, I made marks in red pencil against the ones I liked—those of Watanabe Suiha and about a dozen others, poets writing in the traditional 5-7-5 form—while I gave a fairly wide berth to "free-rhythm" haiku. By some sort of accident, however, I noted two poems of that type, both with the same opening line, on either side of one about snow.

Shigururu ya	Rain in late autumn
shinanaide	managing not yet
iru	to die

Shigururu ya	Rain in late autumn
shigururu yama e	walking in the hills
ayumiiru	with the autumn rain

When I think about it now, it was very much like the way one immediately spots the name of somebody in a newspaper because it's the same as one's own. The two haiku themselves made no impression on me, my response being simply that here was a man who liked the kind of rain that falls in late autumn and early winter, the cold showers, usually nothing more than drizzle, which mist the hills in patches, sometimes hiding them behind a veil, and arouse those feelings of impermanence, vagueness, and time passing which obsess the poetic mind. I looked at the top right-hand corner of the page to see who he was, and found a name I'd never come across before, that of Taneda Santōka. Never having heard of him, I decided to read through all his haiku in the anthology. It was just a whim on my part.

He took up five pages of three columns a page, a total of

around three hundred haiku, selected presumably from his whole output. It may be that I've always been prejudiced against free-rhythm haiku, but I found the constant harping on travelling, loneliness, hunger, and poverty tedious. In fact the stuff really turned me off, and I expect it was only the acquired ability of a literary scholar to force himself to read just about anything, whether it arouses his interest or not, that kept me from giving up. The result was that, when I'd finally waded through it all, I felt horribly depressed. Naturally I'd been able to make the odd red pencil mark above a few haiku, but my overall reaction was that it was no surprise in the least that he should be so little known. My sense of disappointment may have been partly due to the fact that there were only two other poems dealing with autumn rain:

Ushiro sugata no   Whose back going
shigurete   into the autumn rain
yuku ka   fading

Shigururu ya   Rain in late autumn
aru dake no gohan   all the rice I have
yō yaketa   nicely cooked

The poem about going into the autumn rain was one of the few I'd ticked. Of course, the idea that I was looking for something and disappointed at not finding it is only the way I see things now, an interpretation coming well after the event.

When I'd finished reading I had a look at his photograph at the end of the book. It was obviously some amateurish snapshot which had been exorbitantly blown up to produce this blurred portrait of an old man's face against a dark background. Perhaps a self-consciousness about being photographed was responsible for the slight sense of nervousness, even tension, in his expression. He seemed to be bald, but I couldn't be quite sure; there might

123

have been a light directly above him which made a not very abundant head of hair shine like that. He wore a large pair of spectacles, one lens of which appeared to be metal-framed and the other rimless, though presumably this wasn't the case. His eyebrows were thick, even bushy, and he had a rather large mouth and ears. Finally, he had a quite preposterous beard, like a stringy brush dangling from his chin, which seemed more grizzled than white, although that could well have been the fault of the photograph. There was something unpleasantly worldly and vaguely corrupt about the whole thing, a priest who'd failed to achieve enlightenment and was spiritually in total disarray, but still determined not to let on to anybody, assuming this impudent, who-do-you-damn-well-take-me-for attitude towards the world. That the poet was also a priest was an impression I'd automatically received from reading three hundred of his poems, not by looking at this photograph.

I then read the small print of the biographical details:

> Born 1882, Hachiōji, Hōfu City, Yamaguchi Prefecture. Real name Taneda Shōichi. Educated at Yamaguchi Middle School, then Waseda University, Arts Faculty. Leaves without taking degree. 1911 becomes pupil of Ogiwara Seisensui (b. 1884, leader of free-rhythm movement), dedicating himself to haiku. No other profession throughout life. 1924 abandons wife and child to enter priesthood (Zen sect, Sōtō branch). Resides at Mitori Kannondō near Kumamoto, Gochūan in Yamaguchi, Issōan in Matsuyama. A born lover of travel and wine, tours whole country as mendicant priest with "one bamboo hat, one begging bowl". A life totally given over to the creation of haiku, devoid of all material possessions. 1940 dies suddenly at Issōan hermitage in Matsuyama in 59th year. Published one collection during lifetime, *Sōmokutō* (Grass Tree Stupa). Remaining manuscripts

published after death in *Gu o Mamoru* (The Defence of Folly) and *Ano Yama Koete* (Crossing That Mountain).

When I read that he'd abandoned his wife and child I felt it was just what one would have expected of someone like him, although the information that he'd been "a born lover of travel and wine" made no particular impression. However, "1940 dies suddenly at Issōan hermitage in Matsuyama" brought the poem "Whose back going / into the autumn rain / fading" vividly to life, like a butterfly zigzagging across my field of vision, and this in turn led to a new—though at first quite casual—idea. Might it not be that this bald (if bald he was) poet was that same priest my father and Kurokawa had plied with drink? Once the thought had occurred, it seized hold of me and wouldn't let go. A travelling priest who had "dedicated himself to haiku" would naturally have a way with words, and probably the gift of the gab as well; and a "born lover of wine" who was "devoid of all material possessions" would certainly be obliged to cadge his drinks off somebody. The real point, however, was his concern with late autumn rain. Admittedly, four poems out of three hundred is no remarkable percentage, but this was only a selection of his work and there could conceivably be many more among those which hadn't been chosen. Anyway, one could not state categorically that the priest had not been Santōka, so it was certainly possible that it had been him. In fact it was very likely indeed.

This kind of rash assumption was precisely what I never allowed myself as a scholar, yet on this occasion I accepted it with no qualms at all, presumably because I was dealing with contemporary literature, something outside my field, and thus something to which the usual scholarly rigour need not be applied. I admit this probably also reflected a prejudice shared by most scholars of Japanese literature, namely that nothing since the Meiji period really deserves to be taken seriously, which in my case led to the tacit assumption that there was no point in applying strict academic standards to works that weren't proper targets of genuine research. It may seem unwise to admit how much this bias affected my attitude, but I suspect that any literary scholar would regard it as a perfectly normal part of one's intellectual equipment.

Anyway, having come to my unfounded conclusion, I felt sufficiently elated to reread the four autumn-rain haiku, this time adding one more tick to the one about going into the rain. I then came across this towards the end of the selection:

Dōgo Spa

Asayu konkon	The morning bath
afureru mannaka no	water swiftly overflows
watakushi	me in it

Celebrating the simple joys of life (man plops into morning bath, bath overflows) is a theme common to a lot of free-rhythm haiku poets, and these lines by Santōka had nothing in particular to recommend them, being merely dull. Yet they appealed to me. What I liked was the naive image of Santōka, all nice and clean and smelling of soap after his morning bath, setting off along the road to the tea-house, there to rest and make the acquaintance of Kurokawa and my father. I felt (though unfortunately this contradicts my disparaging remarks about modern Japanese literature) that my father's encounter with a poet of sufficient standing to appear in *Contemporary Japanese Literature* added a certain distinction to the life of a man who'd been nothing more than a local G.P. Or it might be that I was performing some sort of act of filial devotion by aggrandizing the priest who'd sponged off him. As the night grew colder I spent a long time savouring this remarkable discovery I'd concocted for myself.

4

Two days later I had to go into the university to teach, and decided to have a look in the library for the three books mentioned
in that brief biography; but the library was very small, so I had no
great hopes of finding anything as rare as they were. In fact, when
I looked up Santōka in the card index, all I came across was the
volume of *Contemporary Japanese Literature* I'd already seen. I
could hardly complain, however, as I expect I would have got the
same result in almost any library at that time. During the fifties
Santōka was a complete unknown, and his appearance in a standard anthology issued by a big publisher was quite exceptional.
For this reason I talked to nobody about the possibility of Kurokawa and my father having met Santōka, because nobody I
knew would have shown the slightest interest. I didn't know
anybody who wrote haiku for a start, and my one colleague who
specialized in the modern period was only concerned with the
novel, theories of the novel, and biographies of novelists.

I had also come to the conclusion that my discovery had been a
late-night fantasy, something that wouldn't stand up to the harsh
scrutiny of the day. It had been a ritual, only half serious, performed secretly at midnight to appease my dead father's shade. So,
having made the gesture of looking for Santōka's works in the
library, I felt no need to do anything more, and came inevitably to
forget all about him. I had my hands full enough with research
into medieval poetry without wanting to bother my head with
Santōka.

Then, in the autumn of 1960, I was obliged to return home
since my mother was ill, and one evening went to visit Kurokawa
at his home. He was seventy, and some time ago had given up lecturing at the university to which he'd gone after retiring from
high school, and now just taught twice a week at a private junior

college. He looked remarkably well. Since we hadn't played *go* for ages we started off with a couple of games, both of which I won with ease, not merely because Kurokawa had never been any good at it but because he seemed to be more concerned with what was going on in the world of beer (which he drank instead of tea), and his mind just wasn't on the game at all. We then switched to saké, talking about this and that, until I suddenly remembered the business at the tea-house in Dōgo. When I mentioned it, however, Kurokawa immediately flushed red with rage.

"That damn priest? What's so interesting about him, then?"

I wasn't sure if this irritated response indicated that he had aged and could no longer hold his drink, or that I'd been unwise not to let him win one of the games of *go*; but it turned out that his rage was directed at his recollection of the argument he'd had with the priest about the conduct of the war in China. It seemed he was still in no mood to forgive the "warmonger", as he bitterly referred to him, for his militaristic opinions.

"All he could do was mouth newspaper slogans at me: 'Chastising Chinese Aggression', 'Spreading World-wide the Imperial Teachings', and other drivel—all in dead earnest. Never met such an idiot. Of course, it was impossible to reason with him. He said Japan was a poor nation, and the only path for a race like ours must be traced in blood, and so on, when it was as clear as daylight that we were poor because all our financial resources were being wasted on armaments."

"Well, you were absolutely right, of course," I chimed in, perhaps a bit too hastily, and Kurokawa went on:

"Funny sort of priest. No danger of him having to join the army, so he could happily recommend war for everybody else. All that talk about national effort, and there he was trudging about with a begging bowl. It didn't make sense."

"Quite."

"Rightist, you see. Probably played with left-wing ideas when

128

he was young, then went into the Buddhist church and emerged way over on the right. Plenty of people like that at the time. Looked just the type."

Kurokawa had said all this at high speed, almost spitting out the words; but he soon returned to his usual quiet tone of voice, and his expression softened.

"He got on my nerves rather, so I gave him a piece of my mind. Your father was really worried. Kept telling me to stop. But I just let the horse have its head. . . ."

"Um. I may be wrong, but I believe you said at my father's funeral that there was no actual clash of opinions between you."

"That's right, I did. Because there were other people present. One in particular, the lieutenant-general or major-general's widow. You know who I mean."

This was the wife of a distant relation of my mother's who'd risen to the rank of major-general by the time the war ended. I didn't know either the wife or the husband, but the widow (as she then was) came to my father's funeral for some reason I wasn't clear about. I couldn't remember if she was actually present in the room when we were having our conversation, but if Kurokawa said so then she must have been. While I was paying no attention to my surroundings, Kurokawa had noticed the old lady and, so as not to hurt her feelings, had kept off the subject of war and restricted himself to the *shōgi* player's hand towel. It was just one more instance of his consideration for others. I felt ashamed of my own insensitivity.

"So you pretended he only told a lot of jokes. . . ," I said, speaking the last words as though to myself.

"I wasn't pretending. He did tell a lot of jokes. He told them very well. He was a marvellous raconteur—very fast. It was eccentric, even weird perhaps, but I'd certainly heard nothing like it. Not just eccentric, either. I'd say he was a real character; he was even quite sensitive in some ways. I just didn't like the way he supported an aggressive war. I couldn't take that at all."

Hearing that he was "quite sensitive in some ways", I was eager to get onto the subject of Santōka, but didn't get the chance.

"It must have been at the end of November, perhaps the beginning of December. A lovely autumn day, just the kind of weather when anyone would have felt like quenching his thirst early on in the day," said Kurokawa, as if the events of that time were coming back to him, and he went on to describe what had happened.

That morning, after breakfast, he and my father had taken the tram into the centre of Matsuyama, done some sightseeing, and then set off back to Dōgo a little after midday. A resort like Dōgo is always crowded with people, so they chose an out-of-the-way tea-house in which to rest. I imagine my father just wanted a light lunch, but presumably Kurokawa had alcohol on his mind.

He wasn't all that clear about what kind of place it was ("it must have been a village shop with a tea-house tacked on, I suppose"), but at least it wasn't some wind-swept, desolate shack. So they sat in the shop, eating *inari zushi* and drinking beer and chattering to each other, when a priest, who had been sitting unobtrusively nearby reading a newspaper, addressed them in a very friendly way.

"I believe you must be from Tokyo. I spent a little time there some years ago, and it's always a pleasure to hear Tokyo speech. Good, precise language, a joy in itself, besides bringing back the past."

Although they had both been students in Tokyo, neither lived there now, but they didn't mention this, replying in an appropriate way to his friendly overture, and the priest responded by relating some peculiar incident which had occurred in Tokyo when he was living there, presumably as a university student as well. This led to all three engaging in general conversation, and, very much as if he were a stranger they'd met on the train, beer was urged on him. The priest declined quite firmly, but at last allowed himself to be persuaded into accepting one small glass, which he drank fairly slowly ("it must have taken him about five minutes"), and then cheerfully accepted a refill, without any outward qualms or hesitations, although he seemed more absorbed in the story he was telling than in the beer. Part of his gift as a conversationalist was that he also knew how to listen (though it still probably consisted of seven parts talk to three parts listening), but it was his narrative skill that was most striking, for he had a real artist's understanding of pace, timing, and form, and knew exactly when and how to bring his stories to a close. It was also completely unobtrusive, with no sense of someone demonstrating a skill, and quite straightforward, as though he were talking to a close friend with whom he felt completely relaxed.

"By the time we'd finished two or three bottles it was as if we'd known each other for ten years or more." So it wasn't surprising they switched to saké, particularly as Kurokawa was normally in the habit of drinking beer only as a brief prelude to getting down to the real thing. The local saké was good, unpretentious and dry, and all three were satisfied with the way the day was proceeding.

Kurokawa felt he was in the company of a drinker of the first rank by the time they'd finished the fourth or fifth flask. He said he could tell by the way the priest, without any interruption of his pleasant flow of speech, kept refilling his own cup and raising it to his lips in a precise, steady, repeated motion; although he stopped noticing this after a while, for his stories were so interesting, so rich and varied, that he just listened, as the laughter, the smiles, and the drinking continued. By this stage it had turned into a solo performance by the priest. My father had stopped drinking and sipped tea instead, occasionally chuckling to himself in obvious good humour. The priest, on the other hand, each time his flask was empty, would call to the old lady of the shop for another, always in a perfectly easy way so there was nothing strange about it. In fact it seemed the most natural thing in the world.

"Pretty remarkable behaviour for a mendicant priest. I suppose he'd had a lot of practice."

"A past master, believe me," replied Kurokawa. "A classic demonstration of the art."

"Did he have other stories like the *shōgi* player's underwear?"

"Masses of them, and all much the same. All inoffensive, amusing, and nothing more. I've forgotten the lot."

"I suppose he didn't talk about haiku at all?"

"I don't think so," said Kurokawa, pondering the question a while and then giving up. "I can't remember, anyway, if he did. It's all gone."

"Didn't talk about free-rhythm haiku, anything like that?"

"Shouldn't think so. I can't remember, of course, but I'm pretty sure nothing of that kind was talked about. Why do you ask, anyway? Have you got something on your mind?"

"Well, I have really. There's a haiku poet called Taneda Santōka. . . ."

"Of the Hekigoto school?"

"A disciple of Seisensui, in fact, and thought of very highly in some circles."

I gave a short account of Santōka, quoting three of his haiku.

Ushiro sugata no	Whose back going
shigurete	into the autumn rain
yuku ka	fading
Massugu na	On the dead
michi de	straight road
samishii	alone
Ame furu	Going barefoot
furusato wa	about my home village
hadashi de yuku	as the rain falls

Kurokawa particularly liked the "Ushiro sugata" poem, and

didn't make the obvious comparison with Bashō but said much more pertinently that it had something almost erotic about it, similar to a popular ballad from the Edo period. I was very struck by that, adding that it did sound remarkably like the opening to such a song, to which he replied that it was probably closer to the sophisticated, slightly decadent haiku of the same period, although he didn't really know enough about such things to say. Since he'd shown this amount of interest, I thought I could introduce my theory that the priest he and Father had met at Dōgo was this very same Santōka.

Kurokawa listened carefully to what I said, then sank into silence as he thought about it. Finally he made a little grunt and muttered:

"Died just before the war in Matsuyama. A priest. Liked his drink. Well, it seems to fit. It's an interesting idea, anyway. Taneda Santōka. Judging from that one poem, he seems to have been a cut above his master, Seisensui. Still, I don't know. The impression I got of him hadn't much to do with people fading into the rain or anything. He was just a worldly priest, common, vulgar. All he talked about was drink and women. I could always be wrong, of course. After all, most poets have something of that about them. In pre-war days, for example, when the big boss of one of the poetry groups went off to the provinces, the people there always had to provide a 'sacrificial maiden' for him from among the local poetesses, or female hangers-on. At least that's what I've heard; it might be a pack of lies, I suppose. Still, in principle it sounds right; there's nothing more awful than a great man of letters. They're all the same—nothing poetic about them; just a lot of creeps on the make."

We'd now deviated considerably from our original subject, but when we returned to it the inevitable conclusion appeared to be that it was very unlikely their acquaintance had been Santōka. I took his word for it, merely justifying the rashness of my assumption by saying that it all seemed to fit, he being a priest, fond of drink, and in Shikoku in the right year.

"Now, what year was it? Ah, that's right, the year of the Konoe Cabinet. That makes it 1940, doesn't it? Yes, November 30th, 1940. I remember because the following day, being the first of the month, was one of those Support Asia Days, so you couldn't drink alcohol, and it was discussing this that led to our quarrel— well, not so much a quarrel as a debate—about the war in China."

"If that's what it was all about I should have thought you'd both have been of the same opinion."

Kurokawa looked almost boyishly embarrassed by this mild fun I'd poked at him, and replied:

"Obviously both of us would have been considerably put out by a day on which saké was prohibited. There couldn't have been any disagreement about that. What irritated me was that he started blabbing away about how shameful it was for us, shouldering as we must the burden of the Construction of a Greater East Asia, to be drinking away like this just because we wouldn't be able to on the following day, which was dedicated to that Great Cause. That got on my wick. Then he went on about owing an apology to our soldier boys in the front line, or some such stuff, but I didn't take much notice. After all, how can you reply to someone who uses phrases like the 'Construction of a Greater East Asia', which was the kind of shit the military were throwing about at the time?"

I was amused to note the slight vulgarity that had crept into his speech as he grew excited, and I asked him what precisely he'd said in reply to all this. Kurokawa seemed a little reluctant to answer.

"Well," he said at last, "you must realize that we'd both had quite a lot to drink. I said that if we didn't make stupid aggressive wars we could all of us have enough to drink whenever we wanted it. I think I probably put it a bit more discreetly than that. After

"No. It goes back to the Heian period. It's been used in poetry."

"Really? It sounds to me like something an old sea-dog might have said. 'Ah, looks like driven rain up ahead'. . . ."

But my father's reflections were put an end to by the priest repeating the expression "driven rain" aloud, apparently in the grip of some powerful emotion. His cup remained untouched, and it was as if he were tasting the words in his mouth in place of the drink, for he said them over and over. He then dipped his finger in some spilt saké and wrote the characters on the table.

"Driven rain. That's absolutely right. Perfect. People in those days certainly knew how to express things. So brief, and yet it seems to sum up everything. It's the first time I've heard it. Is it well known?"

"Not particularly. Minamoto Yorimasa used it. He was the one . . ."

"Who hunted down the fabulous night bird?"

"That's right. Minamoto of the third rank."

" 'And nevermore the blossoms on the buried tree.' That Yorimasa?"

"Exactly."

Here my father butted in to say that it was Yorimasa who committed ritual suicide at the Byōdōin temple at Uji, and this led to their discussing the war between the Taira and Minamoto clans, a subject which, unlike the war in China, caused offence to nobody.

Eventually, in obvious admiration, the priest repeated the two words, closing his eyes and nodding his head a few times. He picked up his cup and flask again, drained the cup dry four or five times in quick succession, then drew himself up into a formal seated position, and placed his hands together in benediction:

"I must express my profound gratitude for the cordial hospital-

137

ity offered me this day. For the wine, and for driven rain, I give my deepest thanks."

After this solemn leave-taking formula, he stood up briskly, slipped on his clogs or whatever, declined the old woman's offer of an umbrella, and—to borrow Kurokawa's words, "loath as we were to see him go"—pushed off into the rain.

I really ought to have pressed Kurokawa at this point about the poem by Yorimasa, but since I was supposed to be an authority on medieval poetry I wasn't all that eager to display my ignorance before someone who, although my teacher, was still only a specialist in Edo erotica and should have known much less about it than me. The implicit suggestion (in his tone of voice, if not his actual words) when he referred to the poem was that I must be well acquainted with it, and I didn't have the courage to say I wasn't. I don't think I would behave like that now, but at the time I was still young, and vanity played an important part in my life.

But perhaps I'm being a bit too harsh on my youthful self, and vanity did not play quite such a vital role in my failing to ask about the poem, for it wasn't so much the priest's extraordinary enthusiasm for those two words that struck me at the time as his abrupt departure, his "back going into the autumn rain, fading", the poem seeming so strikingly relevant that I again became confident that this must have been Santōka. After all, how many eccentric priests of that calibre could possibly have been around in that same place and at that exact time? It seemed the right moment to ask Kurokawa what the priest had looked like, and see if his description corresponded at all with the photograph in *Contemporary Japanese Literature*.

Unfortunately, this part of the investigation didn't go too well. The photograph had not been a good one, and it was also some time since I'd looked at it, so my questions were a bit hazy—as was Kurokawa's memory. In fact he was astonishingly vague. I asked him about the bald head, the beard, and the glasses, and his response each time was to become profoundly lost in thought. For example:

"Yes, he certainly wore glasses. Big fat lenses. Very short-sighted, I should have thought. Quite positive he did."

But having given this firm guarantee, he soon cancelled it:

"No. Wait a minute. No, I'm not sure, not sure at all."

The same happened with the beard:

"A beard?" he said, contemplating the idea for a while. "I got the impression that he was pretty old, so it wouldn't have been strange if he did have a beard. Still, I can't help thinking that he was just ill-shaven; a two or three days' growth rather than a beard. I mean, what I recall of the face is the impression it gave, one of worldliness, of the market-place. Nothing priest-like about it. That's all I can say."

Compared with his fairly precise recall of a lot of the words they'd exchanged, this was absurdly vague and totally unreliable; but since memory tends to be like that, there was nothing I could do except give up on that particular point. We'd both, after all, had quite a lot to drink. Yet, oddly enough, because Kurokawa had failed so signally to remember the face, all the confidence of a few seconds before seemed to drain out of me, perhaps because it had been so excessive. But a much more important objection to the idea that it might have been Santōka now seemed to me the priest's remark about having no adequate words of apology to offer His Imperial Majesty. It simply didn't go at all with the language of Santōka's poetry which, as Kurokawa had said so well, had that elegant, slightly decadent atmosphere of the Edo world about it, the floating world of witty *haikai*, sentimental songs and ballads, of the melancholy sight of the departing hero as he moves slowly away into the misty rain. His inarticulateness concerning H.I.M. suggested a world of drab khaki uniforms, barked-out orders, mud, sweat, and stupidity.

As I got more and more drunk, I began to see two quite different priests at Dōgo Spa, each representing one of these two different worlds; the two images then came together to make one figure, one priest, the urbane poet and the fanatical emperor-worshipper, only to drift apart again, turning their backs on each other. But Kurokawa disturbed these confused images of mine by dropping the subject of Santōka completely, and getting onto a topic much nearer home by complaining about the quality of the saké one had to drink nowadays, so damn sickly sweet, and it was all the fault of the war because it hadn't tasted like that before, and if only all the Christians in Japan had had a bit more guts and really opposed the war it needn't have happened and then we wouldn't have to drink saké as lousy as this. These irrelevant remarks were presumably occasioned by a memory of how good the saké had tasted on that afternoon in Dōgo. I decided it was about time I made a move to leave.

But, despite the remarkable staggers and lurches he made as he saw me to the door, I managed to revive the subject one last time, which must indicate, given the state I too was in, how much a hold my literary guessing-game had taken on my mind. Or perhaps I was still reluctant to lose this opportunity for an imaginary act of filial piety towards my father. Anyway I asked him again, just to make sure:

"It was 1940, wasn't it? November 30th, 1940?"

"Right. Year 2600 of the Imperial Succession," he said, with a large nod.

"Still. You chose a funny time to go travelling, didn't you? In term-time. With the winter holiday still three weeks or so away."

"That's right. Can't remember why now." He shook his head, then smiled and said: "Must have been playing truant."

5

What I probably should have done that evening as soon as I got home—or, if that was impractical because of the lateness of the hour, at least the next morning—was ask my mother or brother why such a hard-working person as my father should have decided to take a week's holiday in Shikoku. The only question in my mind, however, was how a teacher like Kurokawa had been able to go on a trip like that when it was still term-time, and I assume it was because I was in the teaching profession myself. At least that assumption makes sense of my behaviour.

Still, even if it does make sense, I can't work out why I didn't take another look at the only piece of literature I had on Santōka's life, namely the biographical sketch in *An Anthology of Contemporary Haiku*, as soon as I got back to Tokyo. Unlike my other books on modern literature, this one at least hadn't been stuck away somewhere at the back of a cupboard. Of course, it might have been pure laziness, just not wanting to bother, but the fact that I hadn't bothered seems to indicate a desire, albeit a very slight one, not to disturb the almost legendary shape that an event in the past had taken on for me. I wanted the picture I had in my head of Santōka, Kurokawa, and my father happily chatting away in the tea-house in Dōgo to remain as it was. This nursery tale had already been disturbed, sullied indeed, by what I'd heard from Kurokawa about Santōka (?) being a rightist, a warmonger and an emperor fanatic, and my unconscious decision to investigate the matter no further I can now see as having a certain inevitability about it.

Perhaps as some unconscious compensation for what I wasn't doing, I did, in fact, try to look up the poem by Yorimasa that Kurokawa had mentioned, but his *Collected Poems* only revealed four works in which there was any reference to *shigure* (late autumn rain), and certainly none containing the key term at issue, that of driven rain (*yokoshigure*). A further investigation of the massive concordance to Japanese poetry (the *Kokka Taikan*) and the index to the *Great Anthology of National Poetry* (*Kokka*

Taikei) produced nothing either. Admittedly, both these works give only the first and last lines of each five-line poem, but I decided to ignore this limitation, even though it meant that I hadn't been absolutely thorough, and concluded that no Japanese poem made any mention of *yokoshigure*. Kurokawa's memory must simply have been wrong. After looking at the collected works of another soldier poet of the period, Taira Tadanori, and failing to find anything about it there, I couldn't see any point in prolonging the search. Unfortunately, I never found an opportunity to ask Kurokawa directly. The last time I saw him was at the funeral of my mother in the following summer, and towards the end of the same year he suddenly felt unwell when drinking one evening, and while his wife was telephoning for the doctor he died.

So that seemed to be the last of Santōka. The whole thing had only begun very casually anyway, and at the time I hadn't heard the slightest murmur of the fame he was eventually to achieve. My loss of interest, therefore, was natural enough, and for about ten years I forgot the journey and the saké and the poet, the teahouse in Dōgo and the priest.

Even so, there was one minor incident. It was the year when I'd been given a temporary lectureship at my old university, which would be some six years ago now, round about the time the Santōka boom was starting to get into its stride. I was attending a student get-together at a restaurant near the university, and in the lavatory I came across this piece of graffiti:

Oto wa shigure ka   The sound of autumn rain?

It was written in a surprisingly literate hand for a present-day student, and I remember thinking it would make a rather good opening for a song. I have to admit, with some reluctance, that I didn't immediately recognize that this was a work by Santōka, but at least I was impressed by the wit of the person who'd seen fit to write it on a lavatory wall, which isn't bad going for a literary scholar, I suppose.

6

According to the biographical chronology in the seventh volume of the *Collected Works* (published by Shunyōdō Shoten), Santōka first became known to the public at large in the autumn of 1967. The interest in him was triggered by a series of seven articles in the Osaka *Asahi*, written by Santōka's friend and fellow poet Ōyama Sumita. This chronology doesn't record when he was introduced to an even wider public on a late-night radio show, or the date of the appearance of his cartoon life in the *Boys' Magazine*, but obviously all that must have come after the Ōyama articles. Since I don't read newspapers published in Osaka, don't listen to late-night radio shows, and have no interest whatsoever in comic books, I was bound to become aware of what was happening only much later; in fact I remained totally ignorant until the 1970s. Although a full-length biography had appeared in 1967, an edition of his notebooks in 1968, reissues of *Crossing That Mountain* in 1969, and *The Defence of Folly* and *Grass Tree Stupa* in 1971, I missed them all, presumably because I tend to ignore newly published books. I only came across Ōyama's standard edition of the poems, published in 1971, when I happened to accompany my daughter to the local bookshop towards the end of that year.

My first response on seeing it was something close to genuine stupefaction, quite literally not believing my own eyes. It was like meeting an old acquaintance after many years and realizing what a distinguished person he'd become. As I blinked at the fat volume in the glare of the bookshop's fluorescent light, I stood for a while stock-still, feeling both pride and excitement—though I can't think why, since Santōka was no discovery of mine. This excitement, however, was soon followed by a powerful sense of

143

let-down, because when I picked up the volume and turned to the biographical chronology at the end I found this entry for 1940:

> Fifty-nine. Private printing of haiku selection *Karasu* (Crow). Living at Issōan in Matsuyama. Haiku circle, "The Persimmon Group", formed. In May, with the publication of *Sōmokutō* (Grass Tree Stupa) by a Tokyo publisher, travels to Hiroshima, Tokuyama, and Kita Kyushu. October 10th, afternoon, collapses with cerebral haemorrhage. From that evening, members of haiku circle assemble at hermitage. Dies at approximately four in the morning of eleventh. Kubo arrives in time for funeral. Taneda Ken (his son) comes from Manchuria to take care of remains. Ōyama arrives to pay off debts.

Kurokawa had met the heavy-drinking priest on November 30th of that year, so clearly it couldn't have been Santōka, who was no longer alive. With an awful feeling of deflation, and a theatrically wry smile contorting my face, I was forced to admit that the whole supposition had become quite hopeless, consoling myself with the reflection that he was nothing to write home about as a poet anyway. Tutting mildly to myself, I was about to return the book to its place on the shelf, when instead I opened it casually in the middle, presumably because I still wasn't quite prepared to give up yet. And there, to my astonishment again, I saw this poem:

> Oto wa shigure ka   The sound of autumn rain?

immediately followed by:

> Asa kara shigurete   Light rain since morning
> kaki no ha no   the beauty of
> utsukushisa wa   the persimmon leaves

These were the last two poems on the left-hand page, and

when I looked to the right I found these two as well:

Shigurete nurete
matsu hito ga
kita

Wet in the rain
and the awaited
person comes

Watashi hitori no
kyō no owari no
shigurete kita

Today spent alone
and at its close
the rain comes on

Four poems out of fourteen on a page opened quite at random. This wasn't someone who was merely fond of using the word *shigure*, but a man obsessed, even bewitched, by it. Ignoring the extravagance of spending such a large sum of money on something like a volume of free-rhythm haiku, I bought the book without hesitation, telling my daughter, who was still debating what kind of diary she should buy, to hurry up about it.

7

The concept of the *kigo*, or "season word", is so linked with traditional poetics that it may seem comically out of place in the context of a writer of free-rhythm haiku, but there doesn't appear to be anything else one can use. An investigation of the standard *Collected Poems*, however, reveals that Santōka's most frequent season marker is by no means late autumn rain. There is no need to count: a mere flicking through the pages makes it quite clear that the words "snow" or "fallen leaves" occur much more frequently. In the first section of the volume *Grass Tree Stupa* (a selection made by Santōka himself), there are sixteen poems about autumn rain. In the second part, entitled *Gleanings* (a selection made by Ōyama from haiku Santōka had discarded), there are eighteen; and in the third section, a selection from his earliest published haiku in the magazine *Sōun* (Stratus Clouds), there is only one. This makes a total of thirty-five, while the references to snow or fallen leaves are, in either case, at least double that number.

Still, if one decides not to go by the simple yardstick of quantity, but to think of the quality of the poems as well, then it's a quite different story, and late autumn rain certainly predominates in the really good poems. In *Sōmokutō*, for example, there is the poem already quoted as a favourite of mine, the title of which is given in this edition as "Self-Ridicule":

Ushiro sugata no	Whose back going
shigurete	into the autumn rain
yuku ka	fading

That's the only one, I admit; but if one looks at "Gleanings"—the selection made by Ōyama from the discarded haiku—then a striking number of his best poems are on that subject.

Tomete kurenai	Walking through the rain of
mura no	the village where I have
shigure o aruku	no place to stay
Shigururu ya	The rain comes down
michi wa	the road
hitosuji	makes one straight line

Dazaifu

Ukon no	Before the shrine the
tachibana no mi no	mandarin tree its fruit
shigururu ya	wet in the autumn rain
Ōkusu mo	The great camphor tree
watashi mo inu mo	and me and the dog
shiguretsutsu	soaked in the rain
Matsu no otera	Temple among pines as

146

| shigure to natte | rain comes on   here I shall |
| tomarimasu | spend the night |

| Oto wa shigure ka | The sound of autumn rain? |

It's clear from these that he had a passion for this sort of rain, and was obsessed by the images it presented. Also, judging from the high quality of other haiku on the same theme which he decided to discard, this obsession of his was by no means a simple one; it could even be considered perverse in a sense, as though he were almost ashamed of the emotions that were aroused in him. The rain that falls in late autumn—the occasional showers which appear and disappear among the mountains, covering them in a fine mist, then once again revealing their existence—has always been associated with travel in Japanese literature, particularly in the haiku tradition; and the symbolic implications to be drawn from it are fairly obvious. Now, in the case of Santōka, this tradition comes to life again, not as a natural continuation, but as a deliberately willed act, as if he were acutely aware of the tradition and yet determined that his use of it must appear as no stereotyped act of conformity. Thus he allied himself with a haiku school which was vigorously breaking out of the confines of the traditional 5-7-5 form, yet still relied entirely on a sensibility directly linked to the past in which that form had been created. He must, I thought, have felt extremely unsettled in the contradictory poetic role he felt obliged to play.

Those, at least, were my reflections as I read through the volume in one sitting, reading with care and even taking notes as I did so. I don't mean that I only saw Santōka's concern with autumn rain as an attempt to link himself with traditional sensibilities, for clearly much more complex, even mixed motives were at work there. As I thought of his character in general, or at least the one that appeared in his writings, I came to the conclusion that it revealed an overall obsession with images of rain, or perhaps just water itself. The truth is that I would have preferred to continue emphasizing the primary role of late autumn rain in his poetry, but I found that my mind seemed unwilling to work any more along such lines, simply because the text, with its constant images of water (and its implications of flowing, of time passing, of purity, and also of the erotic), provided conclusive evidence which it was impossible to ignore.

Hyō hyō to shite mizu o ajiwau	Floating drifting the wandering water I taste
Mizuoto to issho ni sato e orite kita	With the sound of falling water to the village I came down
Ano kumo ga otoshita ame ni nurete iru	Soaked in the rain that cloud there has let fall
Mizu o hedatete onagoya no hi ga mata takidashita	Across the water the lights in the house of women lit once more

The Public Bath

Chinpoko mo ososo mo waite afureru yu	Cocks cunts all boiling and the bath water flows over

Hiraizumi

Koko made o kishi mizu nonde saru	Having got this far I drink some water then leave

September, Leaving for a Pilgrimage around Shikoku

Karasu tonde	I shall cross this

148

| yuku mizu o | water the crow |
| watarō | flies over |

These demonstrate well enough how much Santōka was stirred by images of water, of rain, drizzle, wintry showers, autumnal rain. Was it surprising, then, that he should have been fascinated on hearing for the first time a word—part of the traditional poetic diction—describing a natural phenomenon which already exerted that same fascination on him: the word *yokoshigure*, which represents the late autumn or early winter rain as it is driven by the wind? The term itself is a remarkable combination of the ordinary vernacular and the elegantly poetic, down-to-earth and yet powerfully lyrical, having both aspects quite unambiguously but with no sense of any conflict between them, a lucky union of what ought by rights to be two discordant tones; and surely that's precisely the kind of word a haiku poet of the free-rhythm school would particularly favour. After all, the very basis of the whole haiku aesthetic is a celebration of the commonplace, the everyday, in a poetic language with traditional, elegant overtones; as in the case of Bashō, for example, when he puts on new sandals, the thongs of which are blue from iris dye:

Ayamegusa	Iris flowers to bind
ashi ni musuban	my feet the thongs
waraji no o	of my straw sandals

This tradition was transformed in the direction of a greater realism by a process that led away from the fixed poetic form towards a much freer one, and the free-rhythm haiku can be seen as a culmination of this process. The dual tendency of the free-rhythm school, to reject the traditional poetic vocabulary while still being irresistibly attracted to it, is almost perfectly exemplified in the word *yokoshigure*. That priest just had to be

Santōka. It all fitted together so well; and as I told myself this, my face was probably wreathed in cheerful, self-congratulatory smiles.

Of course, there did remain one major drawback to this theory, namely that Santōka was actually dead by November 30th, 1940; but I managed to find a solution to that problem. Here is the entry for the year 1939 as given in the biographical chronology in the standard *Collected Poems*.

> Fifty-eight. Volume of haiku, *The Solitary Cold*, published. In March travels to Tokyo on foot, returning home in May. Goes to Hiroshima, saying has premonition of approaching death, and wishes to die in Shikoku. Arrives Matsuyama November 1st, staying with Takahashi, with whom he travels around Shikoku, although on his own from Unpenji onwards. Again visits Hōsai's grave on Shōdojima, begs way to Kōchi. Abandons pilgrimage. Returns to Matsuyama on November 21st. Stays with Fujioka at Dōgo Spa until twenty-sixth, then at cheap lodging house, the Chikuzenya (also in Dōgo), until December 14th. Through good offices of Takahashi finds housing in grounds of Miyuki Temple in Matsuyama, naming this hermitage "Sumita Issōan" after his friend Ōyama.

All that was needed was to make the meeting exactly one year earlier, when Santōka was staying at the lodging house in Dōgo. There could be nothing at all strange about someone in that situation taking an early bath and then going off to a tea-house to read the morning paper. The assumption was, of course, that Kurokawa had mistaken the year 1939 for 1940—and I was able to find reasons for making this assumption. First of all, Kurokawa had said it was in the year of the Konoe Cabinet, and then, after thinking for a while, that it must have been 1940, although he hadn't added the date with much confidence. Confidence had, however, established itself in his mind once he'd said the year, particularly as it was also the year 2600 of the Imperial Succession. "The year of the Konoe Cabinet" is not a specific statement, since it only suggests that something happened to it that year. What in fact happened was that the first Konoe Cabinet resigned in January 1939, and the second was formed in July 1940. It seems more than likely that Kurokawa had confused the two different cabinets in his mind. Again, the Support Asia Day business (whereby one wasn't allowed to drink saké on the first day of each month) began on September 1st, 1939. Now, obviously a really heavy drinker would complain about this, and when the system was only three months old there would still be a certain novelty remaining; but more than a whole year later is a rather different matter. Also, by November 30th, 1940, it had become very difficult to get hold of saké at any time, and it would have been fairly pointless to complain about the one day in the month when drinking was prohibited. There certainly wouldn't have been sufficient quantities at a "tea-house" (assuming there was any at all) to permit that kind of unrestrained imbibing of it.

8

Early the following year I acquired Ueda's biography of Santōka, plus the two volumes of notebooks and diaries edited by Ōyama that I've already mentioned. I also ordered a more recent work, Murakami's *Santōka, the Poet Vagrant*. I then read, as soon as it was published, Koyama's account of Santōka's travels, and whatever was available on the poets of his school, or on those who were in any way connected with him. I even went so far as to buy each volume of the seven-volume *Collected Works* as they arrived in the bookshop, and for a man who possesses no collected works by any writer of the modern period except Ōgai and Sōseki, this can be said to represent a rare enthusiasm. Of course I could have got the university library to acquire a copy, which would certainly have made things easier on my own purse, but when I thought about all the delays it would entail before the books actually reached my hands I decided to go ahead and pay myself. This foraging about in the Santōka literature took up all the time not actually spent in teaching and research; i.e., all my spare time for quite a while, as I'd even begun regretting the hours wasted over incompetent games of *go*, and gradually cut down on them in order to read these books. In the event, the books provided much more amusement than my visits to the *go* club.

One of the results of this rather cursory reading was that I gained some grasp of the economic facts of Santōka's way of life. I should point out that the methods by which those contemporaries of ours who have "retired from the world" manage to make ends meet is a question of considerable interest for the scholar of medieval literature. In the Middle Ages, an actual "withdrawal" (in the proper sense of the word) into the "solitary life" was virtually impossible. The wandering poet Saigyō, for example, was an extremely wealthy man, and it was for that reason he was able to continue his travels. He was so rich, in fact, that the legend about his calmly giving a cat made of gold, which he'd just received from the great Minamoto Yoritomo, to a small child who happened to pass him in the street could very well be true. In the case of Sōgi, Bashō's great precursor, the facts of his acquiring a splendid house and living a life of considerable luxury by sucking up to the people in power have been made quite clear by Konishi's recent research. When one reads things like Kamo no Chōmei's description of life in his tiny hut in the *Hōjōki*, one gets an impression of honest poverty, of straitened circumstances if not actual destitution, but one would do better to think of them merely as statements of the aesthetic ideals of the time. When Kamo no Chōmei describes a visit to the capital which fills him with shame because of his beggar's way of life, whereas back at home in his hut he feels free from all such afflictions, from the dust of this world, there can be little question that he is exaggerating the matter considerably. No doubt he wasn't dressed in the finery natural to his class, and looked quite drab, even poor, by such standards, but he was certainly no beggar, having a perfectly sound economic basis to his way of life.

The question is, what kind of economic bases exist for those contemporary poets who seem to have accepted the fantasies of the past as gospel, and have similarly retired from the world? Even if the way of the mendicant priest, of the begging bowl, provided an answer for one of them, what sort of answer was it? It could hardly have supplied Santōka with food, clothing, and shelter, and surely not with the huge quantities of alcohol he seems to have consumed.

I'd had considerable doubts about this from the start, and yet the diaries provided only a very naive account of the matter. According to them, Santōka lived on the proceeds of his begging and on the charity cheerfully meted out by friends and admirers. This sounded dubious to me, as if the diaries had deliberately been written to maintain this illusion. Since most of the books about Santōka were produced by these friends and admirers, I'd gained the impression they were covering up for him by not mentioning what must have been a very different reality, and I received confirmation of this from Koyama Eiga's *The Wanderings of Santōka*, in which there's the following passage:

> During this period of his life Santōka did very little actual begging, having made up his mind that he was going through a spiritually blank period, or at least one of mental indolence. A young friend (and probably others) sent him saké every three days, and thus in the comfort, not of his own home, but at least a settled abode, he was able to get happily drunk

for nothing and investigate the darker aspects of his awareness of "life". The reason he'd decided not to beg was certainly not because he had become financially secure, for he
hadn't. It was just that he didn't like begging.

Despite this dislike of begging, he still had no qualms
about receiving gifts of food and money from his friends . . .
as described by Tanaka Jun'ichirō in his brief article on the
subject: "Santōka often pestered his fellow poets for money,
and they always responded (with no mean sums, either). He
even got his wife, and the son he'd done absolutely nothing
for, to send him money as well. That sensitivity he showed
when he was involved in other people's affairs, that delicacy,
that vulnerability, were counterbalanced by the barefaced impudence, the refusal to take no for an answer, which he
displayed when sponging off people, and were all part and
parcel of the same infantile egoism that dominated his life."

Both Tanaka and Koyama are writing about the period around
1935, but the chances are that his "barefaced impudence", his
easy ability to cadge off people, were something the "recluse"
had to employ throughout his life. It's hard to believe that, in an
age of only lukewarm religious belief, his begging bowl could have
provided him with much of an income, or that he came into contact with many people who were well enough off to give him
what he needed without being asked.

I certainly wouldn't want to laud a life-style of that kind, but I
can't see much point in taking an attitude of stern moral disap-
proval towards it either. It was merely the inevitable consequence
of a simple-minded yet passionate desire to conform to two images of life which he'd superimposed on one another: that of the
illusory "recluse" of Japanese literary tradition, and the "bohe-
mian artist" taken from Europe.

As I've said, I have no desire to praise any of this, but I do feel one should recognize that Santōka did at least have the strength of character to persist in the way of life he had chosen. This strength reveals itself not only in the undeniable expertise of his poetic writings, but more extensively in his personality itself, in his obvious attractiveness as a person. Presumably, ordinary people who had conformed to the social pressures around them, observing a man who had actually performed what they could only dream about, experienced feelings of half-timid respect, resulting in an awed sense of inferiority towards him, which led in turn to a sympathetic desire to sustain and support him in his poverty. Indeed there seems little doubt that he had a gift for arousing such feelings to a quite passionate degree in the members of his immediate entourage, probably by very out-of-the-way methods as well, methods which would have been ridiculously ineffective if used by someone else. Most likely he shared the same temperament as those other two geniuses in the art of using people, the major twentieth-century novelists Shimazaki Tōson and Dazai Osamu; but in Santōka's case it was an extreme caricature, or, if that seems too strong an expression, a highly condensed version of their devious talent for getting on in the world.

This ability to keep on falling on one's feet is best displayed in his behaviour from the spring of 1936 to the summer of the same year. He visited Tokyo to take part in some get-together organized by the magazine *Sōun* with which he was affiliated, and, after being received by all its other poets with wild enthusiasm (and concrete expressions of the same), he journeyed all round northern and central Japan, not only living off his acquaintances through the length and breadth of the land, but causing them serious inconvenience, too, until he finally reached Hiraizumi, the farthest point north Bashō had gone. Like Bashō, he then turned for home. It was at Hiraizumi that he wrote:

Koko made o kishi   Having got this far

| mizu nonde | I drink some water |
| saru | then leave |

The literal reality this poem is describing (and I'm ignoring its deeper poetic significance) is that Santōka has arrived at a town where nobody knows him and so no one is prepared to ply him with good, strong drink. The fact that he feels this deeply enough to write it down so well shows just how generously he has been provided for elsewhere, and also how much he has come to take it all for granted, seeing nothing at all remarkable in his perpetual sponging off people.

It was before a man of this calibre that, some three years later, two travellers appeared, one a country doctor, the other a high school teacher, with bulging wallets, like two plump pigeons ready for the plucking. How eagerly he must have leapt to the attack, displaying all the many facets of his craft. I brought the scene to mind over and over again, and it was perfect. Before my eyes arose the face that everyone now knows, the bamboo hat, the thick-lensed glasses, the goatee beard; and I thought of my father and Kurokawa with this appallingly energetic alcoholic, of the hours the unlikely trio had spent in cheerful talk. And so I smiled, remembering the past and thinking of the dead.

9

The fourth volume of the *Collected Works* to reach me was the poetry, a book divided into three sections. The first section comprised those poems which had appeared in the selection made by Santōka himself, *Sōmokutō*; the second included those published in the magazine *Sōun*; and the third consisted of some fairly elaborate scholarly apparatus. Using this third section, I put ticks against all the poems that mentioned late autumn rain. This would have been towards the end of January 1972, about a year after I'd come across the standard *Collected Poems*. At the time, I was bringing to completion a major piece of research on the *Gyokuyōwakashū* (Collection of Jewelled Leaves, a fourteenth-century imperial anthology), and hadn't yet been able to get around to reading all Santōka's poetry. But my research did produce something strikingly relevant to his case, for I finally came across the mystery word *yokoshigure*.

I found it in a work called the *Yakumomishō*, a compendium of critical remarks, notes, and instructions in the poetic art written by the Emperor Juntoku in the early thirteenth century, and one of the two major reference works for that period. After listing various terms for rain which were acceptable in poetic composition ("rain", "small rain", "passing rain", "long rain", "evening shower", "passing shower", "driving rain", "fifth-month rain", "late autumn rain", and so on), it gave words for "rain blowing in the wind", saying that "Yorimasa did use the word *yokoshigure* in his verses, but it was greeted coldly."

There is very little I can say in my own defence here, for, as a specialist in medieval poetry, I must have used this book on innumerable occasions, and even read it from cover to cover twice, once as a student and once as a research assistant. I must have looked at it dozens of times, probably more than a hundred in fact, since Kurokawa mentioned the word *yokoshigure* in my presence. Together with the twelfth-century poet Fujiwara Kiyosuke's *Introduction to the Style of Waka*, it is one of the two standard source books on the subject to which any scholar is constantly making reference, and the fact that I hadn't tried to look up the term in this work is an appalling oversight—one I simply can't explain to my own satisfaction, yet alone anyone else's. I know Santōka belonged to the free-rhythm school, which in theory eschewed traditional poetic diction, but that was no excuse, and I could only blush at the thought that I obviously wasn't even competent to direct my own students' research.

What was clear was that Yorimasa had made use of the word in a poetry contest, and the judge had told him off for doing so. All I had to do now was find the account of the contest in question, and this I was able to do easily enough, for it was in the *Gunshoruijū*, a massive, early nineteenth-century collection of poetic records which took the editor fifty years to compile. The contest formed part of an offering to the Sumiyoshi Shrine and took place in the second year of Kaō (1170) on the ninth day of the tenth month. One of the themes was "sheltering from autumn rain while on a journey". Yorimasa's poem ran thus:

Tabi no io wa	Like to a sudden storm
arashi ni taguu	this shower of driven rain
yokoshigure	halts not at the thin
shiba no kakoi ni	brushwood fence about my hut
tomarazarikeri	slight shelter on a journey

The judge at this contest, Fujiwara Shunzei, gave the victory to Yorimasa's opponent, and his comments on the poem were surprisingly severe, singling out the word *yokoshigure* for particular censure, but also condemning the inadequacy of the particle *ni* in that context, and the work as a whole for not being truly moving. Shunzei, who was a great social success as a poet (he was entrusted with the sole editorship of an important imperial anthology some twenty years after this date, and later on seems to have been the poetry instructor of the Cloistered Emperor Gotōba, himself a formative figure in the history of the Japanese poetic sensibility), was clearly not the kind of person who went around deliberately annoying people, and the harshness of his criticism must indicate that his canons of poetic taste had been seriously offended. His objection to *yokoshigure* was that, although the eccentric insertion of such a word (which admittedly referred to a genuine weather phenomenon) might be considered interesting, it lacked the elegance essential to poetic composition.

At the time, I didn't read Shunzei's judgement, or even the poem itself, with any great attention, as I was too preoccupied with feelings of regret, even of guilt, at having doubted Kurokawa's knowledge of these matters. Obviously he'd read a great deal more as a student than the usual stuff I preened myself on, having slogged through the whole of that massive compilation (and probably its awesome supplement, too). I didn't so much admire this effort, however, as find my mind boggling at it; and in the midst of my rueful astonishment I suddenly realized that the word might well be included in the *Ruidaiwakashū*, the work that lists poems according to their themes. My not having taken the obvious step of consulting it before must also be seen, I'm afraid, as a serious oversight on my part.

I hastily flipped through the pages until I came to the section dealing with the large, early fourteenth-century compilation, the *Fubokuwakashū*, and there found two poems about driven rain, one of which, unsurprisingly, was the piece by Yorimasa already quoted; the other was this, by Fujiwara Nobuzane:

Kaze wataru	Brought by the wind across
mine no ki no ma no	the peak brought through its
yokoshigure	trees
moru yama yori mo	this driven rain
shitaba somuramu	soaks but the lower leaves and not
	the mountain that protects

Nobuzane was a man better known for his painting talents, and particularly famous for the portrait he was commissioned to make of the Cloistered Emperor Gotōba in exile. I can remember how struck I was at the time that the two people who had used the word in poetry (apparently the only two to have done so) should have been a soldier and a painter. They must both have taken a genuine pleasure in the term, and it seems likely that in Nobuzane's case, given his keen interest in poetry, he had heard of the public rebuke Yorimasa had suffered for his use of it. That he should himself have chosen to go against Shunzei's authority and employ the same eccentric word argues no ordinary commitment on his part.

The ideal behind traditional standards of poetic decorum is most succinctly expressed in the words of Shunzei's son, Fujiwara Teika, still the pre-eminent figure in these matters: "Language preserves the old when the heart desires the new." Yorimasa's going against these standards was probably seen not just as a threat to the laws of poetic diction, but as a deviation from the general aesthetic principles established by the first three imperial anthologies and the *Tale of Genji*, which had dominated the Japanese court since the late Heian period. A term as blunt, as coarse, as "driven rain" would appear as a direct assault on the world of social conservatism, aesthetic traditionalism, and intellectual formalism which had created, and was sustained by, such standards.

The fundamentally disturbing aspect of the expression was that, if it were accepted, it would mean the introduction of a realistically descriptive element into the formalized poetic vocabulary, and the fact that it should first have been put forward by a soldier, then taken up by a painter, is of particular interest. Although they were both obviously members of the aristocracy, they would also have been brought up with a clear awareness that their role in life was not merely to conform to the dictates of tradition, one being from a family of soldiers, the other from a family of visual artists; and it seems reasonable to assume that at least the conditions needed for a nonconformist gesture were present in both of them. For the normal aristocrat, a shower of late autumn rain being driven by the wind might be a fact of experience, something actually seen, but it wasn't something to be celebrated in poetry, and the idea of using a bastard word like *yokoshigure* would have been too shocking to be entertained. The sort of term that might naturally come to mind would be something in the nature of *yokozama ame* (sideways rain), which was acceptable because it had been used in the *Tale of Genji* to describe a storm in autumn. But, with people like Yorimasa and Nobuzane, the life-style in one case and the everyday habits of an artist in the other would have encouraged a tendency to experience the world as it was, to feel a blast of driven rain as exactly that, and to seek the word that would express it, a word going beyond the limits so rigorously imposed by traditional aesthetic tastes. One can see much the same thing in the case of Taira Tadamori who, according to Tanizawa Shigeru, reintroduced a great number of *uta makura*, or poetical place-names, which had fallen into disuse, and even went on to create new ones of his own, because, as a distinguished soldier (in the opposite camp to Yorimasa), he was used to an unrestrained field of activity both in action and ideas.

While toying with these thoughts, I picked up a felt pen and wrote out the two poems by Yorimasa and Nobuzane on the back of an advertising hand-out which had come with the newspaper. I then wrote down all the haiku by Santōka about late autumn rain that I could remember. I hadn't done any calligraphy practice for years, and my attempts in one or two cases to render the complex, square Chinese characters in the more flowing, abbreviated Japanese style were fairly dubious; but what did result from this writing and rewriting of their verse was a vague feeling that the poems by the two medieval poets, the ones in my field, were really not up to much after all, and that Santōka's were much better by any standards. It was a pity, I felt, that a man who could write like this hadn't produced a haiku about driven rain.

The next moment I jumped up and dashed for the Santōka *Collected Works*, taking up volume 1 and turning to the third section, the one with cross-references. The priest who'd been stood all that drink at the tea-house might very well have written a haiku using the word he had just learnt there. If I could find something on that subject among Santōka's works, then the whole problem would be solved once and for all. (This had always been such an obvious thing to do that, if I hadn't been so excited, I would have been shocked at yet another example of my incompetence.)

But the poem did not exist. Page 497 of this volume recorded all the verse written during his travels around Shikoku, but there was a blank stretch after the point where Santōka settled at the cheap lodging house in Dōgo (the crucial date of November 30th is during this period), and although the poetic record started again on December 15th, it was merely a series of notes and jottings, with nothing in the way of verse until the bottom of the next page. Neither page 497 nor 498 had any poems about late autumn rain, and until his death on October 11th, 1940, he only wrote six on this theme.

Asa hayaku	In the early morning
shigururu	a cold rain falls
hi o taite iru	I light the fire
Shigururu ya	Rain falling and
yūbinya-san tōkute	the postman has
kite kureta	travelled far for me
Tsukiyo	A moonlit night
shigurete haru	falling rain the sound
chikaku naru oto	of spring approaching
Shigure kasa de	Rain falling on my bamboo
otonari e	hat I go next door
mizu o morai ni	to get some water
Shigurete kaki no	Rain falling on the

| ha no iyoiyo | persimmon   its autumn leaves |
| utsukushiku | finally beautiful |

Otata shigurete	Caught by the rain
suta suta	the woman with her load
isogu	hurries onwards

That was all. No matter how much I looked I could find no reference to driven rain, and the quality of these six haiku was also astonishingly poor. I began to feel sorry for Santōka: with only a year to live he had been unable to use the word he'd just learnt and so much valued, and his poetic powers seemed to have fallen off badly during that last year as well. Of course it might have been that in his last two autumns there was only light rainfall in the Matsuyama area, and that when it did rain it came at the wrong time, when the wind wasn't blowing, and thus the phenomenon of *yokoshigure* itself didn't occur. That was one way I attempted to explain the matter to myself, but the fact was that only six poems on the subject in a whole year seemed to suggest that Santōka was nothing like as concerned with autumn rain as I'd assumed. I even began to feel that, in his final days, he took only the mildest interest in it.

As these doubts arose in my mind I went on turning the pages, and made one more unexpected discovery. He had written a surprising number of haiku on this topic just before settling down in the lodging house at Dōgo. In less than a month, from November 3rd onwards, he produced a total of thirteen. Among them, four are worth quoting:

Shigururu	It rains and I
ashiato o	follow after
tadoriyuku	the footprints

| Nami oto | The sound of waves |

| shigurete | in the rain |
| harete | in the sunlight |

Matsu no ki	Rain falling on
matsu no ki to	the pine tree and
shigurete iru	the pine tree

Shigururu ya	In the falling rain
inu to	my way barred by
mukiatte iru	a dog

This wasn't just a question of quantity: the quality of these lines is at least higher than those written after the Dōgo period. Here was something to brood upon, and I gave my imagination free play. First of all, despite the fact that in his later years Santōka retained his enthusiasm for late autumn rain, for some reason he wrote far fewer poems using this motif from December 1939 onwards, and there was also a marked decline in his skill in handling the subject. Mightn't the reason be that his encounter with the word *yokoshigure* had created some kind of tension, or mental block, which contributed to this overall decline? The more I thought about it, the more convincing it became.

I'd felt from the beginning of my acquaintance with free-rhythm haiku that it was the really short poems that were best (an opinion I'm happy to have confirmed by Ishikawa's book on the subject, which I've just read), and towards the end of his life there seems little doubt that Santōka, having spent most of his energy on writing haiku, was thinking in similar terms—and perhaps had always done so. As evidence one can put forward the fact that the number of good, relatively long poems he wrote can be counted on one's fingers; there is also this very interesting entry in his diary for December 4th, 1938, almost exactly a year before the crucial date.

Haiku must be constantly worked at, polished; one should never be enslaved by the original form.

Furu ike ya	The ancient pool
kawazu tobikomu	a frog jumps in
mizu no oto	sound of water
kawazu tobikomu	a frog jumps in
mizu no oto	sound of water
mizu no oto	sound of water
oto	sound

Old Bashō was an auditory poet, *the world of sound.*

At first sight, he might seem to be emphasizing the musical aspects of haiku, but it's surely more of a casual confession of his own method of constantly pruning his work in order to arrive at an ultimate purity and brevity of expression. One can perhaps point to some slight influence from Zen modes of thought here, for he hated the garrulous and longed for silence; yet this is a tendency that appears throughout the history of Japanese poetry, as the long poems in the *Manyōshū* were replaced by the five-line waka, then the three-line haiku, and finally the even shorter works of the free-rhythm school. Santōka's "Oto wa shigure ka" (The sound of autumn rain?) can thus be seen as the natural apotheosis of the tradition, being even briefer than the famous piece by that other disciple of Seisensui, Ozaki Hōsai: "Seki o shite mo hitori" (Alone even when I cough). Consequently it not only serves as a summary of Santōka's poetic intentions, but also represents the kind of work towards which the whole free-rhythm movement tended.

Now, it's obvious that the idea of a poetry of silence is just a rhetorical imposture, for silence itself is no poem. Even the most informal of haiku will still require at least one word. But . . .

one word; the one-word poem: surely that's what Santōka was really after, the ideal he aimed at? And if this seems a reasonable assumption, then what could be more reasonable than to imagine that a poet who was constantly pondering the possibility of a one-word poem (or something close to it) should have thought this possibility had been realized when he heard the expression *yokoshigure*? It seemed to me not only likely, in fact, but inevitable. How else could one account for the extraordinary enthusiasm that priest at the tea-house in Dōgo had shown for the word? Hadn't he kept on nodding and repeating it, saying it was exactly right, that was it, the perfect description, the final word on the subject? In this one expression, in this season marker so rarely used in our poetic tradition, didn't he see the culmination of that tradition, the ultimate form towards which his whole method and output had led?

If we accept that the words most pregnant with implication in traditional Japanese poetry, the most suggestive and sonorous, are the *uta makura*—the place-names whose resonance lies in the imprecision of their referential function—but exclude them from our ideal poetic grammar on the grounds that they are proper nouns, then we must inevitably give pride of place to the *kigo*, or season words. The ordinary season words (*shigure*, for example) are pure givens, however, and merely setting one down hardly calls for the exercise of any poetic skill. But in the case of *yokoshigure* we have a composite word, a word which has been constructed, and in the shades of meaning thereby added surely we see the very act of poetic creation at work. Santōka had at last come across the word he'd always been looking for.

The problem in his case, though, was with the result of his discovery, with what could come after it. He had been enormously excited by the term, had understood intuitively that this was the kind of expression he'd been seeking, and yet he was also aware that the word as it stood did not make a poem. He turned it over in his head, over and over. It was certainly a uniquely beautiful word, and had almost seemed at first to be a poem in itself, a poem approaching total silence. But in fact it wasn't. It was just a fragment, much like the fragment he'd found when he took Bashō's famous haiku to pieces. He would have to throw it away, just as he had thrown the line "Oto wa shigure ka" away; and as he came to this conclusion, perhaps he reached a more radical conclusion somewhere much deeper in his soul, a decisive doubt as to the validity of this quest for a poem of pure silence. To silence this doubt he searched for one word, two words even, that might be added to the perfect one to complete the act of creation, but *yokoshigure* was complete in itself already, resisting in its perfection all attempts to add anything to it. His poetic method thus led him to despair, and he despaired of his poetic method. My assumption then was that the fact that some sort of impasse had been reached with regard to his dealings with the word resulted in a general mental block, about which he could do nothing, so that even if he encountered the phenomenon itself in actual life, a poem on the theme of *yokoshigure* had become an impossibility. Although he wrote a few haiku about ordinary late autumn rain, he was incapable of producing anything of real value on that subject, either.

Plain common sense, of course, would say that I'd been indulging in unbridled fantasy in all this "reasoning", and eventually, as I was travelling home one day on the underground, I did begin to see things in perspective again. I was genuinely astonished, in fact, that I, a literary researcher rigorously schooled in the principle of theorizing only on the basis of hard evidence, should have linked together this long chain of speculation, each part of which ought to have been considered highly dubious. Though there were no reasons at all for concluding that the priest in the tea-house in Dōgo and Taneda Santōka were one and the same person, I had at some time accepted the idea that this had been shown to be the case, and my whole "argument" had taken flight from there. If I went on like this I would soon cease to be a scholar, so I told myself that this fantasizing of mine must come to an end at once. On the dark road back from the station I realized the time was now ripe to break off relations with Santōka, and I decided that when I got home I would gather all the books I had on the subject and stow them safely away at the back of a nice, big cupboard.

10

But stuffing the books away at the back of a cupboard didn't stop more books about Santōka being published, nor could it stop me buying them when I saw them advertised; and new volumes of the *Collected Works* still kept arriving from the bookshop. Even if I didn't read them properly I at least glanced at them from time to time, which only showed that breaking off relations with Santōka was proving to be no easy matter. He had taken on a legendary status for me, and this legend was fixed in my mind, deep-rooted, and there was no way I could just cast it out.

For example, the fifth volume of the *Collected Works*, consisting of the diaries from January 1937 to May 1939, appeared in the following year, and though I was able to put it away unread, I was aware of a glow of excitement at the thought that the sixth volume would include the diary containing an entry for November 30th, 1939. As soon as I read that, the problem would be finally resolved.

Although I knew my excitement would grow as the fatal publication date approached, I was still surprised at the heights it reached. I'm also ashamed to say that within a mere two months I was even indulging in childish reflections on what the diary entry would be like, imagining it in the pure Santōka style, of course, which I'd picked up from the earlier volumes:

<u>November 30th, 1939</u>

Clear turning to cloudy, then showery.
    Up early. Morning cold. Nothing like a hot-spring bath. Saké at a tea-house—put back about three pints. Haven't been properly drunk for quite a while.
    Found the word *yokoshigure.*

But that wasn't how it was. When the book arrived I hurriedly opened it, without removing the cellophane wrapper as I normally do, and skimmed through the pages to find this:

November 28th–December 2nd

I think this is what must be referred to as "dreaming one's life away". There's nothing I want to write down, but I force myself to write this.
    30th. Visited Takahashi at Commercial College. Haven't seen him for ages. He came to my lodgings at night to guarantee my bill, also gave me some money for myself.
    These last few days and nights convince me more and more bitterly of my own uselessness.

That was all. There was nothing about the weather. The entry proved nothing one way or the other. Why on earth had he chosen to be lazy about keeping his diary at this crucial juncture of all times? The disappointment I felt, however, was only slight at first, but as I read the surrounding entries, and then this one again with more care, I realized they were extremely damaging to my thesis.
    From the entry for the twenty-seventh ("Cloudy, then clear. Dōgo Spa. Chikuzenya. / To Dōgo as a pilgrim. Turned away from a number of inns. Finally accepted at this lodging. / Occupied fully with washing, sewing, writing, reading"), it seemed

clear that he was tired from his journey and spent the five days until December 2nd just vaguely recuperating. After all, he was in his late fifties, and no matter how used to it he was, all that travelling on foot must have taken a tremendous toll. There could be nothing strange in his needing five days to recover, nor in his spending that time cooped up in his room, just going to bed and getting up again, "dreaming one's life away". This could only mean that he hadn't met my father and Kurokawa, that it was the plain truth when he said he had nothing to write about, and all that had taken place (which he had "forced himself" to write down) was his visit to Takahashi at the Commercial College on the thirtieth. So I decided meekly to accept the evidence, and let out a long sigh, having at last discarded the Santōka legend, the myth that I alone had cherished for so long, the quaint tale of the poet, just out of his bath and smelling nicely of soap, and his meeting with the two travellers. But while acknowledging the fact that the whole fantasy I'd created had been mistaken, I couldn't help persisting in the thought that, even if my father and Kurokawa hadn't met Santōka on that particular day (if the poet had been back and forth to Matsuyama—the nearest place where there was a Commercial College—he could hardly have done so after spending all those hours drinking in a tea-house, and a heavy shower of rain made it all the more unlikely, the obvious time to go being a clear, sunny morning), there remained a possibility that the three of them had still met casually somewhere else on another occasion. Nevertheless, I knew this was merely a way of consoling myself for my main loss.

So despondent was I feeling that I had an urge to work my depression out on somebody, and this took an eccentrically scholarly form. In the diary entries up to September 26th, each separate entry has the date underlined (in double underlining), but with those beginning on November 1st (none remain for the intervening five weeks) this double underlining does not appear in the printed version; *and yet* a photographic reproduction of the first page of the original diary (i.e., of notebook 24, appearing on page 63 of this edition) shows that the double underlining certainly existed for that entry, and presumably for the other entries as well. Obviously here was a case of incompetent proof-reading, which cast doubt on the editing as a whole, thought I, giving the editor a stern, if imaginary, rebuke.

I need hardly add that I was simply letting off steam, lashing out at whatever came nearest to hand. Editions of contemporary literature are not remarkable for their punctilious reading of the original text, and a deviation of that kind is something one would usually ignore. It would scarcely justify the assumption that there had been some actual tampering with the text, and it gave one no grounds for doubting the fact that the account of the five days in question was printed exactly as in the original. Ōyama Sumita, the editor (and proof-reader), was known as a person of genuine discernment (we have him to thank for preserving the discarded "Oto wa shigure ka", as well as many other haiku) and someone deeply committed to the memory of Santōka. There was no reason at all for mistrusting this edition, even if some of the dates for the diary entries did lack the proper underlining.

Having talked myself into a saner, if sadder, state of mind, I turned to the next entry, that for December 3rd. As I did so, I had the sudden feeling I was remembering something of great importance, though what it was I couldn't tell. The entry ran:

December 3rd: fine.

Feel rather light-headed. My fifty-seventh birthday. One should never celebrate (or mourn) by oneself!

For some reason the remark about being "light-headed" brought me up short. Aware that I shouldn't casually pass this over, I gazed at that exclamation mark for some time, wondering what might have happened to Santōka on the previous day, December 2nd, until the vague idea crossed my mind that he could well have been suffering from a very heavy hangover. I then recalled some circumstantial evidence which seemed to bear this out.

The evidence concerned events which occurred in Yamaguchi in 1937 (one of the two best-known anecdotes about him, the other being the drinking tour of 1936 already mentioned). It was in January of that year, and he spent five days on a binge which ended in his being taken into custody for consuming food and beverages on licensed premises without any visible means of paying for them. The diary record for those five days is similar to that covering an identical period in Dōgo in that there are no separate entries, the whole being included in one general entry. The same is true of the week he spent sponging off his fellow members of the magazine *Sōun* up in the north, and there's certainly one other instance (quite possibly others) when days of unrestrained drinking resulted in a blank of some days which then had to be covered by a single entry. I wasn't able to make any definite judgement on this at the time, since I'd only read through the previous diaries very casually, with no such research aim in mind. But on the basis of this secondary evidence it wasn't unreasonable to think that Santōka had been on a drinking spree during those five days in Dōgo as well. One had to bear in mind that the poet, who had an extremely tough constitution and was almost never ill, was also remarkably punctilious in his habits, particularly in the case of his diary, which he normally wrote up every day with scrupulous regularity; and it was hard to think of any other reason why he should have failed to do so for five days except that of incapacity through excessive intake of alcohol. His life may have looked like a series of aimless wanderings, something without form which became more and more so, but this only meant that its real centre was his desire to write, the desire being for him life itself. Even if nothing happened worth recording, he still had

172

various reflections to write down, and it is this expression of the unceasing everyday life of the mind which his diary records.

Where I seemed to have gone wrong was in my interpretation of the standard phrase *sui-sei-mu-shi*, four characters which commonly mean "to dream one's life away". I had assumed it just meant he stayed shut up in his room vaguely mooning about. I hadn't taken into account the poet's concern with giving life to a stereotyped phrase by going to its source; and in this case it was the literal meaning of the characters, "drunk life dream death", that Santōka had been talking about. The four words were no cliché but a literal description of what had happened during those five days—at least where a life of drunkenness was concerned, even if the dying in a dream was yet to come. Chronic alcoholism, as everybody now knows, was the bane of Santōka's life, and when he didn't have the money to buy a drink he was inevitably obliged to obtain it by methods which probably weren't much to his taste, such as sponging off his friends, buttering up chance acquaintances, or consuming it on licensed premises without visible means, etc.; and no doubt this made his awareness of his problem even more chronic. *"These last few days and nights convince me more and more bitterly of my own uselessness"* (underlined by Santōka himself) is surely the statement of such an awareness. As a mere expression of vague regret about sloth and a sense of futility, the choice of words (in particular the underlining) seems too extreme.

Having reached this point, I began pondering the word "uselessness". What was he being useless at? Was it a reference to his inability to create a poem that embodied the new word he'd recently encountered, and for which he'd wandered about in the rain racking his brains but to no effect? I didn't spend enough time on this particular fantasy to get really absorbed in it, however, because my mind was soon off on another tack. If Santōka spent those five days drunk, then on the thirtieth, from the morning onwards, he should have smelt fairly strongly of alcohol, though as an accomplished tippler he probably handled himself in such a way that the two travellers wouldn't have noticed. I made this assumption because it seemed fair to say that Santōka would have wormed some money out of Takahashi that morning when he visited him at the Commercial College. Probably it wasn't as much as the solid sum he received the same evening to pay for his lodging (the "guarantee" would certainly have taken a concrete form), but enough at least to tide him over for the day; and one can safely assume he would have spent it on drink, even if it only meant the odd cupful, and that this drinking then extended into the next day, November 1st, Support Asia Day, when all drinking was prohibited so that all might wholeheartedly contribute to that project. Consequently, what Santōka might have been reproaching himself for was not his inability to handle *yokoshigure*, but the fact that he'd kept himself cheerfully topped up throughout a day when the mind of the nation was concentrated on higher things. At least this would have added to his already heavy burden of self-reproach, which in turn would probably have made him drink more recklessly as the day proceeded, until his funds ran out. On the following day, December 2nd, he had a filthy hangover, and no wherewithal to calm it down with a bit more of the same, and so on the third he felt "rather light-headed". It all seemed to fit.

In order to go on piecing this little mosaic together, I needed to find out what Santōka's reaction to Support Asia Day really had been, so I turned to the diary entry for September 1st, the first of these special days.

September 1st: calm sunrise, clear.

Support Asia Day. Anniversary of Great Kanto Earthquake. Two hundred and tenth day of the old calendar. A day of considerable significance. Morning bath, Purification of Body

174

and Spirit, Obeisance to the Imperial Shrine, Silent Prayer, Self-Control, Obedience to the Commandments. . . . .

Arrived in Yamaguchi late afternoon. Visited Shimoida at his home, read the paper, and met another unexpected visitor, Hase, who invited me and Shimoida to his home to meet his newly married wife. Then who should turn up but Murata, and the four of us spent some time quietly talking (there was a little to drink as well, but we have to keep that a secret, don't we?), and we got onto the subject of the delicate situation on the Manchurian border, and became suddenly depressed by it all, feeling very painfully that our people must endeavour to raise their efforts to new heights. . . . When I was alone I thought about a number of things: the border situation, of course, then my boy, and my friends. . . . .

There was nothing strange about his discussing the situation in Manchuria, for the "delicate situation" was the defeat at No-monhan which was being whispered about at the time, though no one dared to say outright what had happened. But for a man who was supposed to have cast aside the cares of this world the pompous admonition to "our people" to "endeavour to raise their efforts" seemed most peculiar. His "feeling very painfully" presumably didn't apply to his own behaviour as one of "our peo-ple", since no matter how much a mendicant priest might "raise his efforts" it wouldn't make any difference to the outcome of the war. All the phrase could mean was that Santōka was genuine-ly inspired by the spirit of Support Asia Day, and felt compelled to urge everybody else on to greater efforts, which he could only observe from his lonely vantage point. The earlier clichés about bathing, purification, worshipping the Meiji Shrine from afar, self-restraint, etc., were clearly a product of the day as well, but its true effect on him was more apparent in this private patriotic outburst at the end of the quotation. It was undoubtedly a day he took very seriously.

There is no entry for October 1st. In the introduction to the "Journal of a Pilgrimage to Shikoku" (which starts on November 1st), the editor points out that "the only entries in the diary for the previous month are poems, and these will be found in the haiku section". I then checked them, and it was clear from the haiku written on October 1st that Santōka had travelled from the mainland by boat to Shikoku on that day, and stayed in Matsuyama. Since one tends to have company on voyages like this, he presumably had nothing to drink at least during the journey to Matsuyama.

On November 1st he was staying at lodgings near Hatajima (the place where Minamoto Yoshitsune had landed in pursuit of the fleeing Taira army), and wrote:

> Today is Support Asia Day, only the second [sic] occasion, and yet I have shamefully acquired a little alcohol to comfort the weary heart of a traveller.

That he should have mistaken this third occasion for the second might be considered to indicate a lack of interest, though I'm prepared to concede that it need not be seen in that way. What the entry as a whole does seem to suggest, however, is that unconsciously he chose not to be overly aware of this day of prohibitions imposed by the military establishment. The preceding entry is full of complaints about the lodging house and the man running it, as if he were inventing reasons why he should have been driven to drink, and his very use of the word "alcohol" suggests that he was trying to explain away the indulgence by considering it as a kind of medicine whereby to treat his melancholia.

I suppose I could be accused of making too much out of too little material, but the fact is that, only two months before, Santōka had made it quite clear how seriously he took this day, even if he may have broken the drink prohibition to some extent. He certainly wasn't making any sort of fun of it; in fact it probably required some elaborate mental gymnastics on his part to allow himself to break the patriotic pledge. Now, if he also drank on December 1st at Dōgo (and one is surely entitled to think he did), doesn't it seem rather likely that he would have suffered considerable spiritual pangs about it? Couldn't it at least have led to a bitter recognition of the meaninglessness of his way of life, of his uselessness as a person?. . .

At this point I was feeling quite happy with the way my deductions were going, and I began thinking about how Support Asia Day had been observed in 1939 in the world of my own immediate acquaintance, when I was a thirteen-year-old schoolboy.

Every summer we used to go, the three of us (myself, my brother, and our maternal grandmother), to the seaside for our summer holiday. This custom had been going on for years, and we would leave about a week before the end of July and stay for just under a month. We went to a fishing village called Isohama and took over the whole upper storey of the house of a local municipal worker, although this only meant the use of two moderately sized rooms. The cooking was done by his wife, who had worked as a nurse at my father's clinic before marrying a man of this village—the reason for our coming to spend our summers here. Mother would turn up once a week to make sure our needs were being catered to, cook us one good solid meal of meat, and generally tidy up. Father was always so busy he only appeared once during the whole holiday. That day, of course, would be one on which no surgery was held, and he used to bring the nurses along with him to go swimming, while Mother stayed at home and looked after the house.

But that summer of 1939 was different from the others, because for some reason or other we stayed longer than usual (until September 5th, in fact), and though my mother certainly ap-

177

peared from time to time, Father didn't bring the nurses on any outing, nor did he come himself. I was still only a child at the time, and I can remember feeling seriously disappointed that I wasn't able to play cards at least one evening with a reasonably large number of people. I moaned about this to my brother, who was already a university student, but he didn't seem in the mood to sympathize with me very much, and made only the vaguest of replies, though his teaching me the rudiments of go must have been some kind of attempt to cheer me up. From around August 20th the sea in that part of the world becomes full of jellyfish, making it impossible to swim, so since there was nothing else to do I used to fish from the end of the jetty, but it wasn't much fun, and I remember how I pestered my brother with perpetual complaints about wanting to go home.

I don't know if it was because we spent that September 1st in this fishing village or not, but I was unable to recall anything special about the day. Certainly we all knew that the government had issued a directive that the whole nation should rise at 4:30 in the morning and offer obeisances to the Emperor in his far-off palace, as well as prayers for the safety and success of our soldiers fighting abroad, yet I very much doubt if even the Prime Minister himself behaved in accordance with his own commands. We were also ordered to eat only a one-course meal, but since most people were already doing so every mealtime, or even eating less, it caused them no additional hardship, nor did it cause us any. As far as drink was concerned, the example of Santōka finding saké available on November 1st in Shikoku (he presumably wasn't carrying his own bottle with him) showed that it seemed to have been sold—when available—with no sort of scruples; and on the day itself I can remember quite clearly watching fishermen drinking at noon in the local shop. In fact that very evening, when my brother and I had just finished our dinner and were taking the trays downstairs, our landlord and the local policeman were sitting having a drink together. As soon as he saw us, the policeman made some kind of quip related to the fact that Father was a gynaecologist, the sort of thing to which we were both so accustomed we were able to smile back quite amiably. On our way upstairs again, however, he made the same kind of joke, but this time our landlord's wife scolded him and he suddenly lowered his voice. I found that funny, and giggled, glancing back at my brother, but he didn't look in the least amused. We then played *go* together and I won three games in a row, no doubt because I'd become fairly expert at it through diligently studying a primer on the game which my brother had.

I tried to remember what had happened on the first days of October, November, and December, but could think of nothing at all. I can only presume that in my family and its immediate surroundings practically no attention was paid to Support Asia Day, and this must also have been the case among ordinary people throughout the country. That Santōka should have suffered such pangs of guilt about drinking on that day can only mean he responded to the whole business in a very abnormal way indeed.

At that point I was only thinking of Santōka's "abnormality" in connection with guilty feelings about his alcoholism, and nothing much more than that. When, later on, I was painfully working my way through the poems he'd written about the war in China, I didn't find anything abnormal about them either. I now consider this a gross oversight, though perhaps it wasn't all that surprising that I should have discovered nothing particularly unusual about poems like these in *Sōmokutō*:

Tsuki no akarusa wa	Bright light of the moon
doko o bakugeki	does it know where they
shite iru koto ka	are bombing tonight
Kogarashi no	Beaten by the wind even
hi no maru futatsu	a house like this has given

futari mo dashite iru	both sons as the signs show

Kataneba naranai	We must win all
daichi issei ni	burgeoning together
mebukō to suru	through the great earth

This was pretty run-of-the-mill stuff to celebrate the "China Incident" (as the aggressive war was called), encouragement from the home front for our boys out there, and it seemed to demand no special comment, except a mild expression of surprise that even someone like Santōka had felt called upon to do his own bit of time-serving by writing junk to please the authorities. If the poems revealed anything about Santōka himself, it was a certain sensitivity towards what was written in the newspapers, but little else. I imagine I only gave them a closer reading because I'd been thinking for some time (ideas fostered by my studies of medieval poetry) that any poetry written in really short forms is virtually obliged to produce clichés of this kind if it attempts to touch on genuine social realities.

What I mean is that, if one looks at the thirty-one-syllable waka of the medieval period, one is struck by the richness of expression arising from the allusive nature of a poetry describing a world where such allusions were understood by its readers. A twelfth-century poet will write something echoing a poem in the eleventh-century *Tale of Genji*, a poem which itself has all the weight of the rich world of that novel behind it. In later ages, however, we find that the kind of allusiveness available to earlier poets (even writers of seventeen-syllable haiku) gradually ceases to be possible as the stable, organic society that provided the material for such allusions finally disappears. Instead of the world of the court, one small enough to be comprehended, we find a world growing daily larger and more complex, until it eventually baffles true comprehension, receiving its sole expression in the columns of the daily press. The only knowledge such a society has in common is what everybody reads in the newspapers, and our poets feel obliged to write verse about public events based on the headlines used to proclaim them, whether the date be December 8th or August 15th.*

It was with such ideas in mind that I began to read the poems Santōka had written about the "China Incident" in 1937. Here was this mendicant priest seeking some sense of oneness with the world at large and, since he could find nothing else to serve his purpose, he selected the newspaper as his sole link with society, hoping to assuage his sense of isolation in that way. I saw the poems as a negative exercise in cheering himself up which led to a diffident support of the war effort itself, and I continued to think more or less in these terms until around mid-May, when I was searching through a cupboard for some old notes of mine and came across Murakami's *Santōka, The Poet Vagrant.* After turning over a few pages I found a remarkable passage describing the relationship Santōka established with Hasuda Zenmei. The fact that I'd forgotten it all, despite having read the book before and even underlining the passage in question (I must also have learnt the same facts from other sources), was a complete mystery to me, and I decided to put it down to my gradually advancing years. This is what Murakami wrote:

At nine o'clock in the morning, March 23rd [1934], he [Santōka] landed at the port of Ujina. . . .

He called on Ōyama Sumita at the Communications Centre, then went with him to Ōyama's house. That evening Santōka met, quite by chance, Hasuda Zenmei and Ikeda Tsutomu, who came to visit Ōyama. They were both scholars of Japanese literature, bright protegés of Saitō Kiyoe,

* December 8th (7th by local time), 1941: Pearl Harbor. August 15th, 1945: Japanese surrender.

and had got to know Ōyama through their professor. This was how Hasuda had first come to hear about Santōka, and he had read his second published volume of haiku, *Sōmokutō.* . . .

So, quite accidentally, Hasuda came to know the strange priest he had already heard such rumours about. Hasuda was thirty-one at the time, and one wonders if his clear, young eyes saw Santōka merely as the cheerful, eccentric priest he'd been told about. The fact is that this meeting seems to have been a profoundly moving one for Hasuda, since from start to finish he made notes on what Santōka said, and was deeply influenced by it. *The various studies he eventually pursued were all sparked off by this encounter with the poet, which provided the basis for his own writings* [my italics]. A few years later, Hasuda started the magazine *Bungei Bunka* (Literary Culture), and dominated the world of Japanese literary studies for a while. He was also Mishima Yukio's mentor. A full account of him can be found in Kodaka's massive study, *Hasuda Zenmei and His Death*.

Hasuda Zenmei was a member of the ultra-nationalist *Nihon Roman-ha* (The Japanese Romanticists, although the "Romance" is very much of the fascist kind one finds in Mishima), and if Murakami's remarks are to be believed Santōka's ideas must have been very close to theirs. One can certainly assume that his notion of the sort of body politic to which he wished to belong must have been heavily imbued with their rightist ideology. I started to have doubts about the way I had interpreted his poems on the "China Incident", feeling they required a quite different kind of reading, and these feelings gradually grew stronger. The truth is I had no real wish to follow this line of thought, because the conclusions it seemed to indicate were painful to me. If Santōka really had positively supported what the Japanese were doing in China, if he rejoiced at our boys bombing the Chinese mainland on a moonlit night, if he felt a naive, warm glow within him at the sight of a wretched house, blasted by the cold wind of autumn, where the two metal signs on the door indicated that two boys had been conscripted, then the image I had of him was going to change drastically. It would have helped if I could have interpreted what he wrote as, if not actually anti-war in sentiment, at least showing some awareness of the horrors of war, a poetry that considered what it was like for the Chinese who were being bombed, that sympathized with the misfortunes of a poor, married couple deprived of both sons. But no matter how hard I tried to entertain such ideas, a close rereading of all his poetic output on the theme of war convinced me that an interpretation of that kind was quite impossible. Look at this, for example:

Futatabi wa	Marching firmly on the
fumumai tsuchi o	earth their feet will
fumishimete iku	never tread again

What dominates the poem is not compassion for these men who march away never to see their country again, but a purely aesthetic intoxication with—even a revelling in—the picturesque beauty of the soldier's fate; and this itself demonstrates a disturbing egoism, an almost sado-masochistic callousness, which ultimately amounts to a cruel celebration of the power of the State.

This sudden appearance of another version of Santōka was a major disappointment. It was clear there was a definite connection between him and Hasuda, and quite possibly something more than that. I knew very little about Hasuda Zenmei other than what I'd picked up by hearsay: namely, that at the time of the defeat he was a company commander in the army in Malaya; that he shot his divisional (or perhaps only his battalion) commander, after accusing him of being a traitor to his country, and then committed suicide himself. He had been the most extreme, and obviously the most dangerous, of all the Japanese Romanticists. I had also read a couple of his books during the war (one of them was on the reclusive Kamo no Chōmei), but not thought much of either of them. Of course, I didn't think Santōka himself would ever have been capable of such lunatic behaviour, and had no intention of linking the two together in such terms, but as I read over the war poems again I was obliged to note that not one of them showed a scrap of sympathy for the victims of the war. All they revealed was a complete confusion of emotional attitudes, as if Santōka were finally honouring the very evil of State power, which had provided him with a war he could use to intoxicate himself with brutal images of tragic beauty. Santōka's obsession with the concept of "home" (a lost home) is well known:

Ame furu	In the rain that rains
furusato wa	on my own village
hadashi de aruku	I walk barefoot

His tendency to extend this concept until it comprehended an abstract idea of the State itself, while at the same time escaping from the present (and thus the actual society of his day, the real country) by wandering around villages and small provincial towns begging, indicates a genuine closeness to the ideology of the Japanese Romanticists, making their beliefs virtually the same. Perhaps these ideas were contingent on his way of life, and thus inevitable, as he watched an agriculturally based society having sudden and severe inroads made upon it by an increasingly Westernized present.

The more I thought about this, the more empty it made me feel inside. No doubt this link with Japanese fascism provided evidence in favour of the theory that the priest in the tea-house at Dōgo, who said he had no adequate words with which to apologize to H.I.M., really was Santōka; but the knowledge gave me little pleasure.

11

When the summer holiday started in July, I had to go down to Kyoto to spend five days investigating some ancient documents in one of the shrines, a chore I'd been asked repeatedly to do and eventually could put off no longer. A number of enormous chests stuffed full of old scrolls might have a certain appeal to historians, but for people like us they're just incredibly tedious, and the harvest of my labours was very meagre. To make matters worse, my assistant was obliged to return to Tokyo early because his wife was suddenly taken ill, so I was left to wade through the remainder myself. As a result, on the evening of the final day, I decided to give myself a small treat, and went to dine at a rather nifty little restaurant I knew there.

As soon as I entered the place I was greeted by a man who, judging from his dress, was trying to look considerably younger than his years. He was sitting at the counter drinking.

"Hello, there. At last a man who comes to Kyoto and doesn't bring a girl with him. I also happen to be alone myself, of course."

He was someone I'd met through one of my old high-school companions—a poet who'd read French at university. Some years ago he had published a study of Fujiwara Teika entitled *The Clouded Sky*, from which one might gather that he had an interest in medieval poetry; in fact, recently he seemed to have become better known for that than his own verses. From a scholar's point of view, the book on Teika was full of prejudices, wild assumptions, and unproven hypotheses. More importantly, it was patently lacking in the basic knowledge such an undertaking requires. Still, if one ignores such failings, his work did show the occasional sharp insight, and, so far as such productions by novelists, poets, and their ilk go, it wasn't bad at all.

"Hot here in Kyoto, isn't it?" I replied and, assuming it wouldn't sound all that affected in this kind of company, added: "It would be rather nice to be 'Surprised by autumn / in dreams of a summer night'."

I then sat down beside him. We seemed to be the only customers, perhaps because of the summer heat.

"From the *Shinkokinshū*," he said. "Doesn't it begin, 'Near to my window / the small grove of bamboo / moves in the wind'? Who's it by?"

"Kintsugu, Lord Steward to the Crown Prince. Still, you seem to be well up in these things, I must say. With a memory like that, in the Muromachi period you could have . . ."

". . . made a living as a teacher of linked verse, no doubt."

We talked about mutual acquaintances, the various things he'd brought back with him from a trip to Italy and Spain the previous year, and so on, until he suddenly started on a series of anecdotes about Saitō Sanki, a writer of rather surrealistic haiku, so it was a fairly natural progression from that subject to Santōka. The drink had already gone to my head, and since my audience was a literary acquaintance and not a scholar he seemed just the sort of person to tell everything to. So I told him about my father and Kurokawa meeting a priest in Dōgo and standing him drinks, about the poet's pro-war enthusiasms, about *yokoshigure*, and my suspicions that the priest might well have been the aged Santōka. I only gave a general outline of things, and didn't speak with much confidence, as I'd already discussed the matter vaguely in casual coffee-shop conversations with a colleague (an assistant professor specializing in modern literature) and one of the brightest of my graduate students—neither of whom had shown much interest. I suppose they both thought I lacked sufficient evidence for my assumptions, because the assistant professor kept getting off the main point by raising general questions as to the way one should interpret blank spaces in a diary, the life-style of the *poète maudit*, and how any treatment of wartime literature should bear censorship conditions rigorously in mind; while the graduate student talked very intensely about the relationship between free-rhythm haiku and *vers libres*, before finally telling me that Santōka's life had appeared in cartoon form and had also been talked about on a late-night radio show. Having gone through that kind of experience twice in coffee shops in Tokyo, I was wary about the response I might arouse in a smart little restaurant in Kyoto. But the poet reacted quite differently.

"That was Santōka, all right. There can't be any doubt about that. It must have been him. After all, who else could it have been?"

I was obviously thrilled to hear this absolute judgement, but still saw fit to retain a certain caution.

"It certainly seems so, but the trouble is there's nothing in the diary."

"Poets don't write what they don't want to write. Look at Teika. Look at me, for heaven's sake."

He seemed to be putting himself on the same level as a major poet, but he added with a laugh:

"Admittedly I don't keep a diary anyway.... I must say, though, *yokoshigure* is a marvellous word. Hasn't it been used in Edo *haikai*?"

"Once by Issa, but it's a pretty dull poem—so dull I've forgotten it. And that's the only example I've come across so far."

"When you turn up a really good word, it's hard to know what to do with it; particularly hard if you're writing things as short as that. You want to use it but you can't, so the thing starts to irritate you. That's why it wouldn't have got written down in his diary."

The poet said all this with (and after) much deliberation, then fell silent, as if he were thinking deeply about something, or had

187

even conceived so great a liking for the word that he was now in the process of embodying it in some small creation of his own. I decided to ignore whatever he might be preoccupied with, and went on with my relation of the facts about Santōka, confident that he would be interested.

"Actually, he had encountered just that kind of wind-driven rain not all that long before."

"Santōka had?"

"That's right."

This was something I'd discovered when reading the 1939 diaries through from the beginning, the entry being for November 4th:

> Raining when I set out, and so I begged in the rain (today it really felt like begging for the very first time). Then the rain came on heavily. The wind started to blow fiercely—I walked on, up hill, down dale. Through breaks in the storm I could see the long, winding beaches, and the bay, and hurried on, visiting Sabadaishidō temple to pray, my bamboo hat blown off by the wind, my glasses, too, and I didn't know what to do, but a small boy who was passing picked them up for me, so kind of him, so kind. The rain thickened and the wind became more frightful, so there was nothing for it, I thought, but to spend the night at Okutomochō, yet none of the lodging houses would give me a room, so on I trudged, looking like a drowned rat, but reached a point where I could go no further, stopping under the eaves of a storehouse to wring the water out of my clothes and eat my lunch, not moving for a couple of hours.

Up to this point the writing is good, clear, and vigorous—remarkably so, perhaps; but then comes the important passage (in which the underlining is Santōka's own).

A total downpour! That's exactly what it was—blown in by this violent wind, blown up like a bamboo blind, and pouring in from the side; *and I felt as if I were being struck and beaten by the heavens, and the feeling was good.*

The underlined passage demonstrates an excitement about a natural phenomenon that one might almost call sado-maso-chistic, and it is clear from the rest of the entry and the style in which it's written that the rain, "pouring in from the side (*yo-kosama*)", had affected him in an extraordinary, an abnormal way. But what's particularly worthy of note is that, of the nine haiku he wrote that day, not one deals with this experience. Which means that the experience wouldn't take poetic shape. The most he seemed capable of producing was this mediocre effort:

Aruku hoka nai	All I can do is
aki no ame	walk the autumn rain
furitsunoru	falls furiously

Santōka must surely have seen that his prose description was superior to that, and one can well imagine the state of mind of a poet who, after a month's mortification at not being able to write what he wanted, suddenly receives the gift of a totally expressive word, and yet is still unable to compose the right poem. Isn't it at least very likely that it would have led to intense spiritual anguish?

I was quite carried away by my own eloquence as I reported these findings to the man beside me—even putting in that final bold inference—and although it was three months since I'd read them I managed to quote the words "blown in by this violent wind, blown up like a bamboo blind, and pouring in from the side" verbatim from memory. Certainly the style was vigorous, and the material itself was important for the maintenance of my thesis, but I think the principal reason it remained so vivid in my memory was that, after all the worries I'd had with those dreary (and, as I now saw it, quite irrelevant) war poems, the discovery of this passage in the diary, with the rain being driven by the wind, had been of the utmost assistance in allowing me to return to the cheerful ways of literary speculation.

When I came to an end, the poet nodded.

" 'Like a bamboo blind' is a pretty rotten comparison. The slats in a blind are horizontal, not vertical, so when the blind was blown up they'd be pointing in the wrong direction. He's got his image mixed up."

He shook his head with a grimace, then went on:

"The reason he left the tea-house first was because he wanted to be alone to write his poem. But no matter how much he walked through the rain it just wouldn't come. So he walks and walks, he goes on walking. . . ."

Having muttered this in a deeply serious voice, he asked the man behind the bar for some paper, whereupon the aproned cook produced a memo pad and a ball pen. On this the poet wrote *shi-kure* in kana script, then ripped the piece off and wrote the same words in Chinese characters over the imprint made on the page beneath. *Shigure*, or late autumn rain, deprived of the voicing of its second syllable, had become *shikure*, and the rewriting in characters had given it a new meaning as two words, "death" and "ending".

"Well, I'd never thought of that," I said, reflecting how this type of verbal play, whereby new interpretations are produced, was one of his critical specialities much in evidence in *The Clouded Sky*. There is, of course, no question that the *kakekotoba*—the pivot word in which one word fades into another, an elaborate form of punning—is a basic device in traditional Japanese poetry, and this habit of his would have been acceptable if directed at nothing else. The trouble was, his

190

heuristic approach sometimes seemed to get totally out of control, resulting in wild flights of the imagination which ignored the simplest and best-established conventions. As an extreme example I can cite his reinterpretation of a proper noun, the name of the Cloistered Emperor Gotōba (written with three characters meaning "after", "bird", and "wing"), as *kotoba*, written with one character and meaning "diction". None of the considerable evidence we have will allow this reading, and clearly it's a purely fanciful view of the matter with which no sensible person could agree; yet his response to such objections when politely pointed out to him was to remain perfectly indifferent, claiming that the objector's awareness of the problem remained on the superficial level of written characters, whereas he was sounding the lower depths of the mind, that deeper consciousness at work when a man chose a name for himself. Obviously there was no way one could argue with him.

In the case of *shigure* turning into *shikure*, however, despite my initial dismay, I felt almost immediately a direct intuition that he was right, that this interpretation could be made to fit perfectly, allowing the whole pattern to be completed. It was as if the life and works of a haiku poet were being reduced to two basic images, and what could be more basic than the idea of death, and that of an ending, be it the twilight close of day or the year's end? The poet sitting beside me, a cigarette perpetually unlit between his lips, went on talking, this time in a quiet, persuasive whisper quite unlike his normal hectoring tone, as if he were carefully delineating the process of my own ideas.

"I can't help feeling that must be right somehow. It's just like a puzzle falling suddenly into place. And because the meaning stayed at the bottom of his consciousness he spent his whole life writing poems about autumn rain which were really about death. Because he was a man perpetually obsessed by death."

"He tried to commit suicide once. It was . . ."

"It was hopeless from the start, always wanting to die, a way of life focussed on death. But, of course, he couldn't do it; he couldn't die so the obsession with death became all the greater. So he gets this image fixed in his mind, a compound image of his own death, the twilight close of the day, ending in darkness, the ending of the year and the wintry rain. The terrifying image of death concealed behind the rains of early winter. But just remove that veil, and this is what you find:

Ushiro sugata no	Whose back going
shi kurete	into the closing day
yuku ka	but that of death

He watches the dead Santōka; watches his own back going away from him, fading into the dusk. The living Santōka watches the dead, seeing him off. . . ."

"Just like the last scene in a film."

"He probably did get some kind of hint from the cinema. After all, wasn't he a great fan of the moving pictures?" said the poet, using the old-fashioned term as an informed gesture towards the age in which Santōka lived.

"Yes, he was. The diaries have a number of entries about the 'kinema'."

"There you are. He was really up to date. Right in the swing."

We both laughed. Then, using the image of death as a natural point of entry, I got onto the subject of Santōka's relationship with the Japanese Romanticists, emphasizing that, though it might seem casual enough at first sight, it was in fact extremely deep, and that there was a theory that he'd had a profound influence on the ideas of Hasuda Zenmei, for one.

"Well, the combination certainly makes one's mind boggle initially, but somehow they seem to match all right. It's a fascinating idea."

"They both believed in practising what they preached. Santōka expressed his misgivings about the nature of capitalist society by begging, and Hasuda's emperor-worship took the form—when the war was already over and, indeed perhaps for that very reason—of killing a superior officer because he wasn't pursuing the now non-existent war positively enough. Of course, with Hasuda it was just a pretence of practice rather than the thing itself. But, anyway, he did something. That naive brooding over things, that obsession with form, it's the same in both of them."

The cook struck a match, and the poet at last allowed his cigarette to be lit, muttering his thanks before continuing:

"Practising what you preach; the unity of thought and action. Well, in literary terms our Japanese Romanticists seemed to do so—probably as a result of their obsession with the distant past. But, of course, ancient literature is extremely simple-minded in its attitudes, so there was bound to be a good deal of similarity between what was expressed in a literary work and the actual behaviour of the writer. And then, the Japanese Romanticists didn't know much about what ancient literature was really like; indeed they were ignorant, quite lacking in discrimination, ignoring the obvious fact that the whole body of literature could hardly have consisted solely of works where the writer had actually done what he said he'd done, and so they created a convenient fantasy about it. Don't you agree?"

"Absolutely," I said, and gave three examples off the cuff of "their ignorance and lack of discrimination", which the poet listened to with a smile, though he suddenly interrupted me during the third and began to give his interpretation of the "Oto wa shigure ka" poem. Unfortunately I paid almost no attention to this analysis, not because I felt it would be tedious, but because I was thinking of something else. At a convenient break in his flow of remarks, I showed him the result of my reflections, a slip of paper on which I'd written the characters *yoko* (side) and *shi* (death), meaning (when read as ō-shi) an unnatural, untimely, or violent death, an out-of-the-way death, by the roadside; a dog's death.

The poet showed real interest, so I said:

"You see. Following your example, and assuming that San-tōka really was bewitched by the word *yokoshigure*; only assuming that, of course . . ."

"Well, there's no doubt about that. Go on."

"Then it might well have been because this truly dark image existed somewhere in his mind. Just an application of your method, though it's something I've been thinking about vaguely for some time. I mean, why are poets who've died an unnatural, preferably violent, death given such preferential treatment in the history of Japanese literature? Is it a sort of leftover from the very distant past? Whatever it is, it's a clearly established tradition."

I went on to explain in more detail, saying that Japanese literature seems to welcome some kind of unnatural death in a poet—whether by another's hand, or in some calamity, or even, taking its wider meaning, simply in unfortunate circumstances—as a final accolade set upon his life and work. If the death of a literary figure is particularly striking, its tragic nature will bestow on his work a preposterously high value, and his fame becomes eternal. Minamoto Sanetomo's assassination at Tsurugaoka Hachiman Shrine, and Kobayashi Takiji's death by torture at the Tsukiji police station, have wrapped their names in a good deal of additional glory by reason of the existence of this tradition. Thus it is that a form of spiritualism, a belief in the powers of the souls of the dead, has had a profound effect on literary appreciation, since this honouring of their names is really a placating of their tortured souls. Now, this interpretation might seem all right in the case of the assassinated Minister of the Right, but it can certainly sound a bit odd, if not absurd, when mixed up with twentieth-century Marxism, as it must be with the proletarian writer Kobayashi; yet one only has to think of the mummified carcass lying in state in the Lenin Mausoleum to realize it doesn't have to be all that peculiar. In backward countries revolutionary ideologies often get entangled with the local religion.

To find the first example of a poet meeting an untimely death we probably have to go back to the fourth century and Prince Yamato Takeru, who pronounced an inappropriate spell when he encountered a sacred white boar in the foothills of a mountain. His health was impaired by a hailstorm during the subsequent climb, which led eventually to his death, though not before he'd composed a poem bewailing his fate. This event gave dramatic expression to a naive sentimentality already implicit in the idea of the poet, something latent in the native literary sensibility which became the real centre of the literary experience itself. Thus an automatic response to the poetic life became fixed over the centuries, and this resulted in a heavily idealized image of what the Japanese feel a poet ought essentially to be. That the soul of a great departed poet was something not merely to be admired but also solemnly placated can be seen in the case of the early Heian poet, Sugawara Michizane, who not only died in exile while gazing in a melancholy manner at the moon, but sadly failed to achieve his proposed visit to China, something as important for a famous writer of Chinese poetry as the death in exile itself. After his unappeased spirit had plagued the capital with thunderstorms and other misfortunes, shrines were set up all over the country, dedicated to Tenjinsama (the heavenly person) as he was dubbed, it being his new fate to become the god of learning. Learning itself was basically a question of literary learning, and of poetry in particular; and, as one can see in the case of Fujiwara Teika paying a formal visit to the Kitano Shrine to pray that he might be included in the first of Gotōba's hundred-poem anthologies, the religious implications of poetry and the poetic act were considerable. Poets and the readers of poetry became votaries at the various shrines in order to placate the departed soul of Michizane, now a god and yet still disgruntled with the death he suffered in this worldly life.

It is in the Kamakura and Muromachi periods, between the thirteenth and sixteenth centuries, that one finds the most complete expression of this aspect of the Japanese literary tradition, for there the aim of placating the spirits of the dead takes its most striking forms. The *Shinkokinshū*, an early thirteenth-century anthology, includes sixteen poems by Michizane, and at least twelve of them are placed in a group at the very beginning of the eighteenth volume, which is devoted to "poems on various topics"; a remarkable phenomenon if one considers that Japanese poetic anthologies tend to group poems by theme rather than author. I don't see how one can interpret this as anything other than an essentially incantatory gesture to appease the vengeful deity. This tendency to be primarily concerned with the fetishistic nature of what should be the act of literary appreciation is also shown in the way that, even when major poets died perfectly normal deaths, totally bogus legends were created in order to demonstrate otherwise, as if it were felt to be a form of disrespect towards the poet's output, an undervaluing of it, indeed, if one didn't construct some kind of fantasy to glorify the manner of his death. It's impossible to understand what was going on unless one takes this approach. If one looks at actual examples, the death of someone like the Cloistered Emperor Gotōba, who spent his last years in wretched exile on a remote island, needed no embellishment, but what was one to do with Fujiwara Teika? Here was a man living to the ripe old age of eighty-six who, after exercising dictatorial authority over the world of poetry for years, died in the capital by what could only have been the natural ageing process. Obviously this created real problems, which were solved by the eccentric device of having him reappear in the form of a creeping plant entwined about the grave of his mistress, the Princess Royal Shokishi (who some claim wasn't his mistress anyway), this being about the best they could do for him. If one is to believe a fairly reliable historical source, the woman in fact died about forty years before Teika (there are other opinions about the date, however), which implies that this passion for the deceased had continued all that length of time; an unlikely story, to say the least, though the fact that nobody at the time saw fit to raise any such objection is a good indication of the reverence in which his poems were held.

A tale as patently risible as that one can be dismissed with a cheerful smile, of course, but this fantasizing habit is often a perfect nuisance, as is shown in the case of Teika's master, the Regent Fujiwara Ryōkei, who died in 1206 at the youthful age of thirty-seven. Three versions were given of the way in which he died. First, it was claimed that he had become too friendly with the powers that be in Kamakura; or at least too friendly in the eyes of the Cloistered Emperor Gotōba, who had him killed. The second version was that his death was brought about by Teika, who was jealous of his poems; and the third was that it was done by Sugawara Tamenaga because he had a grudge against Ryōkei, who he thought had used his influence to prevent him being allowed to write the preface to the *Shinkokin-shū*. What stands out in all these fairy tales is the quite irresponsible way in which they were created, and though one can see a simple motive of regret for the fact of one dying so young at work here, undoubtedly the true driving force behind it all is what can only be considered a psychological abnormality, the wish to bestow the added glory of a wretched death on a poet who had written many fine poems before his premature death.

I concluded this long preamble (all material previously used in lectures, except for the example of Kobayashi Takiji) by saying that any consideration of the history of Japanese literature is obliged to take into account the fact that the arts of literature and incantation, the act of writing a poem and that of intoning a spell, have never been made completely distinct from each other. I also said it was hardly likely that a poetic tradition which placed so great an emphasis on untimely death could have failed to permeate Santōka's consciousness, and thus it seemed inevitable that a poet so obsessed with suicide should have seen the apotheosis of that traditional urge in the word *yokoshigure*; at any rate, that was how it looked to me.

My companion, who had kept quiet all this time, just listening and occasionally nodding, announced his agreement.

"Yes, there's certainly something odd about seeing modern Japanese literature solely in terms of European romanticism, as we always tend to do. Mishima Yukio is probably another case in point."

I was slightly taken aback by that final comment, putting in a hurried word of protest, but the poet remained unperturbed.

"I know, people claim the act was essentially political, or sexual, or lots of other things. I wouldn't say they're wrong to do so, either. Still, when all is said and done, he was a man of letters, and I would have thought that a literary motive was the basic one."

"Well, if we do interpret it that way, the connection with Hasuda Zenmei comes in very nicely."

"It does indeed. The unity of thought and action; practising what you preach. The only trouble is it certainly makes Japanese literature look pretty unhealthy."

198

The poet pondered this awhile, his face becoming remote and serious, even melancholy; but he soon recovered.

"I must say it seems ridiculous to commit suicide because you're determined to be a major writer. Absolutely daft. Much better to be like Ryōkei. Suppose, for example, that I were suddenly to pop off in my sleep in my room in the Kyoto Hotel tonight. People of a later age might cook up the theory that Hagiwara Sakutarō had poisoned me because he was jealous of my poetry, though some nosey scholar might then find out Sakutarō had died decades ago, and publish an essay in which he claimed that the poison theory was quite untenable. That's something to look forward to, surely?"

I smiled briefly.

12

Pathetic though it may sound, I gained real confidence in the value of my ideas by having them endorsed by a man who had not only made a name for himself as a purveyor of the irresponsible, but was also under the influence of drink at the time. Still, that was the way it was, and I'm obliged to record the fact. The truth is that, ever since I came across the passage in Santōka's diary describing his drenching in the storm, his awakening to the reality of *yokoshigure*, I'd been quite desperate to believe that my theories were true, and on the super express back to Tokyo I virtually reached the point of announcing to myself that the priest in the tea-house and Santōka were indisputably one and the same person. This definitive judgement would result in no article on the subject or any conference paper, so I was in the same happy-go-lucky position as the irresponsible poet, at least insofar as this particular question was concerned; and yet by the time I arrived at Tokyo Station my old tentative, questioning state of mind had returned, and again I wasn't sure.

Then, as luck would have it, while I was messing about investigating this and that, I came across some new material which only added to my confusion, a confusion presumably caused by the fact that I'd been too deeply imbued with the scholastic standards of the university from which I'd graduated and where I was now employed: that solid method whereby one tests every inch of the ground before taking the smallest step forward. Of course, this isn't in itself something necessarily to feel ashamed of.

The first piece of new information to cast an awkward light on my assumptions was the strong likelihood that when Santōka visited Shikoku he wasn't dressed as a priest but as an ordinary beggar. Presumably if I had been a poet who'd graduated from some department of French I could have laughed this off by saying they'd have looked pretty much alike, surely; but the fact is a mendicant priest and an ordinary beggar just don't look the same at all, and the problem this raised simply couldn't be ignored. My habit of fussing over things that might seem to be very minor matters of detail to an ordinary bystander is one I'm incapable of shaking off.

According to Ueda's *Santōka the Poet*, in September 1939, when he abandoned his hermitage at Yuda in Yamaguchi, Santōka also discarded his religious clothes, because he felt he wasn't the sort of person who had any right to chant the sutras and wrap himself in priestly robes.

> He believed that mendicity as a religious act, the use of the begging bowl, etc., were no longer relevant to him. He was merely a lay mendicant, a beggar, a vagrant; that was what he was and that was what he should look like. . . . In a dirty, unlined kimono held about him by a thin belt, with his skirts girded up about his loins, a towel dangling from his waist and *jikatabi* on his feet, he looked exactly like a real beggar.

On October 1st he visited the house of Professor Takahashi of the Matsuyama Commercial College, with an introduction from Ōyama Sumita; "and the old beggar with his one towel was warmly received by the whole household". He next paid a call on Kawamura Miyuki, a fellow member of the haiku magazine *Sōun*, who recorded that:

> Musō, a priest from the Ittōen in Kyoto who occasionally visited me, turned up, and a passionate conversation was held about Ozaki Hōsai. Musō took off his own black over-robe and gave it to Santōka, who no longer wore priestly garments. Santōka intended to do a pilgrimage around the whole of Shikoku, and he certainly looked much better dressed for the part than he had in his former wretched outfit.

If one is to believe all this, one has to imagine Santōka in the peculiar costume of an ordinary kimono with a string-like belt, a towel dangling from his waist, and a priest's black robe on top of everything, while on his feet he wore rubber-soled *jikatabi*, the kind workmen wear on building sites. It was certainly an eccentric way to dress for a man who "intended to do a pilgrimage", even if he might not have meant to beg as a mendicant priest but merely as someone who did it in order not to starve. The detail about the *jikatabi*, however, is confirmed by the entry in the diary for November 7th:

> One of my *jikatabi* has been broken these last few days, so I've been troubled by sores on my left foot, but luckily I found a discarded gumboot and was able to use a piece cut out of that to resole it.

The existence of the towel, and the importance it had for him, can also be seen in the entry for the third: "I seem to have lost my towel somewhere, but found a poem in its stead." And my guess is that the poem he mentions is this one:

Shigurete nurete	Soaked through in the autumn
tabigoromo	rain I wring out my
shibotte wa yuku	travel garment and go on

The question, however, is what this "travel garment" actually was, for it is by no means clear. In his notes to the sixth volume of the *Collected Works*, Ōyama Sumita maintains:

> He was not dressed in the manner of a Zen priest, or a properly appointed pilgrim, but simply wore a kimono and a thin sash, with his skirts gathered up behind, *jikatabi* on his feet, no bamboo hat, and a small bag dangling from his neck, looking for all the world like a mere beggar, a lay mendicant.

This seems to fit in well enough with Ueda's account, but it still varies slightly in certain places. Even if we accept that Ōyama's omitting to mention the towel presents no great problem, we can hardly dismiss his failure to refer to the black over-robe in the same way, as this would have made a considerable difference to Santōka's appearance. Unfortunately, further investigation of the matter is hampered by the fact that the diary itself, from September 27th to October 31st of the year in question, contains no entries at all; so at this point speculation must begin, principally because research so far has overlooked the importance of this large blank in the record. My own view is that, given the undoubted fact that Santōka usually kept up his diary quite scrupulously, the other undoubted fact that he left nothing but poems for a period of over a month must mean one of two things: either he stopped keeping a daily record (and had reasons for doing so), or he continued it and later destroyed it, retaining only the verse he'd written (and he must also have had reasons for doing that).

For comparison, it is worth looking at the diary of another poet, one altogether different in status as a writer and, in that sense, offering a slightly awkward, even laboured, analogy, but no matter. All that we have now of the diary of Fujiwara Teika for the three years of the Jōkyū era (1219–1221) is two entries in the intercalary month of February 1219, on the second and the twenty-third. I have always wondered about this long hiatus, assuming that it was either a period during which Teika was in no mood to keep a diary, or that whatever he wrote (assuming he wrote anything) had to be disposed of later for some unknown reason. What we do know is that the politician on whom Teika had particularly relied for support, the Shogun and poet Minamoto Sanetomo, was assassinated in January of that same year (which should really be referred to as the seventh and last year of the Kenpō era rather than the first of Jōkyū, since the era names changed officially in April). This marked the beginning of a series of set-backs for Teika: in February of the next year he suffered imperial censure for his famous poem about the willow by the wayside unfeelingly putting forth new shoots, and in the third and final year of that era, 1221, there was the culminating disaster of the Jōkyū Rebellion. It isn't hard to imagine how wretched this period must have been for him, how much it must have weighed on a nature as sensitive as his. Consequently, he failed to keep a diary of that time or, if he did, then in later years he destroyed what he'd written as something potentially dangerous. Either eventuality seems feasible, and much the same would apply in Santōka's case.

In the critical introduction to his edition of *The Defence of Folly* Ōyama Sumita has written that "a pilgrimage around Shikoku in autumn, with no hat, when it can still be very hot during the day, and in the plain clothes of a beggar, was not only a rather bold thing to do but suggests a state of mind where the traveller was prepared for, even expecting, death". Ōyama's claim may seem a little bold itself, but he had already explained that Santōka had previously given his priest's robes and begging bowl (those passports to nourishment) to a friend, which certainly looks like a deliberate attempt to make life hard for himself; and Koyama in *The Wanderings of Santōka* agrees with this point of view, going on to say:

> Santōka's pilgrimage in Shikoku was not the standard one of visiting the eighty-eight holy places and praying there. In fact he only visited about ten of the temples. Referring to it as a pilgrimage is misleading, too, for he had no spiritual need to do anything of that kind and his real motive for setting out was that, with no settled place to live, having just lost his home, all he could do now was walk. This pretext—of having nothing else to do in life but wander about—was there from the start.

It is a fine insight, but I would alter it slightly and suggest that, when Santōka was deprived of his hermitage (or deliberately abandoned it), his journey to Shikoku was yet another attempt on his part to die; or an attempt to encounter death, if you prefer—no conscious aiming at suicide, perhaps, but a gradual drifting towards his own end. This desire was not fulfilled, however, because of his rugged constitution, an emotional clinging to life, and probably other reasons as well. He kept no diary because there was no need for one on a journey where he had already determined to die like an outcast in some desolate place.

One can find confirmation of this assumption in the haiku written on October 23rd and 24th.

Nakanaka shinenai	Unable yet to die
higanbana	flowers of the other shore
saku	in bloom

In Memory of the Priest Hōsai

Shi o hishi hishi to	Hurrying on to
mizu no	death the water
umasa ka na	tastes so good

And the following three, written on the twenty-sixth, make particularly interesting reading if one bears in mind the remarks of my companion in Kyoto about *shigure* and *shikure*.

Shigurete	Rain falls on one then
yama o mata yama o	another mountain
shiranai yama	unknown mountains
Karada	Striding out urging
nagedashite	my body onwards cold
shigururu yama	rain falls on the mountain
Shigurete michi	In the cold rain
shirube sono ji ga	the signpost and I
yomenai	cannot read it

Despite their technical competence these poems are somehow lacking in energy, peculiarly unhappy in tone, and seem to provide corroboration of the thesis being put forward. Given this state of mind, one can only assume that the decision to take up his diary again (from page one of what's referred to in the *Collected Works* as "coverless notebook 24") must have been a decision not to die for the time being. At least that's how it appeared to me. I was unable to ascertain if "notebook 23" had been abandoned because it was full, or if blank pages remained (a matter not mentioned in the *Collected Works*), which would have been further evidence that he was making a new start. But I think it's fair to say that Santōka decided to go on living, though he was no doubt just as obsessed by the idea of death. Since the diary begins again on November 1st it seems likely the decision was made on that day and, given his patriotic feelings, the fact of its being Support Asia Day had some influence in the matter.

Whatever the reason, then, he chose to go on living, and returned to his begging ways, but apparently as a mendicant priest again. On the day he encountered the storm with rain "pouring in from the side"—November 5th—his diary records: "Raining when I set out, and so I begged in the rain (*today it really felt like begging for the very first time*)" [my italics]; and that surely must be seen as evidence. Exactly how he was dressed, however, remains unknown, and Ueda, after quoting the diary entry for that day, only has this to say:

> Santōka at this time theoretically had nothing to do with religious mendicity or the begging bowl, believing that his true nature was that of the lay beggar, the vagrant in fact, and that he should look like what he was. Yet, to go by this entry, he was wearing a bamboo hat and begging in the style of a priest. Was he wearing priestly robes, or just the black over-robe given him by the priest from Kyoto? It is impossible to say. Again, if he was begging in the formal way, then he must have had a bowl to receive the offerings of rice and money, and presumably he chanted the sutras as he did so. What had happened to the Santōka with the ordinary kimono and belt, the towel and girded loins? Where had he disappeared to? There seems no point in asking.

No point in asking, of course, because there's no hope of an answer. Certainly at this remove there is no way one could really investigate the matter, and one sympathizes with the person who just gives up trying; but as far as I was concerned, Ueda had thrown in his hand at a most unfortunate point. What it came down to was that, if Santōka hadn't been dressed as a proper priest, then the man my father and Kurokawa had met at the tea-house in Dōgo just couldn't have been him. I suppose he might conceivably have acquired the right clothes somewhere, but there was no record of any such thing in the diary wherever I looked, and common sense argued strongly against it. There was certainly no suggestion that he had somehow got back the vestments he'd given away to various friends. Perhaps, then, one could ignore the question of clothing and say that his priestliness resided in his undoubtedly priest-like behaviour, in the way he talked, for example, or in his general manner. (The man in question had, in fact, placed his hands together in a priestly gesture when he took his leave.)

Yet both the accounts given me by my father and Kurokawa made it quite clear that he was not simply a priest-like person but unmistakably a priest at first glance. One might claim that a round-shaped head would give this impression (and probably it did appear that way), but this wouldn't have been because it was clean-shaven, as most of the various photos of Santōka I've seen show him with the same sort of hairstyle, just close-cropped, the kind of severe trim that was compulsory in the armed forces and thus common among a great number of men at the time. It would be absurd to believe this haircut could have convinced anybody that its possessor was a priest. If Santōka was not dressed as a priest, then he couldn't have been the one my father and Kurokawa ran across, and so the additional material I'd unearthed had done me no good at all.

Still feeling a great desire to make the story seem plausible, I toyed with the idea that the two of them had mistaken a black over-robe for the proper garments, so I decided to investigate the kind of dress they wore at the Ittōen in Kyoto. The Ittōen (Garden of the One Light) was a religious organization set up in the early years of the century. Its main emphasis was on choosing poverty as the road to spiritual development, and there were a number of books about it. But when I searched through these, including the writings of its founder, Nishida Tenkō, I could find no mention of any such over-robe, and there were no photographs of the dress worn there. The only clue was in a book on Ozaki Hōsai, which described a visit paid to the Garden of the One Light by Ogiwara Seisensui (both Santōka and Hōsai were his disciples) when Hōsai was working there as a temple servant. Hōsai was "wearing a tight-sleeved kimono which seemed to be their standard dress, and washing a pickles tub". Was this tight-sleeved garment the over-robe in question? There was no way of knowing; and even if it were black, even if it might give the impression of a priest's clothes when looked at briefly from a distance, it was impossible to imagine anyone continuing to think so after hours spent drinking with a person dressed like that. There was nothing for it but to abandon this idea as well.

As if this wasn't sufficiently depressing in itself, I then came across some even more damaging evidence which finally cast what seemed to be conclusive doubt on my theory. While I was investigating the question of Santōka's clothes, I discovered that the man from Kyoto who'd given him the black over-robe, the man called Musō, was the same kind of wandering priest as Santōka. Murakami refers to him in Santōka, the Poet Vagrant in precisely such terms: somebody "he met occasionally, living under similar straitened circumstances, the vagrant priest Kimura Musō". I had read the book before, but somehow had stupidly overlooked this. According to Murakami, Santōka had urged Musō, "as though concerned about his own child", not to become a vagrant like himself because "one was enough". A long letter addressed to Musō in volume 7 of the Collected Works confirms this. It starts by saying:

> I have read both your letters with much soul-searching. I am truly sorry. I only sent that postcard because I had reached the end of my tether, and all I can do now is look back on it with shame. I think we should both forget that the card was ever sent, or ever read.

Later there is this passage:

> Think about it carefully. I will also. This is a very important

period in both our lives. If your first plan doesn't work out, there's always a second, and a third. But vagrancy is no good; it won't do at all. I could never accept your doing anything like that, though I understand only too well how you must feel.

The letter ends:

I am awaiting your reply. We must consult together about this. What I have written here is just my first thoughts. Take care of yourself.

Taneda

(October 31st, morning)

The date should not be overlooked, being the very day before he began to write his new diary, "Journal of a Pilgrimage to Shikoku", and by using the information provided in this letter we can, I think, arrive at a more detailed account of why Santōka should have abandoned the idea of suicide.

Until he met Kimura Musō, Santōka had presumably thought he was the only really individual vagrant of his day, the one exception to the current social order, confident in his unique importance. Certainly he had associated with Saitō Kiyoe, a professor of Japanese literature who had thrown in his job at a national university to wander the length and breadth of Japan, and he knew what he had done and must, to some extent, have respected him as a person, perhaps feeling a certain kinship with him. But Saitō's journeying could hardly have seemed the real thing, since it was only a form of amateurism involving no real risks or economic hardship, being essentially a gentleman's grand tour. Santōka may even have despised it. I may be slightly prejudiced in my own views on the matter, but, generally speaking, poets and novelists (even those employed at universities), from some excessive confidence in the rightness of their calling and an inflated view of its perilous nature, tend to criticize scholars of literature in terms similar to those I've suggested Santōka would have felt (and with infinitely more justification) towards the travels of ex-professor Saitō. In fact it seems inconceivable to me that he would have thought of Saitō except in such terms, which thus allowed him both to take pride in being the one genuine vagrant in existence and to feel reassured that, since he'd given rise to no imitators, he was having no harmful effect on the orderly running of society. The average admirer of Santōka's work seemed quite happy to restrict his nonconformity to the writing of incompetent free-rhythm haiku, making no other attempt to deviate from the workaday life of the ordinary citizen, and thus imposing no burden of guilt on Santōka. Obviously one should be careful about making conjectures as to what's taking place in somebody else's mind, but at least there must have been something of that sort going on there, even if only at an unconscious level.

Then Musō appears on the scene, another vagrant priest, apparently determined to go on imitating Santōka's life-style, and to an even greater extent. The disconcerted Santōka, aware that vagrancy, the rejection of the world, can only lead to suicide, anxiously pleads with him to give it up, and is so worried he even sends him an insulting postcard (one can read this between the lines of the letter just quoted). But in forbidding vagrancy to Musō, he has also condemned himself to go on living. It may seem to require a huge mental leap to arrive at this conclusion, but it's reasonable enough, surely, if we accept that Santōka had convinced himself that vagrancy was no more than a drawn-out form of suicide. And it explains why he abandoned the idea of death and began to keep a diary again, though this in no way diminished the desire for death itself (in fact the decision to stay alive probably made it even stronger). It also makes clear why his encounter with the rainstorm, the punishment he received at its hands, should have moved him so profoundly.

I was aware that, at least in terms of conventional scholarship, this hypothesis relied too much on guesswork, but I still felt there was some justification in my conclusions, and was pleased that the image I was attempting to form of Santōka during his Shikoku pilgrimage had become appreciably clearer. Yet I have to admit that a general feeling of uneasiness about my position was much greater than any satisfaction I took in it. The basic cause of the unrest was a suspicion that, if this Musō was also a vagrant priest, there was an off chance that the man my father and Kurokawa had met and enjoyed drinking with was merely an imitation of Santōka rather than the poet himself. In point of fact, it seemed rather more than likely, which would mean that the one colourful incident in my father's life became very drab indeed, as the discovery could hardly be said to add any kind of lustre to his days. I wasn't just disheartened at the prospect but quite desperate about it. Even so, I told myself that this attitude was ridiculous and that I'd have to investigate the matter further.

This took the form of going over the letter again. It wasn't clear where it had been posted (it was simply headed "while travelling"), but the address it had been sent to was written on the letter, a rural district called Shūso in the prefecture of Ehime. There was also the name of a village and what seemed to be a temple in it, although this could have been a place-name. Aware that there was always the possibility that the name of this village had changed, I had a look at the area map in my daughter's atlas, using a magnifying glass. I couldn't find the village (as I'd assumed from the start with a child's atlas), but luckily there was an index and the name of the district was in it; and it was quite clear that the place in question was fairly close to Dōgo. This meant that Musō could well have been in the tea-house on the vital day. In his letter, Santōka had written that he "should be able to visit Mr Takahashi on the tenth" (of November: in fact he visited him twenty days later), so it was possible Musō had come to the Dōgo area around that date in order to fit in with Santōka's plans. From the point of view of mere geographical proximity, then, he couldn't be ruled out as the other person.

What allowed me a way out of this unfortunate quandary, however, was the question of the age of the person they'd been with, and this did seem to furnish a strong argument against its being Musō. According to Murakami, when Santōka was trying to persuade Musō that vagrancy was wrong for him, it was as though he were "concerned about his own child", and the style of the letter itself suggested someone considerably younger than the writer. To put it in the vaguest possible terms, Musō was apparently a young man or, at the most, only middle-aged; and it is worth remembering that Santōka's only child, his son Ken, had reached the age of thirty in 1939. Now, according to both my father and Kurokawa, the priest appeared to be somewhat older than themselves, so on the strength of these two independent judgements there was good reason for thinking that a much younger Musō wouldn't qualify. I realized that if I could get some concrete evidence on this question of his age, then one thorny problem would be disposed of.

I need hardly say that I immediately set to work; unfortunately, I was able to discover not only nothing about his age at the time, but simply nothing about the man at all. The only letter addressed to him in the Collected Works is the one already mentioned, and his name never even appears once in letters written to other people, nor in the diary. I must have gone through a dozen books about the Garden of the One Light in Kyoto to which he belonged, either borrowed from the library or picked up cheap in second-hand bookshops, and about the same number on the free-rhythm haiku poets and their world; but I found no trace of him whatsoever. The only exception in this general silence was the passage in Ueda's book from which I've already quoted, but by some unhappy irony the more I read it the closer I came to thinking that he was actually the same age as Santōka, if not slightly older. There was something in that scene where he puts his black over-robe on Santōka which seemed to suggest this. So all that my research had done was enhance the possibility that it was Musō they had met.

Being now at my wits' end, I returned to my former fantasizing, deciding that the address Santōka had sent his letter to must have been a temple, and that Musō had kindly brought a whole priest's outfit from that temple and given it to the poet, which was how my father and Kurokawa had been able to meet him in his proper priestly guise.

Then, late one sultry summer night, I was leafing through a book called *Glimpse* [sic] *of America*; and as I gazed idly at a photograph of Nishida Tenkō, the founder of the Garden of the One Light, noting what an oily, vulgar pig the great man looked, and yawning, a clear idea of just what I'd been up to finally got through to me. It wasn't a new perception, but simply a sense of how wrong I'd been. Obviously I hadn't undertaken these researches in any professional way; only half seriously, as a means of somehow honouring my father. That was something in my favour, I suppose. But I was still a man whose trade was the study of literature, and to have lost myself in such irresponsible musings was unforgivable. I rebuked myself as I would a student in a graduate seminar who hadn't done his homework, and I can't say I enjoyed the experience. Then my melancholy gaze returned to the photograph of Nishida, to note the bold figure at his side: a man of far more refined features—the boss, in fact, of all Hawaii's gambling joints—who stood there quite justifiably full of his own importance.

I heaved a deep sigh. Even if I did manage to clear up the

point about Musō to my own satisfaction, another more insoluble problem would remain. Though Musō might actually have been a young man and therefore not the priest at the teahouse, the very fact of his existence meant that other priests like him could have been in Shikoku at the time. After all, the event had taken place before the war, when the pace of life was a bit more leisurely than it is now, and Dōgo was not only a popular hot spring but a place to be visited on the standard pilgrimage, so there was no reason to suppose there wouldn't have been other travelling priests around—probably quite a number of them, in fact—from all parts of the country.

The priest in question was a product of the pre-war educational system, so he would have known about someone like Minamoto Yorimasa, for the latter appeared even in primary school textbooks at the time. The whole edifice of conjecture I had built was suspect even on a simple point like that, and thus untrustworthy overall. I was finally obliged to admit that in all likelihood the priest had not been Taneda Santōka.

It was on August 10th or 11th that I reached the point where I knew there was simply nothing more to be done. I can't say that, in my heart of hearts, I had truly grown resigned to the fact, for I was still reluctant to admit final defeat to myself, a defeat which had been forced upon me rather than consented to. But it did mean that, throughout that long summer, as I worked every day on my annotations of Botanka Shōhaku's *Shunmusō* (Spring Dream Grasses), I was also watching the decline and fall of the Santōka legend, like a castle built of sand gradually crumbling away.

13

One sunny afternoon in November I went out for a walk, saying I probably wouldn't be back for dinner. I'd had a rather rough handling from some of my students on the previous day, then a row on one of the faculty committees, and I was feeling pretty fed up with everything. I took the underground, and looked up from the Chinese paperback I was reading to note we'd stopped at a station I'd never been to before, so I promptly got off and wandered about for a couple of hours. I noticed a house with an enormous garden, in one corner of which was a persimmon tree with amazingly brilliant vermilion fruit. Just beyond it there was another house with a stone wall, and on top of the wall stood a huge wire and metal cage, like a small room, full of birds of all sorts, colours, and sizes. I tried to work out how many there were, but lost count halfway through.

I had a cup of coffee, went on reading my book, and decided it was time to go home. Up to that point the idea of playing *go* hadn't crossed my mind—I hadn't done so for over a year—but I noticed a *go* parlour near the station and suddenly made up my mind to enter. I suppose I felt that just taking a walk was an inadequate response to the mood I was in.

The old woman in charge asked me what grade I was, and I mumbled that I was third, perhaps fourth; whereupon she bawled out, "Any third grades?" howling it again when no one answered.

After the second call, an elderly man with a bald head and a leather jacket crept forward.

"Third grade, eh? Well, you'll do, I suppose. I'll give you a six start, all right?"

I didn't like the cocky way he spoke at all, but I agreed to take him on. I felt I had seen him somewhere before, though I didn't give the matter much thought as I was soon totally absorbed by the contest taking place on the board. Even when he took me off to a local *oden* restaurant to have dinner, I still hadn't realized that this leather-jacketed ancient was none other than my old high-school geography teacher, Yagizawa. This wasn't all that surprising, really, since the baldpate before me used to have long hair which he was always irritatingly brushing away from his forehead; and a man who only spoke in the most perfunctory, slip-shod manner to us students was now using at least a form of polite speech. So I thought he must simply resemble someone I knew yet couldn't call to mind. It finally got through when we'd both finished our first bottle, and the cook asked:

"Any of the fried, Mr Yagizawa?"

The name brought immediate recall, a confused yet vital link-ing of the present and the past. When I looked to my side, there was the teacher of thirty years ago, now enveloped in the various odours of giant radish, devil's tongue, and octopus bubbling away in the square iron pot, as he debated whether to have fried *tōfu* or not. It had taken me thirty seconds, perhaps slightly longer, to discern beneath the wrinkles and sagging flesh the face of the mid-dle-aged man (as he had appeared to me then, though he was probably still comparatively young), and when I was absolutely sure, I announced who I was. He seemed quite used to meeting former pupils under conditions of this kind, apologizing without any apparent embarrassment for being unable to place me, and giving a brief account of his subsequent career. Almost immedi-ately after I'd graduated he was invited to join a mining company: he had been ill for some years but eventually recovered and was able to go back to work, and now had some kind of advisory post at the same place. This meant he only went into the office twice a week, and spent most of his time playing *go*, so it was no wonder he was so good at it.

He congratulated me on being employed at my former univer-sity, saying how pleased Kurokawa must have been, and then recalling that he was dead. On his initiative, the conversation then dwelt on reminiscences of Kurokawa, of how much trouble they'd all been caused in the teachers' common-room and else-where by his constant anti-war and anti-militarist opinions, de-

216

livered in a lowered voice, of course, but still easily overheard. The leather-jacketed old man raised his cup to his lips and said:

"What a business it all was. I'll admit he did at least keep quiet when the Cadet Corps C.O. was around, but he still went on about it even when the Head was right next to him. It made it all very awkward for the Head, you know. In the end, he took to leaving the room whenever he caught sight of Kurokawa. It sounds funny enough now, but it was deadly serious at the time, I can assure you."

Even so, he said, he had to respect Kurokawa for being absolutely right about the way the war would turn out. In the summer of 1943, they'd been discussing the fall of Mussolini, not at school this time but at the home of one of the teachers, and Kurokawa had said that Korea, Taiwan, and Sakhalin would all be lost. "What about Manchuria?" Yagizawa had then put in, and Kurokawa had taken him apart for asking such an idiotic question.

"He really let me have it, you know. He was so serious he scared the life out of me. It was a pretty stupid thing to ask, though, I'll admit."

"Well," I said, "one has to remember that he had no ordinary dislike of the military and of war in general. It was all based on his Christian beliefs, so it was bound to be rather passionate, I suppose. . . ."

"Not just that, mind," grinned Yagizawa. "He also had a grudge about this," he said, indicating the flask of saké, meaning that Kurokawa's anti-militarist stand had been fostered by wartime shortages of alcohol.

I must have got onto the question of Kurokawa and my father's trip to Shikoku when we were ordering our third. Not surprisingly, Yagizawa knew all about the encounter in the tea-house at Dōgo.

217

"That priest was bound to have been taken aback. After all, you hardly expect a complete stranger to come out with opinions like that."

His sympathies seemed to lie with the priest and his political ideas, rather than with the pacifist Kurokawa, but the focus of our conversation shifted to the relationship between Kurokawa and my father, about which he seemed pretty well informed.

"Naturally your father would have been used to things like that, so he'd have known how to handle it, but it must have caused him a lot of trouble all the same. I can just imagine."

He asked after my father and, on hearing that he was dead, seemed to be deeply moved, though I assume quite a lot of it was put on for the sake of politeness. He showed, however, very little interest in the idea that the priest at the tea-house might have been the poet Santōka who'd become so popular in recent years; he merely listened to what I said, nodding occasionally, putting in the odd question from time to time, and cocking his head to one side in mild surprise. I did, in fact, give him a fairly detailed account of things, although it was all rather wasted on an audience of an old teacher who'd had nothing to do with haiku at any time in his life and had never heard of Santōka. I suppose I thought that by talking to someone like him I could get the whole thing off my chest, and possibly learn something new about the priest at the same time.

That second aim was soon disappointed. All Yagizawa had to say about the priest (and he said it several times) was that he must have been a truly accomplished consumer of alcohol if he'd been able to astonish Kurokawa. Since there was nothing more to be had on that subject, I mentioned that I'd always been rather surprised that Kurokawa had been able to take a trip to Shikoku at the end of November when it was still term-time, to which Yagizawa made a slow, non-commital reply. As an afterthought I also expressed surprise that my father should have gone with him, but he claimed not to know anything about it because it was all before his time.

To say he didn't know because it was before he'd been employed at the school seemed oddly evasive, since he appeared to be so well up on the rest of the story, but that in itself probably wouldn't have aroused my suspicion. What did was his abrupt announcement that he didn't want any rice to end his meal, and when I naturally replied that I didn't either, he suggested we go back and have another game. This certainly seemed to imply that he didn't want to discuss the matter because he had something to hide, an impression I found it very hard to dispel, although I agreed to his invitation in as unconcerned a manner as I could manage.

Things went pretty well for me on restarting, but despite a comparatively good performance I was still obliged to resign during the middle game. Since he'd paid for the meal I felt I ought to stand him a drink, suggesting we might have a whisky before going home. He could hardly refuse, and we went to a cheap so-called "snack bar", a place which gave the impression it was out to attract the younger generation.

"Kurokawa used to say some funny things. Used to explain that all Japan's misfortunes stemmed from America being the Western country closest to us. When I asked him if he was thinking about the Greater East Asian War, he said he meant nothing of the sort, but that we'd received our version of Christianity from America, and that's why we'd got it wrongly connected with the idea of teetotalism."

We both laughed loudly at this reminiscence, and I ordered refills. We were the only customers, and the bartender had apparently fallen asleep in front of the television, which remained switched on. Music from a radio station seemed to have got mixed up with the voices on the T.V., and our laughter only increased the confused racket, so I thought it was a good moment to edge our way back to the relevant subject.

"When was that business, then? You know, the great row about raising the flag in front of the church, and Kurokawa was all against it."

"Ah, now, when was it?" he replied, narrowing his eyes as if he were looking far off into the distance. "It was the year after the 'China Incident' started, so that would make it 1938."

"Are you sure it wasn't 1939?"

"Positive. 1938."

"I see."

At this point the music suddenly ceased, and one could also no longer hear voices from the T.V. drama, presumably because the man and woman in it weren't speaking to each other. In the profound silence my brief reply sounded extraordinarily sincere, and what should have been a casual acknowledgement echoed like a groan of disillusionment (like something in a T.V. drama, in fact), resounding dismally about the empty bar; so it perhaps wasn't surprising that Yagizawa should have asked me if there was something wrong. I thought for a moment of trying to bluff my way out of it, but assumed he wouldn't be taken in and decided to come straight out with it.

"Well, you know that man Santōka I was talking about, the one they might have met on their journey to Shikoku? I was wondering why they should have gone there at such an odd time, the end of November, and thought it might have had something to do with that trouble at school. Kurokawa had been very upset by it, and my father took him to Shikoku as a way of helping him out of his depression, something of that kind. It would have fitted if it had all been in 1939."

Yagizawa just grunted and nodded in understanding, then fell into a heavy silence. I felt it was wrong of me to induce this kind of gloom in him, and tried hard to sound cheerful with my next remark:

"If you don't play along with me the whole thing falls down, you see."

He grunted again, then put down his glass and spoke to me in a quite different tone. Now he was serious, almost grave.

"I suppose there's no reason to hide it from you. You'll soon be fifty, after all. Can't see any reason why you shouldn't be told now. It was probably unwise to have hidden it from you in the first place."

I put down my own glass and assumed what I felt to be a suitable gravity of expression, to listen to my old teacher's secrets. As the strains of the broadcast music started up again, however, what I heard to their shabby, cheerful accompaniment was a story about my father.

"I'd better make it clear from the start that I don't really know all that much about this. It's just the little that Kurokawa told me. There may well have been all sorts of complications I don't know about. Still, as a general outline of what happened, what I'm going to tell you is the truth."

Having made this point very deliberately, Yagizawa then told me that in the summer of the year in question my father had given an unsuccessful abortion to a patient who'd consequently died, and had suffered the penalty of a month's suspension of his medical license. The patient who died was a widow who'd formerly had a relationship with him, although it had all been broken off ten years before, and she'd been made pregnant by a young man with whom she'd been intimate. By the time she'd become aware of the pregnancy, though, the man had already been drafted into the army and sent to Manchuria. The woman first went to another gynaecologist, but in those days abortions were strictly illegal, and if a doctor was found to have performed such an operation it was normal to have him struck off the register; so she was turned away.

As a result, she came to my father. In fact he was the first per-

221

son she had thought of asking, but because of what had happened in the past she had decided not to. Now she was hardly in a position to have scruples of that kind. She was only three months gone at the time, and if she'd had the operation then it would probably have been all right. But the problem, as far as my father was concerned, was the operation itself, there being no guarantee that the police wouldn't get to hear of it. The danger was so great, so obviously great, that he couldn't undertake it.

Whether the woman had come to his surgery on this occasion or had asked him to visit her was something Yagizawa didn't know, although the second alternative seemed more likely. Still, he had heard that my father had been so moved by the behaviour of the woman, who said not one word of protest or accusation on being refused, that he was overcome with pity for her—a point which Yagizawa made twice at some length, whether because of the drink he'd had I wasn't sure.

Two months later the woman, who had tried everything and was at her wits' end, pleaded with my father again (it still wasn't clear where this took place), and this time he was unable to refuse. Obviously it was extremely rash to attempt an abortion with a five-month pregnancy, but presumably Father believed he could do it, or it might be truer to say that his sympathy for her made any calm judgement impossible, with the result that she was admitted to his clinic, had the operation, and died.

Father told the police that his patient had tuberculosis and he'd been obliged to operate, but the operation had been unsuccessful. This cover-up story seemed at first to work very well, due mostly to the efforts of the chairman of the Medical Board, who got his colleagues to accept the tale and obviously did all he could with regard to the press. Unfortunately, the editor of one of the two local papers was a man who'd just arrived from Tokyo, and either because the message hadn't got through to him from the paper's proprietor (who was also the vice-mayor), or because he was eager to make a name for himself, the business was given a great splash in his columns. The article made the point that the woman had not been ill at all, thus, as the saying goes, cutting the ground from under my father's feet; it also provided the fulsome misinformation that the woman in question was his *current* mistress. So the police hadn't much choice but to suspend his practice.

Of course, he should properly have been deprived of his medical license, and the fact that he got away with a mere suspension, was not prosecuted, and had the suspension itself lifted after only a month, could be attributed mainly to all the running about that the Medical Board chairman did on his behalf. But there was another "mitigating factor," ridiculous as it may seem: the man responsible for the pregnancy was no ordinary person but an enlisted soldier at the front, and this also appeared to have had a lot of influence. So the whole affair seemed to have been settled; but the problem was the effect it had on my father, the emotional shock he suffered. There was no decline in the number of his patients, and he remained as busy as always, but whenever he was alone he seemed to withdraw into himself, given over to heavy bouts of depression. Kurokawa couldn't bear to watch him in this state, and as he was due to go back home on business of his own, he invited my father to come to Shikoku with him. This wasn't only out of pity and affection for a friend, but the result of feelings of deep obligation. In the previous year, at the time of the raising of the flag affair, my father had exerted as much influence as he could on the headmaster, despite the fact that he had nothing whatever to do with the school, and Kurokawa saw this as one way of paying off part of a serious debt.

The journey itself had a remarkably beneficial effect. Although he didn't return a completely restored man, my father was healthy again and in good spirits by the New Year, and there could be no doubt that the trip had started him on the road to recovery. My mother sent a set of antique China teacups to Mrs Kurokawa as a mark of her gratitude.

"That's about it; the main story, anyway," concluded Yagizawa, and ordered two more whiskies. "To borrow Kurokawa's words, 'she had a warm, soft beauty, and love was in her eyes and in her walk'. 'Love in her eyes and walk', for heaven's sake, it's straight out of a piece of Edo pornography. She was around thirty-five, apparently."

"Where did she come from? What kind of family had she married into?"

"No idea. I don't think I heard that much. No, he didn't say."

"What sort of work did she do?"

"He didn't tell me that either."

"In 1939 Father would have been . . . fifty-three, I suppose."

"That's right, so your father's relationship with her occurred in his early forties, when she would have been twenty-five—newly widowed, it seems. I suppose I shouldn't really say this to you; it might appear a liberty on my part . . ."

"I don't mind.

"Well, if it hadn't been for your father she might have remained an ordinary widow, stayed in that household, even become head of it sometime. She could have spent her whole life without another man. But he gave her a taste for it, you see; then left her. His good lady made a lot of trouble about it, I heard— was really jealous, so he just had to give her up. He must have felt responsible for what happened later, which is why he did the operation. Sounds feasible, anyway."

I had no reply to that. The drinks arrived. I assumed it was out of sympathy and consideration for me that Yagizawa hadn't suggested that my father went ahead with the operation because he still had some interest in the woman. I took one sip and said:

"It's certainly an eye-opener. I'd no idea he was a ladies' man."

"No idea at all?"

"None. All very upright, I'd always thought."

"Apparently it was the one and only romance of his whole life."

"First I've heard of it."

"Not even about the month's suspension?"

"No. I was only a schoolboy."

Yagizawa seemed only half convinced, so for emphasis I told him I'd been at the seaside while it must have been going on, though I did clearly remember staying there longer than usual, until the beginning of September, which must have struck me as a bit odd even if I didn't know why; but when I got back home nothing out of the ordinary seemed to have occurred. It felt just the same whether I was at school or at home, probably because I didn't spend much time with my parents anyway, and my father tended to be irritable and depressed when he was having trouble with a patient, so if he had been rather gloomier than usual I wouldn't have noticed. Yagizawa nodded.

"Which means you were very cleverly deceived by your parents."

"That's what it comes down to. I was pretty slow as a child, too; not noticing much of what was going on about me."

"Your mother must have been very wise, as well, very calm and collected."

Since I again said nothing, he went on:

"That's the best way to bring up children. Not like me and my wife, having our rows right there in front of them all the time."

I'm not sure if I managed to smile appropriately at his little joke or not. Fragments of memory had been assailing me like sudden bursts of snow; one in particular of that same summer, on the day my mother had come to the fishing village, and my grandmother had grown very anxious towards evening when she couldn't find her anywhere, searching all over the place for her, and telling my brother and me to go to the sea front and look for her. I realized now that Grandmother had known about the affair and must have been afraid she might have killed herself. Then there was that time on September 1st when my brother and I had taken our trays downstairs and were just going up again, and the policeman said something about Father which made the landlady tell him to be quiet. He must have been making a joke about what had happened. Had my brother looked so stern then because he already knew, or because he'd suddenly grasped something intuitively at that actual moment? No, he knew already, because on that evening ten days before, when Mother had disappeared, he just ran off to the shore without a word and I raced after him, and when we got there you could see along the whole length of the long, white, gentle line of the jetty. It was clear at a glance there was no one on it, but he ran right to the very end, and I watched him go, feeling half scornful of his wasting so much time and energy over nothing, yet also feeling a peculiar anxiety and excitement, so that I finally chased after him; and clearly my brother must have been afraid Mother had committed suicide, and who knows just how much of that same fear may not have been transmitted to me? But when we finally got to the rough, grey tip of the jetty and looked down at the sea, there was nothing but a rope and an empty cardboard box being tossed about by the choppy waves, and I went home first as my brother told me to, and there was Mother in the dark kitchen cooking pork cutlets for our dinner. Then later, when I talked to boys older than me at school, and even in the same class sometimes, or to grown-ups in town, there were moments when my father was mentioned and they said things I somehow couldn't quite follow, quite a lot of them, or the expressions on their faces were odd, or they seemed to be looking at me to see how I would react.

From the time the war with America began, Father seemed to be a much more cheerful kind of person, even when he was dealing with patients who were dangerously ill, and I'd put that down to old age and the attaining of that settled calm which is supposed to accompany it; but I now thought it was more likely he had finally recovered from the pain of that disaster, and at last managed to forget the woman who had been "the one and only romance of his whole life". This sole love affair must have started just about the time I was born, and my father's constant bad temper, something I had grown up with and always been used to, could well have been an expression, perhaps not of actual desire for the woman, but at least of a constant discontent at having to be tied to this house, to this wife, these children, this child; and no doubt it had been very wise of my mother to tell me that it was all caused by the heavy responsibilities a doctor has to shoulder. Probably, in fact, she had been trying to convince herself that it was so, and when this strong mother of mine occasionally stopped her knitting, becoming lost in thought, presenting that sad profile which I thought so calm and sweet, perhaps she was brooding about her husband, suffering bitterly inside because there was another woman he couldn't forget.

I also remembered that no newspapers were delivered to our lodgings that summer, and how I'd said rather cheekily that I wouldn't be able to keep up with world events if things went on like this, and my brother, who was even more of a newspaper addict than me, told me loftily that such things were of no concern to me anyway, and casually changed the subject, and Grandmother gave me a very old-fashioned look. Then there was that incident a few years ago now, when I was bullied into making an appearance at a gathering in Tokyo of distinguished people from back home, and the ancient Diet member who was running it asked me my father's profession; and when I told him, he blurted out, "Ah, the famous case of . . .", stopping abruptly and looking embarrassed, but managing with a true politician's aplomb to glide smoothly on to safer ground, as if a cloud had suddenly drifted across his face to hide its perpetual beams, then just as suddenly faded away to reveal double its former splendour. There was also that time, about two years after the disaster, when I told my mother I wanted to become a newspaper reporter, and her face changed colour, and she gave me an awful telling-off. All these memories came back to me, one right after another, like the street lamps coming on as dusk descends.

"But he was a fine man, your father," said Yagizawa, trying to comfort me, "both as a person and as a doctor. I never knew him all that well, but if Kurokawa thought that highly of him it must have been so. I don't see why we shouldn't consider him a good husband as well. That's how I see it, anyway. What happened was just a piece of very bad luck."

"Um."

"A situation like that now, there'd be no trouble at all."

"I suppose not."

The old man in the leather jacket was about to light a cigarette when he suddenly let out a huge cry like some plaintive night bird, but it was only the preliminary to a lengthy yawn. I waited for this enormous yawn to come to an end, observing the tears it had brought to his bleary eyes, and suggested it was time we both went home. It certainly was a good time to leave. Yagizawa had told me all he had to tell, the appropriate polite exchanges had all been made, and at some point a group of six young people, of both sexes, all gaudily dressed, had come in and were now making a cheerful racket.

There was little hope of being able to get down to work as soon as I got home after hearing so disturbing a tale. I sat at my desk, chain-smoking and trying to think. It was ironical that a half-serious attempt to solve a riddle, a detective game whose object was to bestow a little glory on my father's life, should have ended by uncovering something that was supposed to remain hidden. Had Kurokawa been afraid my father might try to kill himself? Hadn't he, perhaps, already tried to? A doctor's trade allows him easy access to tools for doing so, and even if he hadn't tried, the people around him must have been in a constant state of anxiety that he might. Was that why Kurokawa had planned the trip to Shikoku? If that had been the case, and the mendicant priest they'd met at the tea-house in Dōgo had in fact been Santōka, then it would have been an encounter between two people both preoccupied with the idea of suicide and both fighting against it, while neither would have known they shared each other's turmoil. Other things crossed my mind as well, among them thoughts of the young man who had made the woman pregnant. He must have been in his twenties in 1939, and now, if he had managed to get through the war, if he hadn't died in Manchuria or the Philippines or a camp in Siberia, and had somehow endured the years that followed, he would be in his fifties or sixties, and I could well have seen him somewhere on one of the occasions when I went back home; or it might be that he couldn't live in his home town with a past like that, and was now in Tokyo, and perhaps I'd even passed him on the street. An idle, childish fancy, but it sent a cold shiver through my body, and the cold clung to me, like the oil draining from a fishing boat, trailing a long wake and only very gradually growing thin, faint, and finally dispersing.

Now I remembered why I'd wanted to be a journalist. It was because there was a wonderful character in an American detective story I was crazy about, a reporter called Lefty, and when Mother had shouted at me my immediate impulse had been to say I didn't want to work for any Mito newspaper; but I didn't because I knew instinctively that for some reason it wasn't good to mention our local papers, so I kept quiet. This must mean that unconsciously, or in fact half consciously, I knew even at that age there was something about the subjects of my father and newspapers which forbade their being linked together. It finally crossed my mind—something I'd never thought of before—that I might well have become a scholar of Japanese literature because my first choice of a profession had been so flatly turned down. So

229

I hadn't followed in the bold footsteps of Lefty, but was directed smoothly onto a quite different path where I would associate with the great medieval poets instead, and this had perhaps been determined for me by the existence of a woman of thirty-five, a "warm, soft beauty" whose face and name, even, were unknown to me. If she hadn't existed, I might even now be working for a newspaper, not presumably in the style of the dauntless Lefty, but as a staff writer on the local news desk taking down stories over the telephone, or in the editorial section dreaming up eye-catching headlines every day.

Reminiscences mingled with regrets, with interpretations of those regrets, forming new emotions; and then one quite unrelated idea began to take shape, like a thin line of oil drifting from some other boat, forming another glittering chain, surprising and new: that the third member of that trio at the tea-house, Kurokawa, might have been just as possessed by the desire for death as they. At first I approached it like a baseless rumour I had somehow overheard, rejecting it out of hand as totally inconsistent with such an open, cheerful lover of life as Kurokawa. But the idea wasn't so easy to dispose of. He had, after all, been betrayed by a member of his own church to the Military Police over the business of raising the flag, and nearly lost his job. The very stupidity of the affair would have made it only more painful, becoming a scar, a deep residue of melancholy and despair, which could hardly have healed in a year. Also, the situation of the whole country was getting worse all the time, and he knew it would go on doing so, and for a Christian who believed in the total separation of the Church and the State, life must have become bitterly hard. It would have been a tortuous journey before he arrived at the point where he could make ironic protests against the regime by bowing excessively low before the imperial portraits, and one of the blind alleys on that journey, from which he managed to turn back, could well have been a contemplation of the idea of suicide, considered at least once or twice. No matter how much one may claim that suicide is sternly forbidden a believing Christian, the very fact of its being forbidden presumably only emphasizes the power of its attraction. It might even have presented itself to him in the guise of a form of martyrdom; and certainly the spiritual labyrinth into which this world had led him, the conflict of ideas and feelings that had been aroused, would have made him particularly sensitive to anything similar going on inside someone else, like my father. It was surely not unreasonable to imagine that an awareness of the suicide wish in another, recognized because it was also inside himself, resulted in his inviting my father on that journey. But the man who would nurse the patient was more ill than the patient himself, leading to the sudden outburst of anti-war feelings when he met an unknown priest on his travels who turned out to be an ultra-rightist; an action as reckless as that of a priest making a pilgrimage in Shikoku with no bamboo hat and dressed only in an ordinary kimono. Surely this demonstrated at least a fervent desire, though perhaps only a fleeting one, to be made to suffer, to achieve his own downfall.

Finally I began to feel I must get other versions of what I'd heard from Yagizawa that evening. This wasn't because I thought he'd told me a pack of lies, for I was sure the basic outline of his story should be accepted just as he had given it. And yet, since Kurokawa had probably only spoken about the matter briefly to him, what he had passed on to me had quite likely been transformed into something very different from the original, through the effects of time and the gradual decay of memory, and no doubt there were many possible ways of looking at what had happened. Indeed, he had said as much himself at the outset. Yes, there had to be other views of the affair, other versions of the same original tale. If I could get hold of at least one of these, a means of unravelling the various threads of this reality would be in my hands, and a many-sided view of the truth could be attained. People who had lived in Mito all their lives would inevitably have a different interpretation of this story, of the way in which it should be read, from either Yagizawa or Kurokawa, who were both essentially outsiders. I thought for some time about contacting this schoolfellow or that cousin, but because I couldn't think of anyone who seemed right for the task, eventually I decided to telephone my brother.

It would be wrong to say I was motivated by no trace of pure, even vulgar, curiosity, for there was undoubtedly a bit of that— perhaps quite a lot of it—involved. But it does seem that my strongest desire was to know the truth about something which had played a part in forming my character, and which had been completely hidden from me for so long, on the assumption that acquiring as detailed a knowledge as possible of its origin and development would throw a new light on my boyhood and adolescence. Or, to put it in a slightly exaggerated way, I believed I would find something which would clarify what I was, feeling an emotional involvement as though I were collecting material for a biography of myself. I was hoping that the blurred outlines of the ambiguous picture I had of my own existence would immediately become sharp, clear, precise. What I had been and was, what I had not been and was not, would suddenly become intelligible.

Yet there was another motive at work, perhaps the most decisive one. While listening to Yagizawa, I had been surprised how close I felt to my father, how strangely intimate a figure he now seemed; but with the passage of time this had given place to a different feeling, one of guilt at the way I'd thought of him up to now. Hadn't all that respect I had paid him been based, not on affection, but on mere reverence mixed with awe, even a kind of dread? Couldn't the same also be said of the love I thought I had borne towards my mother? The doubt came over me slowly, drifting like smoke, then enveloping me; but this isn't to say I meant to blame my vanished self, the self I had been and was no more, or to hold my parents responsible for what might have and had not been. What they'd done had been right. There was no reason why I shouldn't be grateful to them for that. Only the manner of what they'd done, the skill in the planning of the operation and the brilliance of its execution—it was this that had put a barrier between us, and made me grow cold and distant to them. I knew this interpretation was correct, but it could only confirm my sense of isolation, and I thought I might be able to bury that solitary feeling by talking to my brother.

I went into the living room and switched on the light. The clock showed it was already 11:30, but he wouldn't have gone to bed yet. So long as he hadn't been called out on an emergency, he would be sitting beneath the portrait of my father, pouring out his second glass of brandy. He might be in conversation, laughing in that low voice which was so like Father's. I found the number in my notebook and began to dial it, but when I reached the ninth of the ten digits I put down the receiver. I was wondering why my brother had never once mentioned the matter over all these years, not even after I'd grown up, not even after both our parents were dead.

To awaken these distant memories would surely only cause him pain. He was a much more old-fashioned person than myself, and I could hardly imagine he'd be eager to discuss Father's mistress with me. The story itself was about things that were, after all, scandalous: a failed operation, a sensational newspaper article, the intervention of the police. The affair was something that a local G.P. who had inherited his father's practice would obviously want to forget, as far as that was humanly possible. To raise it now would be bad medicine.

If that were the case, then I shouldn't do it. My brother had made up his mind about this years and years ago, or circumstances had just made it up for him. Whichever the case, I had to respect his decision about the proper way it should be handled. I had, in fact, already been respecting it for years, if only unconsciously, and there was no reason why I couldn't go on doing so. My picture of myself would remain unclear, but could some new investigation of a time already decades old produce the desired clarity? No, it would remain as vague as ever, like my isolation, my solitude, for no awareness of the past could bury that. The past lacks that power.

So I didn't telephone my brother, and I told myself that no one else would be questioned either. What I had heard that evening had been enough for me to know my father's sufferings and my mother's grief. It was enough, I told myself; enough.

Certainly to leave the affair in this state conferred on it the vagueness, the incompleteness, of the few remaining pages of some tale that has been lost. But the lesson that truth need not appear in response to our utmost efforts to discover it had already been adequately impressed on me during my investigations into the case of Taneda Santōka. Wiser to leave the scattered pieces as they are than make rash efforts to assemble them. We lead our lives surrounded by innumerable fragments of the truth, and now at last to recognize that fact was no cause of shame for me, nor one of pride. The year 1939 was for the driven rain, all its days laid open to the wintry showers, the wind rising and driving the thin rain onwards, a fine smoke drifting, a mist.

DEMCO